THE DESERT SAINT

A Maria Varela Mystery

A.M. PASCARELLA

BAY
ROAD
PUBLISHING

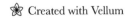

Contents

Chapter 1

You had believed you were done with killing.

Yet here you are.

A gun in your hand.

A body slumped over a desk.

Two bullet shells on the floor.

The last was decades ago, and killing was much easier back then. That's not why you stopped, but it's something you've thought of. If you had to kill again, how would you evade detection in a world of DNA and wireless cameras? You don't think evasion will be an issue with this one. This man chose a house on a street without cameras for a reason. You're sure he never thought that decision would make him an easy target. He probably never thought he'd be hunted.

Still, this killing doesn't feel like the others.

This killing leaves you feeling dirty.

Sometimes, doing the right thing doesn't make you feel clean.

You take the keychain, red and shaped like Alaska, and place it on the dead man's left hand, the loop on the thumb, keys hanging to the side. You turn away from the body and make your way to the bookshelf in the living room. It takes a few minutes to find the hidden switch, an indentation a third of the way down on the right-hand side.

You slide the bookshelf to the left and head down the stairs.

Chapter 2

What an asshole.

Detective Maria Varela looked through the one-way glass at Preston Millicent III. Even without the evidence, which they had a mountain of, Maria would have figured him for the guy anyway, and not because of the suit which probably cost more than Maria took home in a month, nor the face lift so well done, she could barely tell he'd had work done, or the watch, some brand Maria had never heard of and probably worth more than her car, no, none of the trappings of his substantial wealth were what had her feeling this way.

It was his eyes.

Maria had interrogated hit men who'd killed so many people the corpses blended together and human life had become equal to that of an ant. Those men displayed no emotion, just a flat stare, and they never confessed unless an attorney convinced them it was in their interest. But Preston looked around the world like he was judging whatever he saw, and everything he saw came up short. That was what had Maria sure he was the perp before all the evidence came in.

But could she really be sure that was why?

She wanted to believe she wasn't judging him because he was born rich and had soared through life on family money and now believed everything he had was on account of his own intelligence and talent. Wanted to believe that badly. But a part of her wondered if her time on the job and her own arrogance were causing her to think she could scan people and know the truth. She didn't want to become one of those detectives who was so sure of themselves they'd ignore evidence if it went against what they knew in their "gut." She wanted to stay rational, rationality mattered, kept her from putting away the wrong guy just because it felt right.

Michael, her partner, opened the door and stuck his head into the room. He was about six foot two, with the athletic, lithe frame of a boxer. The nose broken too many times to count confirmed his boxing past. He never talked about it, but Maria had seen pictures of him, hands raised in victory, some oversized belt around his waist.

"Just finished the deposition with the wife. D.A. says we have enough to arrest," Michael said.

Maria turned back to the window.

Preston looked at his watch. Tapped it as if it had stopped working.

The door opened and an attorney came in, his suit as expensive as Preston's.

"Where the hell have you been?" Preston said.

"I got here as soon as I could," the attorney said.

Preston opened his mouth to speak, but the attorney waved for him to be quiet.

"Not a word. They're probably listening from next door," he said.

"Smart guy, that attorney," Maria said.

"How do you want to go about it?" Michael said.

"You go at him hard."

"You figuring that ol lily white Preston is going to have an issue with the uppity black police officer questioning him?"

"No, not really. I think he'll have a bigger issue with me being forward, but I want to play it coy, draw him in. See if he'll confess."

Michael walked up to the glass. Looked through.

"He's barely holding it together," he said.

"Nah, that arrogance is real. I doubt he even thinks he should be punished for killing her."

"Fifty bucks says he gives it up," Michael said.

"You're on," Maria said.

"But winner has to do paperwork," Michael said.

"Only a scared man hedges his bets."

"Yeah, well, you've been on a bit of a run with these, so maybe some fear is in order."

PRESTON BARELY LOOKED at Michael as they entered the room, but he couldn't keep his eyes off of Maria. She was used to it. No matter how hard she tried to look severe, no makeup, hair pulled back, men always needed to make some big deal about the good-looking police detective interviewing them. Like complimenting her looks was going to get her to go easy on them. Maria couldn't decide if all men were this stupid or just the ones she ended up interviewing.

"I admit, I'm flattered that the Las Vegas PD sent their reigning beauty queen to interview me, but traditionally, I prefer blondes. So many Mexicans around here, it makes me really long for a good old-fashioned American bombshell," Preston said.

"I apologize for my client," the attorney said.

"You have to do that a lot?" Michael said.

"Seriously though, Officer..." Preston leaned forward to read the name on the badge hanging from Maria's neck.

"Detective Varela," Maria said.

"Of course, Detective, Detective, how could I not have labeled you properly? But seriously, Detective, you shouldn't have that black hair back in a ponytail. I'd probably be much more talkative if you let it down, maybe let it pool at your shoulders. And look at that lovely complexion. Was your father or your mother Mexican? Or both? One hundred percent beaner, are you?"

"Preston, be quiet."

"My attorney disapproves of my behavior. Shocking." Preston made a big show of putting his hands together and sitting upright. He put on an overly polite smile and inclined his head at Maria. "You were saying?"

Maria let the silence sit there. What she wanted was for Preston to be comfortable and chatty, but she couldn't decide if it would be better to challenge him or to be slightly submissive. Maybe let her hair down, something to make him believe he really had control. She decided against it. He'd grow bored with her if he thought he could control her. She needed to keep him interested. Needed to keep him thinking he had something to prove. She looked up at Michael and nodded.

"Oh, so you're the boss?" Preston said.

Michael reached into a folder and pulled out a photo, a glamor shot of a woman. Her name was Maribel Skinner, and she was originally from Ohio. She had moved to Los Angeles fifteen years ago to try to make it big and, after failing, had moved to Vegas to work as an escort. She went by the name Eva. In the photo, Eva was standing against a wall in a low-cut evening gown with a long slit up the left side. She was looking into the camera with what was probably supposed to be a look of desire, but to Maria, Eva looked scared, and Maria couldn't blame her. So many women trying to become famous for their looks. So many women driven to misery by the pressure. Probably why Maria's father had threatened to divorce her mother when she tried to enter Maria in a beauty pageant as a child.

"Do you know this woman?" Michael asked.

"Looks like some hooker to me," Preston said.

"We never said she was a sex worker," Maria said.

"She's not pretty enough to be a real model, and where do all the failed models end up? On their backs," Preston said.

"So, do you know her?" Michael asked again.

"Why is my client here?" The attorney asked.

Michael pulled another photo from the file. This one was also of Eva but had been taken a few hours earlier. Eva naked and lying in a dumpster, her open eyes staring up at the camera, the bruises around her neck and the tearing of three fingernails revealing that she'd spent her last moments gasping for air and fighting to survive.

The photo, as stark as it was, couldn't convey the brutality of the scene. The stench of spoiled milk leaking from a carton next to Eva's shoulder would be circling Maria's dreams for months. A part of Maria wished she could be one of those cops who walled off her emotions behind bravado, sarcasm, and cynical jokes, but she just couldn't. Her father worried about her burning out. Maria only worried about closing cases.

"Dangerous job being a whore," Preston said.

"Why do you keep saying that she's a sex worker?" Maria asked.

"Who else ends up in a dumpster?" Preston said.

"Not another word," the attorney said. "Is my client under arrest?"

"We want to know where he was last night," Michael said.

"At home with my wife, all night," Preston said.

"I'll get an affidavit from the wife and make her available at her earliest convenience. Now if there is nothing else, my client and I are leaving," the attorney said.

Maria let them both stand up before speaking. She enjoyed letting Preston have that moment of believing he was walking out of that room before taking all of that smug certainty away. Maybe she shouldn't have relished it so much, but God, he was such an asshole.

"Do you know what I love about extremely wealthy men?" Maria said.

"We're not interested in your personal opinions, Detective," the attorney said.

"Oh, but I am," Preston said.

"Wealthy men always overestimate their own intelligence," Maria said.

Michael pulled out another photo, a front and back shot taken by a traffic camera. The front photo showed Preston at the wheel, the back photo showed the license plate: WLTHY.

"This was taken last night around one in the morning near an apartment you own. It's on the other side of town from your house. Apparently, you weren't home with the wife all night," Maria said.

Michael pulled out a computer-generated map of Las Vegas with a blue line snaking across it.

"Your wife hired a detective who put a GPS on your car. Apparently, your prenup is void if you're caught cheating," Michael said.

"Good lawyer she must have had. What's she, the second wife?" Maria said.

"Third. Looks like I might be searching for a fourth soon," Preston fixed his eyes on Maria, "Perhaps, I'm growing tired of blondes."

"Think this blonde was a little smarter than you gave her credit for. By the way, your car stopped where we found the body," Maria said.

"And the victim shared all of her booking information with a friend," Michael said.

"She arrived at your apartment at 10:00pm," Maria said.

"Do you really think anyone cares about some whore?" Preston said.

"So you're saying what? Because she was a sex worker, you had a right to kill her?" Maria said.

Preston opened his mouth to retort, but his attorney placed a hand on his shoulder.

"My client isn't admitting to anything. He's a pillar of the community-"

"Pillar of the community? That's what we're calling murdering rapists now?" Michael said.

"Rape? I've never had to rape anyone. Women have always begged me for it," Preston said.

"Interesting that you aren't denying the murder, though," Maria said.

"Not another word," the attorney said.

For the first time since Maria had laid eyes on him, Preston seemed to realize he was in serious danger. He crossed his arms. Looked down at the table. All that cockiness was gone, and watching the shock spread across his face felt so good that Maria wanted to bottle that feeling up and save it.

"We didn't need a confession. We just wanted to see if he was man enough to own up to it, and just like I thought, he wasn't," Maria said.

MARIA SETTLED into her desk and turned on her computer. Michael was standing against the wall behind her. The fifty dollars he'd lost was sitting on the desk. Maria hadn't touched it yet. She was just letting it sit there, crisp and green. As she clicked on the link for an arrest report, she decided Michael had gotten the better of this deal. Writing a report was worth a hell of a lot more than fifty dollars.

"That guy might have been the biggest asshole we've ever arrested," Michael said. He wasn't looking at her. His eyes were on the ceiling, and his jaw was tight, his cheekbone bulging.

"The Pakistani who killed his daughter was worse," Maria said.

"The one who called you a stupid lady? Yeah, but that was a cultural thing."

"Does that make him any less of an asshole?"

"I'm just saying that guy honestly thought he was doing the right thing. That's messed up on a whole different kind of level, but this guy today, this aristocrat asshole, he knows better," Michael said.

"Does he?" Maria said.

"Yeah, he does. He just doesn't care," Michael said.

Maria's phone beeped, a reminder. She looked at the screen.

"Shit, I'm supposed to be having dinner with my brother tonight. He invited me and my girlfriend over, and I just totally forgot." She looked at the fifty dollars sitting on the desk, totally untouched.

"I see you staring at that fifty like it's going to go back in my pocket, but a bet is a bet. Besides, he's your brother. He has to forgive you." Michael pushed himself off of the wall and headed out the door without another look back.

Maria knew he was right. The desert was full of shallow graves for people who'd thought they could welch. In Vegas, you paid your bets. She'd have to cancel dinner. She sent a text message: can't do dinner. on a case. i know i suck. no my gf can't go w/out me. 😂😂 talk l8tr.

Maria turned her attention back to the arrest report. An hour later, she realized her brother had never even read her message.

Then the call came in.

Chapter 3

She looked like a kid's idea of what a hardass should look like.

Dominic Varela settled into the metal seat in the choir room of Our Lady of Eternal Peace Church and smiled at the young woman sitting across the table. She went by Naomi, but her name was Nina Maria Velasquez Ramirez. She had been born in Las Vegas to two undocumented parents, a father, Rodrigo, who fell off of a roof and died twelve years ago, and a mother, Maria Luisa, who had returned to Mexico when Naomi was thirteen. Naomi had stayed on, living in an uncle's house. Her rap sheet had her down for a petty theft charge, but the nuns said she worked the streets for a pimp named el Dueño. His real name was Mauricio Alejandro Vargas, but that didn't roll off the tongue like el Dueño, did it?

Naomi had been in the shelter almost a week now, and she looked a lot better than she had when she came in. A client had beaten her pretty badly and tried to imprison her, but Naomi had gotten away. The nuns had hoped Dominic could talk her into pressing charges against her attacker, but Dominic had taken one look at her and known that was hopeless. This woman didn't trust the police and wouldn't be willing to tell her story to one. She'd only told Dominic what happened because one of the nuns sat in and filled in details from what Naomi had told her. Naomi's participation had mostly been head nods and one word replies, yes or no. No way she'd fill out a statement, much less testify. But Dominic had seen something to the end of their last meeting, a brief glimmer she'd be willing to talk to him. Maybe not about the attack, but about other things. So here he was, taking another shot. Maybe he could help her turn things around, and as for the scumbag who attacked her, well, fucked up lives end in fucked up ways, of that Dominic was sure.

"You're a cop, right?" Naomi said.

"Retired."

"So if you was a cop, how come you told me all that stuff last time, like what cops can and can't do?" Naomi said.

She wasn't looking at him, but she wasn't not looking at him either, and Dominic knew that this was a good sign. The last time they'd talked, her eyes hadn't drifted much above his feet. Right now, they were chest high.

"The sisters say you're smart," Dominic said.

"They say that about everybody." Naomi rolled her eyes and went back to looking at the floor, but there was a hopeful tone to her voice. Inside this street smart young woman with the jaded facial expressions was a kid just dying to be told what she could do rather than what she couldn't do, Dominic was sure of it.

"Not to me, they don't. The sisters don't introduce me to everybody," Dominic said. It was true, the sisters didn't introduce him to everybody, the sisters only introduced him to the hardest cases, the ones they thought would never make it out from the streets. But Naomi didn't need to know that.

"So why'd you tell me all that stuff?" Naomi's eyes were back up to chest level.

"Because one day you might want a regular job," Dominic said.

"Like flipping burgers? Yeah, right." Her eyes were back to rolling, her breath shot out of the right side of her mouth as she leaned back in her chair, crossed her arms, shook her head. All the defense mechanisms firing, trying to hide the fear that she wasn't good enough for the regular world, not smart enough, not normal enough, not fit for day-to-day society.

Dominic wanted to reach out and shake the fear right out of her, but he knew that would only make the fear settle in. No, he had to act like Naomi being in the regular world was absolutely normal. This woman wasn't going to be convinced by words or pleas. She'd only be convinced by nonchalance.

"Flipping burgers. Working in a casino. Answering phones. Could be a lot of things. But if you catch a solicitation charge, changing up your life ain't going to be so easy," Dominic said.

The door to the choir room opened up, and Larry Moyer walked in.

"This is Larry Moyer, Naomi. He's still a cop, so what do we do?"

Naomi looked at all six and a half feet of Larry. His bald head, the drooping mustache and eyes red rimmed from lack of sleep.

"We smile, we be polite, and we don't tell him shit," Naomi said.

Dominic laughed. Naomi turned to him and her eyes came all the way up to Dominic's face for the briefest moment. The genuineness of his laugh brought a smile to her lips, the first smile Dominic had seen. She might end up all right out of all of this, Dominic thought. That client attacking her might end up being the thing that set her free.

Larry Moyer wasn't smiling, though. The news that he had to share with Dominic was weighing on him. Dominic had broken Larry in and paved his way to the head of homicide. Larry owed his whole career to Dominic Varela, and now he had to be the one to break the news.

"Got a minute, Dom?" Larry said.

Dominic realized something was terribly wrong.

"Something happen to Maria?" Dominic asked.

"Not Maria."

Chapter 4

The flash of a camera lit up the backyard.

Maria stood beside Tommy's pool, looking at the Las Vegas Strip glowing in the valley below. She tried to remember what it had looked like when she was a child but couldn't. Everything had seemed just as grand and majestic then as it did now, but there had been half as many hotels, and they hadn't been nearly as large or colorful. Pale shades of the current goliaths.

Everyone here knew that inside was her brother's corpse, and nobody was speaking above a low mutter. She should appreciate their concern, their discretion, but she didn't. She would have preferred that everybody acted how they did on every scene. Then again, she'd probably be pissed off no matter what anybody did, something to think about before she opened her mouth.

Michael walked up to her. He stood there silently, waiting for her to notice him, as if she hadn't heard his footsteps come across the concrete.

"Afraid I'm going to go to pieces if you talk?" Maria turned around.

Michael just looked at her, unsure of how to respond.

"My brother's dead. I'll cry later. Let's work the scene now."

"You sure you want this to be the last memory you have of him?" Michael asked.

"No, I'm not sure. I'm not sure at all," Maria said.

"There's no need for you to go in there," Michael said.

"There is no way in hell that I'm not going in there. My father is going to want to know about the scene. He's going to have questions," Maria said.

"I'll bring the whole case file to him. I'll show him everything," Michael said.

"The only thing worse than looking at my brother's corpse is spending the rest of my life accepting that I was too much of a coward to look at it," Maria said.

Michael knew she was right, but he'd needed to give her the off ramp, and he had. He was a good partner, and Maria wanted to punch the look of concern right off of his face. Maria headed for the house before she said something that she'd have to apologize for later. As she came around the pool, she caught sight of a tech, a new guy named Milton. He was focused on his task, camera to his face, breath even and calm, the camera settling as he picked his shot and then the flash, then the repeat of the same motion.

Routine was a calming thing.

Calm was what she needed.

In the kitchen, she sat down in a chair to put on booties and gloves. She pulled her hair back into a ponytail and covered it with a cap. She looked through the doorway into the hall and thought about the last time she'd been here, maybe a week ago, maybe two. Tommy had been distracted. Something about a business venture going poorly. The two of them were so different he always joked that he must have been adopted, her looking like their mother and acting like their father, Tommy with the same olive toned skin of their mother but their father's height and neither of their parents' dispositions. A ball of motion was how her father described him. All that energy focused on a bunch of get rich schemes that mostly failed miserably, but the latest, a YouTube channel, had apparently gone well. Well enough that he had bought this house a little over a year ago.

Now he was dead in it.

Maria didn't want to get out of the chair.

Two patrol officers stood in the doorway watching her, and she was convinced if they weren't there, she might give up, go back outside, stand there trying not to sob, but she wasn't going to show any weakness here. Not in front of them. When she was home with Carla, she could curl up in a ball and cry her eyes out, but not in front of all her co-workers.

She forced herself up and down the hall.

The first thing she noticed as she entered the home office was the video on pause. Tommy's face, mouth open mid-sentence and the dried blood clinging to the screen, speckling his face. Maria had to stop right there. Tears were trying to force themselves out of her eyes, and she shut them tight and breathed. In, out. In, out. She stood there like that for what felt like an hour but couldn't have been more than five seconds, and she opened her eyes. The monitor speckled in blood was still there but didn't have the same power. Maria fell back on her own routine. Her eyes roved.

Her brother slumped across his desk.

His face resting on the keyboard.

His right hand bent awkwardly against the bottom of the monitor.

His left hand resting on the desk edge, two inches from falling off.

Looped around the left thumb, a keychain, red and shaped like Alaska.

The top ray of his sun tattoo showing above the neck of his blue t-shirt.

Blood stains pouring down his back. He'd been shot while sitting down.

American flag boxer briefs. He hadn't been expecting anyone.

His flip-flops, black and brown, side by side next to the desk.

His left foot bare, pressed against the wheel of the chair.

His right foot pressed up against the wall.

Two small caliber shells, marked by yellow triangles, numbered 1 & 2.

None of the windows were open.

No signs of a struggle.

Just her brother shot twice in the back of the head while reviewing one of his videos.

An assassination.

Then, next to the monitor, she saw a picture of the two of them as children, a weekend trip to the beach in California. Tommy probably about five or six and Maria about three. Tommy had his arm around her, and Maria's eyes squinted in the sunlight, her nose lightly burnt, a waterlogged Minnie Mouse doll in her hand. Maria had the same photo on a bookshelf at her home, and she knew that if she didn't get out of that room right away, she was going to break down, and they'd hear her wails all the way in Phoenix.

When she turned to go, she saw her father standing in the doorway.

MARIA STEPPED OUTSIDE and sat on a chair to pull off her booties. Dominic followed her and walked off a few feet. He stared up at the moon. Inside, he had just stood there taking in the scene in the same way Maria had and when he finished, he'd turned around and walked out without saying a word. Maria wanted to give him time to process his emotions, but she had to ask him one thing.

"Does Mom know yet?"

Dominic shook his head. The lines on his face looked jagged in the moonlight, and his hair was longer than normal and the gray shone dully. Maria wanted to hug him, but he wouldn't have allowed her to. He had taught her to be reserved at work, to hide your emotions. He'd always believed that good leaders hid their feelings, so their subordinates could stay focused on their jobs. When he'd told her that, Maria had thought it made sense, and she still did, but right now, she thought that rule was bullshit.

Larry Moyer walked outside, followed by Michael.

"We should start with his cellphone. Where is it?" Maria said.

"You can't work this case, Maria," Moyer said.

"You can't be serious?" Maria said.

"The vic is your brother," Moyer said.

"He's right. Any defense attorney would have a field day if you interviewed witnesses or touched evidence," Dominic said.

"Nobody asked the retired detective for his opinion, and if you think I'm not in this, you are out of your goddamn mind," Maria said.

Moyer took a long breath before he spoke, a calming technique he used when he was about to confront one of his detectives, tell them something they didn't want to hear. Old timers said Moyer had been famous for his temper and been told he needed to calm down if he wanted to move up. When Maria saw him take in that breath, she knew no matter what she said, he'd never let her near this case.

"I am sympathetic, believe me, I am, but I have a responsibility to run this squad the right way, and we have guard rails in place to protect us from ourselves. You know as well as anyone, a detective has to have emotional control in order to investigate effectively, and nobody, no matter how well trained, no matter how talented, nobody can investigate the death of a family member in a controlled manner. We aren't robots. Nor does anyone expect us to be. And for all those reasons, there is no way you are going to work this case," Moyer said.

"She has essential background info on the vic. I need that knowledge. She'd be a major asset to me," Michael said.

"You can interview her tomorrow, after you're done working the scene," Moyer said.

"We need to go tell your mother anyway," Dominic said and then turned and walked toward the front of the house. Moyer followed close after. They both knew how stubborn she was, and nobody wanted to be here arguing for an hour.

"Before you go, the techs want a DNA sample," Michael said.

"Ruling me out?"

"There were some unwashed glasses in the sink. They want to have some samples to compare them to," Michael said.

Maria nodded and stood up.

"Look, I'll be by tomorrow with the reports and we can go over everything. We'll work it together no matter what the old guys say," Michael said.

Chapter 5

One dead body. So much pain.

Maria could tell her mother, Esperanza, knew something was terribly wrong the minute her husband and daughter came through the door at the same time. Dominic sat her down and told her what had happened. He held her hand as he told her, leaned in so their foreheads touched, so his voice could be low and soft, but she'd still hear him. Maria watched them and wondered what life was like when you spent so much of it with one person. Her parents had just celebrated their thirty-eighth anniversary, and now the man she'd spent her whole adult life with was giving her the worst news a person could ever dread hearing.

Did that make it easier to take? Maria doubted it.

Esperanza stood up and said she was going outside for a cigarette. Her smoking had been the only thing Maria had ever seen her parents fight over, but Dominic wasn't going to argue with her about it now. After Esperanza had walked into the backyard, Dominic looked at Maria and said, "What are you waiting for? Go with her." Not for the first time, Maria wondered why she was so clueless about life at the most important moments.

Her mother didn't even look up as Maria walked outside.

Maria grabbed a chair and dragged it over next to her. Maria reached out for the lit cigarette, and her mother handed it to her. Tears shone on her cheeks. Maria took a drag. The smoke tickled her throat. She wasn't a smoker. Maybe once in a while when she was drinking, but if smoking was how her mother wanted to work her way through this, Maria was game. She handed the cigarette back.

Dominic came to the sliding glass window and slid it halfway open.

"Vino?" He said.

Esperanza shook her head.

Dominic slid the door back shut.

"That's something I've always loved about your father," Esperanza said.

"What?"

"He never tries to fix things through words. Doesn't try to tell me everything is going to be ok. Tomorrow, I'm going to have fifty voicemails from people trying to tell me everything is going to be ok. I won't be able to answer the phone for a week or I'll end up calling them all cabrons and hijos de putas. Then I'll have to call them all back again and apologize and listen to them tell me it's ok. They understand. They don't understand shit," Esperanza said.

Maria had never thought about it before, at least not how her mother described it, but she was right. Her father had never tried to talk her down from anything or change her mind. He'd always just asked her what she thought and let her work through things herself as he listened. He'd always focused on actions. What she could do, what she couldn't do. What the consequences would be on both sides.

"Did you see the body?" Her mother asked.

"Yes."

"And?"

"And what?" Maria asked.

"What the hell do you think? Was he tortured? Did he suffer?"

"He didn't suffer. He probably didn't even see it coming," Maria said.

"Yo soy tu madre, no me mientas," Esperanza said.

"It's the truth. No suffering. No torture," Maria said.

Esperanza started to rock. She was trying to hold the tears back, trying to keep from wailing, but a low hum came from her throat.

Maria put a hand on her mother's shoulder and leaned into her vision.

"We'll find whoever did this. I promise," Maria said.

"Don't you fill me with false hope. When your tio Tomas disappeared, your father looked me right in the face and told me I'd probably never know why or how. I fell in love with your father right there. How could I not? He respected me so much that he didn't lie to me like everyone else. You be like your father."

"Mom, we have a lot more tools now. A lot more ways to find people."

"Don't do that, not ever."

MARIA SAT for a full fifteen minutes in her car out front of her apartment. She was dreading explaining to Carla what had happened. Dreading the tears that were coming, but her dread was wasted. In the apartment, she found a note on the kitchen table from Carla explaining that she had picked up a shift at the Bellagio, where she was a cocktail waitress and would be home later than normal. The note, written in oversized cursive writing in red ink on a yellow legal pad, ordered her not to start any news shows without her. Carla could have sent all this via text, but she thought notes were more thoughtful, and she was right, and Maria felt guilty for dreading seeing her.

After she'd showered and changed, Maria grabbed a bottle of Jameson and a glass and filled it halfway. She sat down on the couch and turned on the television but muted it and sat there drinking. She thought of her brother, him sticking her tongue at her as she sat on her mother's lap, her earliest memory. Him diving off of the roof of a friend's house into a pool and spraying her and all of her friends with water. Him using her window to sneak out of the house because his bedroom was right next to his parent's room, and their father heard everything. Him wrapping their mother's car around a telephone pole and coming home with his face wrapped in gauze. Them watching all the Star Wars movies back to back to back. Her telling him she was gay, and him acting like it was the most natural thing in the world and how grateful she'd been for that reaction.

Was she feeling the right things?

Remembering the right memories?

Should she be angrier?

Sadder?

The front door opening and closing snapped her back. Carla's keys clinked in the bowl by the front door, and Carla bounded around the corner yelling, "Baby, where are you?" She was vibrant, all five feet ten inches of her. Her blonde hair was pulled back in a ponytail that she was pulling a scrunchy off of and shaking out, and her blue eyes absolutely glowed with the excitement of whatever story she had to tell Maria. A story was the last thing Maria could handle, no matter how funny. But instead of telling a story, Carla flopped down on the couch and exaggerated the effort necessary to reach into her pocket of jeans, so she'd have to raise her hips and expose her flat stomach, something that would normally draw all of Maria's attention but tonight just made Maria realize how destroyed she was.

Carla pulled out a yellow one thousand dollar chip and threw it on the table.

"Some guy decided to send you on vacation," Carla said. "A thousand bucks for a smile and drink. How do these rich guys become so rich if they're so stupid?" Carla leaned back into the couch and looked over at Maria, expecting a reaction that wasn't coming.

"Baby, what's the matter?"

"Somebody murdered Tommy."

"Oh my god, come here," Carla said.

Carla reached over and grabbed Maria in both her arms and pulled her across the couch into her lap and wrapped her up and held her tight and for the first time in for as long as Maria could remember she let go and really sobbed.

Chapter 6

Michael looked like he'd slept less than Maria which was not at all.

At the kitchen table, Michael turned on his laptop and flipped the computer around to show a video. Tommy's face was on the screen. His black hair neatly parted, he was wearing a button-down shirt with an American flag tie.

"Do I look like a racist? How's that liberal trope going to work on me? Not so well, amirite? The thing is, when my grandfather came to this country, he did it the right way. He waited his turn. Does it make me a racist to expect these people overrunning our borders to follow the same laws my grandfather did?"

Michael paused the video and looked up at Maria.

"This was what he was watching when he was killed," Michael said.

"He's got hundreds of them. All of them almost the same. That was his niche, the anti-immigration Mexican-American."

"You think that could be what got him killed?" Michael said.

"I doubt it, but Tommy was always hawking something on his YouTube channel. Maybe there's something there, something different from his supposed political views," Maria said.

Michael placed a black flier in front of her. In stark white letters: Climate Coin.

"We found a lot of these in his house. Some type of new climate change friendly cryptocurrency," Michael said.

"He really knew how to hit the sweet spot, didn't he?" Maria picked up the flier. Laughed.

"It flopped. We found some messages from an Anatov who lost a substantial sum of money."

"That sounds much more likely. I'll go talk to Harold. See what he can tell me about it."

"Want me to go with?" Michael said.

"Harold will probably be more open if I go by myself, especially if he and Tommy were up to something really shady," Maria said.

"Fine, I'll try to get a line on Anatov and see what I can find out."

"What did the techs get from the scene?" Maria said.

"So far, not much. They're still processing fingerprints and DNA samples, but nothing looks out of the ordinary. The canvas came up with squat. The houses on either side of Tommy's were empty. The other two houses, nobody saw or heard anything. TOD was estimated to be between 2pm and 4pm," Michael said.

"Who called it in?" Maria asked.

"Food delivery. Directions said to leave the food in the backyard on the table by the pool if no one answered the door. Driver came around and dropped the food on the table and saw him through the window," Michael said.

"I assume the driver has been ruled out," Maria said.

"They tested him for gunshot residue and took his prints and DNA to compare to the scene. So far, his story checks out. Besides, he's nineteen years old and seemed genuinely broken up."

"What about the keychain?"

"Techs say it was placed postmortem, no blood on top, just on the bottom. The keys were his house keys, nothing out of the ordinary."

"Placed after the shooting?"

"That's what the tech said, but maybe they screwed up."

Michael put the laptop in his backpack and gathered the papers together. He looked at her and opened his mouth to say something but changed his mind.

"What's up?" Maria said.

"Didn't all that anti-immigrant stuff bother you with your mom being Mexican and all?"

"Everything he said was bullshit. My grandfather died in a car accident in Yuma when my mother was twelve. He had crossed the border to work on a farm and surely didn't have papers. It was all just a scam. And while I didn't like him being a scammer, he was my brother, and he never wavered in supporting me, so I've never wavered in supporting him."

"Fair enough." Michael slung the backpack over his shoulder and turned to go.

"Moyer tell you not to talk to me?" Maria said.

Michael stopped. Looked over his shoulder and smiled.

"He told me he knew I was an intelligent guy and wouldn't allow anything to happen that could damage the integrity of the investigation. I didn't ask him exactly where he wanted me drawing lines," Michael said. "Speaking of which, he's going to be pissed if he finds out you're interviewing witnesses," Michael said.

"I'm just going to talk with an old friend. Nothing more," Maria said.

HAROLD LOOKED like his soul had been ripped out.

His hair hung down over his face. His skin was a pasty white like he hadn't seen the sun in weeks, and he looked heavier than the last time Maria had seen him. He was sitting at the kitchen table in a pair of jeans and a white t-shirt with some obscure band name on it. The type of band that only got played by their friends on Spotify. It wasn't even noon, but he was already hammered. The bottle of vodka on the table was hall full. The glass next to it was empty, and he looked to be on the border of screaming or crying but just couldn't decide which way to go.

"I know, I know, I don't look so hot," Harold said.

"Are you supposed to?" Maria said.

"Your dad, he called me last night. He wanted me to know what happened, how it happened, he wanted me to know. Told me I was Tommy's best friend, and I should know exactly what happened, and I just, I just can't get out of my head, how calm his voice was," Harold said.

"What did he say?" Maria asked.

"I thought I was listening to an episode of Law and Order where everyone is sitting in the Lieutenant's office talking about a case. He didn't even say Tommy, when he described the scene, he said white male, late thirties. What is that?"

"A defense mechanism. Falling back on his training in order to keep from falling apart. I did the same thing. I processed the scene like any other scene. Was the only way I could keep from going to shit right in front of everybody," Maria said.

"I don't ever want to be able to do that. I'll go to shit. Let 'em think what they want."

"Harold, we don't have much to go on. Anything you know that we might not?" Maria asked.

"You think I have a clue? I'd have already told you if I did. I'd a told your father last night, but I got no idea. I hadn't seen Tommy in weeks. At least a month, maybe two. We'd talked via text, but he was caught up in his YouTube channel and whatever other shit he was working on and we just hadn't talked," Harold said.

"There was something about a cryptocurrency, a Russian guy, Anatov, lost a bunch of money. Could that be it?"

Harold poured some more vodka into his glass.

"Anatov? Never met him. Never heard Tommy talk about him. I mean, he'd been distant lately, you know? He wasn't like he used to be. I can't remember the last time we went out to a club or even a damn brunch."

"That doesn't sound like my brother at all," Maria said.

"I know, right? Tommy loved being around people, and then he didn't. I never could get a straight answer out of him about why he changed. Shit, who knows, maybe I'm just making something out of nothing. Maybe he just got older," Harold said.

"Did you guys have a fight?"

"I wish we had. Then I'd be able to understand what happened and I could let go of the feeling all of this is my fault somehow. But there wasn't no fight, no argument, no nothing. He just became distant. And never explained why to me. I don't know what hurts more. Him dying or him disappearing on me these last few months. I mean, we were inseparable for so long and then bang, it was over. How does that even happen?" Harold said.

Maria's phone buzzed.

A message from Michael: *Something came up. Moyer wants us both in. ASAP.*

Chapter 7

Las Vegas 1983

A problem free shift. Was it possible?

Dominic Varela couldn't believe his luck because the 1980s was no one's idea of an easy time to be a cop. Especially in Vegas, a city of empty hotels and aging singers. There wasn't much to draw tourists here anymore, and the streets and the people knew. Las Vegas was sure it's best days were behind it, and a city without hope could be a vicious place.

Dominic turned right onto Rexford. He liked to cruise the side streets on his way back to the station. The chances of anyone being stupid enough to do something arrestable on a main street while not zero, also wasn't all that high, and just the last week he had stopped a pair of men trying to break into a house less than a block from here. They'd tried to claim it was their house, but who uses a sledge-hammer to knock in their own door? That's what he was thinking about as he turned onto Rexford.

Then Serena had come running out into the street screaming about the Desert Saint.

The thing was, every cop, hell everybody in Vegas, knew who the Desert Saint was. He'd started by killing Anthony Scarvale, an attorney for Benny Binion. Anthony was a tall looker who was often photographed with showgirls entering high-end restaurants. He straddled Vegas's mob past and what people hoped would be its corporate future, the kind of guy whose rough edges were sanded enough to go back and forth between polite society and the mobsters. His cleaning lady found him face down on the floor.

Two .22 bullets to the head and a call girl flier laying on top of his left hand.

First everybody figured it for a mob hit, but word got passed around that not only was it not a mob hit but also Anthony's buddies were offering a substantial reward for the name of the killer. The homicide detectives joked openly that finding Anthony's killer could lead to a promotion or a nice new house but not both.

The investigation was comprehensive and brutal. The detectives were pulling twenty hour shifts and pushing the limits of the law and their own consciences, and the mob guys, well, they didn't have consciences. An ex-business partner of Anthony who'd had a falling out over a proposed apartment building was found dead in the trunk of his own car. According to the streets, he hadn't known anything, but that hadn't been figured out until it was too late.

After about a month, the spectacle wore off. People returned to worrying about whether or not Vegas's best days were behind it. Crime was still all over the papers, just not Anthony's, and even the mobsters' arms were tired of swinging crowbars. The homicide detectives were now commiserating on how none of them had gotten either a new house or a promotion, and people figured that the mobsters must have done it and all the leg breaking, well, it was almost as good a show as when Elvis performed at the International in 1969.

Then the priest got killed, in a confessional.

Two .22s to the forehead and a Stages of the Cross pamphlet placed on his left hand.

Anthony's murder had been sensational because Anthony was sensational, but the killing of the priest, Father Michael McGuire, was a made for the front page event, and when the ballistics report came back matching the slugs from Anthony's killing to the priest's, well, Vegas hadn't been this intrigued with a murder since Bugsy Siegel took three to the face in Beverly Hills.

The mayor was a fairly devout Roman Catholic, at least as devout as a man could be, being not only a politician but a politician in Vegas. As much pressure to make a case as had been felt for Anthony was multiplied by ten for the priest's case. Everybody wanted results, but none were coming. No suspects. No leads. No nothing. Just a vague feeling that this thing wasn't over by a long shot.

Four weeks later, a pimp, Mississippi Johnny, was found by his mother. Two .22s to the side of the head and a pack of Pall Mall placed on his left-hand post mortem. Ballistics were a match to the priest and Anthony. While most of the cops could have cared less about a dead pimp, the politicians were worried about a public panic, and with good reason, because when the press interviewed one of Mississippi Johnny's girls, a southern blonde named Delilah, whose left and right eyes had been blackened by Mississippi Johnny not two days before his killing, the last remaining ingredient for a full-fledged panic arrived: a catchy name.

Reporter: Who do you think killed Johnny?

Delilah: No idea, but whoever he is, he's a Saint.

And the name was going to stick, but the Saint didn't have enough of a Vegas feel, so the next day, the headline read, The Desert Saint Kills Again, a nod to the buried bodies surrounding Vegas that would eventually be discovered by excavation crews building new apartment complexes. The national news networks started sniffing around as did the FBI, and the homicide detectives instead of joking about promotions were placing bets on who'd get demoted first.

Still, the case went nowhere.

Then two weeks after Johnny, then a nurse, Muriel Williams, was killed.. Two .22 bullets to the head, but no shells left by her side. A newspaper left on her left hand. The change in M.O. bothered the detectives but not the press. If Muriel, a woman nobody had anything bad to say about, could be killed, well, anyone could.

Then a week later, Muriel's husband, Donald, was found dead

right where they'd found Muriel. Donald had changed the carpet but not his address. On his left hand, a business card for an ammo and gun store, and by his body, two .22 caliber shells that matched the shells from Anthony, Father Michael, and Mississippi Johnny.

Five victims, and a killer who was heating up.

The Desert Saint was all anyone could talk about. So when Serena came running out of the house screaming about the Saint and waving her arms at Dominic, he knew exactly what she was talking about. Making a bust like that could move a cop out of the patrol car and up into the detective ranks pretty quickly, so Dominic pulled out his sidearm and headed around the house to where Serena said the Desert Saint had run.

He was halfway to the backyard when he realized Serena was following him.

"What are you doing? Get back," Dominic said.

"I ain't staying out front by myself. What if he comes around?"

"Run down the block. There's a gas station on the corner, you'll be safe there," Dominic said.

Serena didn't seem sure.

"If I find this guy and lose the gunfight, do you really want to be standing right behind me?" Dominic said.

That convinced her, and she turned and ran as fast as a woman in a miniskirt and stilettos could run. At the sidewalk, she pulled the stilettos off and took off around the corner, and Dominic turned toward the back of the house.

That's when he saw the gun pointed right at him.

———

"HE SHOT YOU?" Maria said.

"It was a scratch," Dominic said and pointed at his shoulder where Maria knew there was a scar, a jagged line across the upper arm. "But it felt like someone took an ax to my arm. I let loose a few, but he had already moved back around the corner. I figured he used the time I needed to get my wits about me, to go around and head across the street. The backyard had a big fence. Maybe he climbed it, but it's a lot more likely that he went around. Serena had been right about not wanting to be out front."

Dominic, Maria, Michael, and Moyer were all sitting around a conference table in the police station. The ballistics report for Tommy's murder had come back a match to the Desert Saint shootings. On a corkboard, photos of the previous victims had been tacked up. As he spoke, Dominic had gotten up and gone photo by photo, as if looking at the faces brought back the memories in a way that the words of a case file couldn't.

"He disappeared after that. We figured the close call spooked him," Dominic said.

"Why couldn't this be about money?" Maria said.

"So why does a killer come back after almost forty years?" Michael said.

"Seems obvious to me. Revenge," Moyer said.

"You think he targeted Tommy because he's Dominic's son," Michael said.

"That makes no sense," Dominic said.

"You know how publicity hungry they are. You spooked him. It's probably been eating at this guy for decades, and now he knows that the end is near. He's come back to get revenge on the guy who stopped him," Moyer said.

"But I didn't stop him. He got away," Dominic said.

"You did something worse. You showed him that he wasn't the all powerful hunter that he thought he was. Who could he possibly hate more?" Moyer said.

"You do bring out the best in people," Maria said.

"We don't even know if he's alive," Dominic said.

"We know the bullets match, and we think know his motive, which means that we probably know his next victim," Moyer said.

"Who?" Maria asked.

"You," Moyer said.

"Get out of here with that," Maria said.

"No, it makes sense. Everything he says tracks," Michael said.

"We're going to have to get you a protective detail," Moyer said.

"You going to wrap me in bubble wrap next? I'll be fine," Maria said.

"We can't take any chances," Moyer said.

"Take any chances? All the dead are civilians. You really think some creaky old guy is going to get the drop on me," Maria said.

"Might be more likely some old guy than someone young," Michael said.

"He's right," Moyer said.

"Right about what? My inability to protect myself?" Maria said.

"Nobody doubts your ability-" Michael said.

"That's exactly what you're doing right now," Maria said.

"We just have to cover all the bases, prepare for the worst. This isn't about you," Moyer said.

"She can protect herself. She'll be fine," Dominic said.

Michael and Moyer looked like they wanted to keep arguing, but Dominic was more than just Maria's father. He was the one cop every cop up to the Chief respected. If Dominic said that she'd be fine, what right did they really have to argue? Maria couldn't decide what pissed her off more, that they felt like they had to protect her or the fact they were backing down to her father rather than to her.

"Are you assholes done pretending it's the 50s and you have to save the lady in distress? How about we do some real police work? How about that?" Maria said.

"She's right," Dominic said. "What would cause a killer to start up again?"

"Do we know that he stopped?" Michael said.

"Well, he wasn't dropping bodies around here," Dominic said.

"He had to have some kind of trigger. Maybe he was married and his wife croaked. Freed him up to get the revenge he's been thinking about," Moyer said.

"Or maybe he's on the clock himself," Michael said.

"What do you mean?" Dominic said.

"Maybe he's got a terminal diagnosis and is tying up loose ends," Michael said.

"That could be it," Dominic said.

"Good luck getting into anyone's medical records," Maria said.

"I know a guy who survived cancer and still goes to those support meetings. Maybe I can ask him if he's seen anyone new who fits the profile," Michael said.

"It's much more likely he got busted for something and just got out," Maria said.

"I'll get someone to look through newly released convicts, and Michael, you keep on working Tommy's case like any normal case. There has to be some physical evidence that will lead us to this guy. It's not the 80s anymore. Maria, while you can't work on Tommy's case, nobody can object to you going back through the old case file and seeing if you can find anything we missed," Moyer said.

"Are any of the detectives who worked the case still alive?" Maria asked.

"Jack Wilson. He lives down in Henderson," Moyer said.

"Jack broke me in, you'll like him," Dominic said.

"What about the witness? The one who ran out of the house," Maria asked.

Moyer pawed through some papers on the table. He picked one up, looked at it, and handed it across the table to Maria.

"Serena Alivari. We have an address for an assisted living home off of Valley View," Moyer said.

"I'll go talk to Jack and then Serena," Maria said.

"Maybe I should go with you," Michael said.

"For what? To interview an ex-hooker on social security? You worried she's going to beat me to death with her cane?" Maria said.

MARIA HEADED FOR HER CAR, and Michael followed. She gave him a look to let him know she was in no mood for a conversation, but he didn't seem to notice. He was in his own world, his head was down, chin almost touching his chest, as he walked. When they were outside, he sped up so that he was walking alongside her.

"Fucked up development, huh? Did not see this one coming."

"Which development? The one where you guys treat me like I'm a seven-year-old? No, I definitely saw that one coming," Maria said.

Michael stopped. His face scrunched up, and he looked back

toward the station as if he couldn't recall what Maria was talking about.

Maria kept walking. When she got angry like this, she was liable to say whatever was on her mind, and she knew it. Her car was only a few spaces away. If she could get in and drive off, she wouldn't end up owing anyone an apology.

"Are you talking about the protective detail?" Michael said.

Maria took a breath. A deep breath. Two more spots to the car.

"Moyer was right about that," Michael said.

She wasn't going to make it.

Maria spun around. Michael had been jogging to catch up to her and had to stop short so he wouldn't barrel into her.

"How exactly was Moyer right about me needing a protective detail?" Maria said.

"Why else would this guy come back after so long if it isn't revenge against your father?"

"What does that have to do with me needing protection?" Maria said.

"The guy shoots people in the head," Michael said.

"So what? How is that different from any other day when we go out to do our job?"

"When we go out to do our job, the trouble is in front of us. We go looking for it. This guy could walk up to you in a store and bam, it's over," Michael said.

"He could do that just as easily with a protective detail," Maria said.

"This isn't about you or anybody doubting you. It's about wanting to make sure you're safe."

"I don't need you to keep me safe. Last I checked, it was me who saved you from a pine box last year. And we were both facing the trouble then, focused on what was going on. At least one of us was," Maria said.

Michael winced. Maria was hitting him with a kidney shot, and she knew it, and she felt bad about it as soon as the words left her mouth. They'd been looking for a suspect in a string of kidnappings, some of which ended with murder. Michael had allowed himself to be distracted momentarily by a woman with a walker who was trying to get into a store, and the suspect had come around the corner, made them, and opened fire on Michael. The suspect missed the first shot, and Maria hadn't let him get off a second. The first and only time she'd fired her weapon in the line of duty. Blaming Michael for that poorly timed lapse in concentration wasn't fair though. Anybody would have gotten distracted.

"Well, I'm glad you played that card over something so small rather than saving it for later," Michael said. He turned around and headed back inside.

Maria felt like an asshole, which pissed her off even more. She was going to have to apologize. She knew it, but she wasn't doing it today. There was only so much one woman could handle in a single day, and apologizing to her partner after he hadn't backed her up was a bit too much for this day.

Chapter 8

Las Vegas 1983

Sometimes the real victim isn't the corpse.

Jack Wilson stepped out of his unmarked car and started across the Our Lady of Eternal Sorrow parking lot. The asphalt looked like it had been laid not but a month earlier, and the white lines demarcating the spaces practically shone in the sunlight, but heat waves shimmied up off the black surface as if trying to remind the churchgoer what was waiting for him if he went astray. Jack wasn't a churchgoer nor was he a fan of asphalt parking lots in Nevada in August. What was wrong with dirt?

Sometimes progress wasn't all it was cracked up to be.

Jack took in the amount of cars, the news vans half a block away, the gathering crowd of onlookers, and then he stepped inside and saw Father Michael McGuire's legs poking out of the confessional booth. His feet were clad in leather sandals and underneath his vestments, bare legs. On his right ankle, three dots, an Indian ink tattoo, and blood, black and sticky, against the wooden floor. The remnants of a human being always had a tendency to drive away whatever small thing Jack was stewing about, and this day was no different.

Inside the confessional, the priest was laying face down but his left arm was reaching up, the hand resting against a ledge like he'd been trying to raise himself up when he'd been shot. Not likely, the body falls in weird ways, but the impression lingered. Blood dripped down a portrait of Jesus in the manger and pooled around the priest's face and ran out the doorway. Maybe we had souls, maybe we didn't, but if a person was inclined to look, they should start in our blood because if we were made up of anything, it was blood.

Steven Brooks, eleven years old, was waiting for Jack in the rectory kitchen, an open can of Pepsi sitting on the table in front of him untouched. Steven was trying to hold it together, but the effort was getting to him. He wasn't but four and a half feet tall, maybe seventy pounds, just a little wispy thing whose brown hair was running a little long and hanging down over his eyes, and this kid was broken, Jack could sense it. While some people like to say that everyone has their fair share of problems in life, Jack, he didn't know if that was really true. He felt like plenty of people had it a lot harder than others, and this boy was a good example of that.

Children are taught that the church was a place of worship and love and to have that shattered by a random act of violence by a faceless killer, how in the hell is a child supposed to overcome that? Worse, Steven's father was not much of a father, and everybody knew that the priest had taken on a mentoring role for the boy, a stability that the boy's home life didn't have, and now that was over, and the last thing Steven would remember of the man who had been so kind to him was a corpse. As Steven answered Jack's questions, Jack knew the image of the dead priest in the confessional was going to be stuck in that kid's head forever, and he was never going to be right again. After Jack heard his story, he reached over to give him a hug, and the boy practically climbed into his lap and started to sob, and before too long he was just caterwauling, a high keen, more animal than boy.

Steven had looked up at him through those brown bangs and said, "Are you going to catch whoever did this to Father Michael?"

"Damn right I am," Jack said, without even thinking about it.

But what cop didn't think they were going to get the guy? If he didn't think he was going to catch him, shit, why even try? But that time was the last time Jack answered that question in the affirmative because Jack never caught a sniff of the Desert Saint and as the bodies continued to pile on and on, he became damn sure he never would either, and Jack wondered what his failure did to that boy. Not only was the church a place of death but the police couldn't even catch the killer.

How does a child survive double blows like that?

Jack kept tabs on the boy, from afar, ran him from time to time to see if he was showing up in the system, and a few years later, there the boy was, now sixteen, arrested for possession of stolen property. Jack had a hard time believing that the slight eleven-year-old of his memory had already become a hardened criminal, so he talked to the arresting officers, and they saw it how Jack figured, a kid on the edge, a kid who could go either way, so Jack made his way over to the boy's house, now a tall string bean with a green mohawk and a mother at wits end on how to deal with him, and Jack tried to sit him down and talk to him.

But something was different about the boy.

An underlying rage, like magma bubbling up from beneath a volcano, the boy barely looked at him, rolled his eyes when Jack talked about throwing away his potential, laughed when Jack said that he had a mother who cared for him, and then the strangest thing, when Jack was done, the boy, well not really a boy anymore, the teenager with the green mohawk leaned forward and put his hand on Jack's knee.

"You really are one of the good ones, and I've never forgotten that. But this world don't have many like you," Steven said.

Maybe Jack shouldn't have, but he got them to drop the case against Steven. He hoped the reprieve would give the boy a chance to do something, but Jack had a feeling it was hopeless, and it was. What followed was a long series of arrests for all types of things, assault, breaking and entering, drug possession, solicitation, Steven was the Olympian of low-level felonies. Jack wouldn't get them to drop the charges anymore, but it was known, if Steven got arrested, call Jack, and Jack would get up whatever hour of the night, head on down to the holding cell and talk to Steven through the bars.

What struck Jack most, and what he figured kept him coming back arrest after arrest after arrest, was that Steven never asked Jack to get him out. He'd just smile and lean against the bars and ask Jack how he was. Tell Jack stories about friends doing stupid things or random road trips he'd taken to California, or movie stars he'd seen at penthouse parties where they passed young men around like joints. Jack had a hard time with the gays, at least he had before, and maybe he should have tried to counsel Steven to give up that life, but Jack didn't really think Steven would listen, besides he felt like Steven just needed someone to talk to, so Jack just sat there listening and let Steven be whoever he was, and in the process, Jack saw a young man in all his flawed and tortured humanity. Kind of hard to hate something when there's a human being behind the label.

That all stopped though when Steven stuck a .45 in his mouth and pulled the trigger.

The motel they found him in was a rundown place along the side of I-15, not too far from the main police station. Steven had his feet up on a coffee table whose white surface had been lined with burn marks. He could have been a man relaxing in front of a television except for the brain and blood splattered across an aerial photo of the Grand Canyon hanging on the wall. As Jack stood there looking at Steven's corpse, he knew it was time to retire. A human could only take so much death in one lifetime, and Jack had seen as many dead bodies as he could take.

Steven would be the last one.

He wasn't listed as one of the Desert Saint's victims, but he should have been.

⊏⊐

MARIA LEANED back in the rocking chair and looked Jack over. She had liked him the minute she'd pulled up to the curb and seen him sitting on the porch, a big cowboy hat on his head, a cigar between his teeth.

"When all those things with the priests touching boys came out a while back, I of course wondered," Jack said.

"Steven never hinted at anything like that?" Maria asked.

"There were rumors at the time. But I didn't pay them no mind. I was raised to think priests were saintly, and I tend to change my views slowly. Sometimes it's a good part of my character, other times, it causes more trouble than it's worth," Jack said.

"But Stephen never said anything to you? Never hinted?" Maria said.

"There was a suicide note. It said: 'I'm looking forward to kicking his ass in hell." Jack winced as he spoke, and Maria knew he was both on that porch and in that hotel room seeing Steven's body, and she felt a little bad for putting him through this.

"Could have been a lot of people he was talking about," Maria said.

"You don't have to sugarcoat it. I'm old, not sensitive," Jack said.

"I don't really know how figuring that out earlier would have helped," Maria said.

"For one thing, I would have considered Steven and his family a suspect. Might have changed my relationship with the boy, and maybe that'd a been better for me in the long run, but I still can't figure Steven for the crime. All those arrests, nothing for violence. If he had been capable of murder at ten, he'd have killed someone else later. Only person he was capable of hurting was himself. Might want to talk to the sister though, she probably would know," Jack said.

"Sister?"

"Only other person at his funeral. Supposedly there was another brother too, but I never met him," Jack said.

"What about the Desert Saint? How long did you work the case?"

"Few weeks. When he killed that couple a few weeks apart, they started a task force and seeing as how I hadn't made any progress, they left me off. Told me the case needed fresh eyes. The FBI sent some people and whatnot," Jack said.

"That must have pissed you off," Maria said.

"Hell, no. I was grateful. All the political pressure on that case and no evidence. Tell you what, the Desert Saint killed more than a few careers, but I was in and out early, so I came through unscathed. Getting shoved aside was one of the best things ever happened to me," Jack said.

"And they never found a solid suspect?" Maria said.

"They had a ton of suspects, but nothing ever panned out. I had a theory I think might have been what really kept me off that task force. I thought the Desert Saint was a woman. A .22 is a small gun and none of those scenes had signs of forced entry or a struggle. How was this person getting in? I thought a woman was more likely to be able to charm her way into people's homes. Hell, ol Anthony Scarvale was a known skirt chaser who had a rep for getting aggressive if the woman wasn't as interested as he was. So I figured it for a woman, but everybody thought that was just plumb crazy. One of them FBI guys practically laughed in my face," Jack said.

"You thought the killings were revenge killings?"

"I didn't know what to think. But in hindsight, doesn't seem any of the victims were angels with the exception of the nurse. I met your father right before that task force started up. He had a theory that the woman hadn't been killed by the Desert Saint. We all had our suspicions, you know? Why would the M.O. change? Where were the shells? So your dad, who was just a patrolman but obviously had ambitions to move up, he went running around to ammo stores on his own time with the husband's picture and sure enough, the husband had bought some ammo for a .22 from a store on the other side of town from where he lived. But the husband supposedly didn't have a gun. So I tell your dad that he done good, and I head over to go for a run at the husband. I knew he and the wife had issues, and he was supposedly a jealous kind of man, so I go there and what do I find? A dead husband with two .22s lying right next to him."

"So you figure the Desert Saint killed him for being a copycat?"

"Just about the only thing that makes sense. You see, we didn't know much about serial killers back then, but whoever the Saint was, he wasn't publicity hungry. No calls to the press. No calls to the police. But I figure it had to be bothersome to have someone pretending to be you so he could kill his own wife, wouldn't it?"

"What about the tokens?"

"The things left by the body? Your guess is as good as mine what connection they had. We all figured it was how the killer was picking his victims but the connections for most of them were too tenuous to help much."

Maria folded up her notepad. The sister, she'd have to find her. If she was still alive. Someone who hadn't been interviewed before might be useful. Or maybe not, maybe Moyer just had her running around in circles so she wouldn't be chasing around after Michael. Either way, it felt good to be doing something, rather than just sitting on her hands.

And Jack had given her color the case files couldn't.

"Got to tell you, the whole world was on fire back then. It was the 80s. Crack cocaine was everywhere, people were getting murdered left and right, I mean, Las Vegas was thirty percent of the size as it is now and had the same amount of murders as we do now. I listen to the news. People are complaining about the war on crime, the war on drugs, they didn't have to sift through the bodies. We had a war on us, shit, going out on a shift was no joke which was another reason I took a shine to your father. He could handle himself in the streets. I started requesting him whenever I was out looking to make a dangerous arrest. Wanted him at my back when I went through doors. That was a man you could depend on. Tore my heart in two when I saw that his son, your brother, was killed. This world, some-times, it just don't make no sense. I can't decide if that's better or worse. Reckon it just is what it is. That sure as shit don't help, but then again, some things, nothing helps, does it?" Jack said.

"No, not really," Maria said.

"I don't envy what you're going through, but I do envy the time you live in. When I had a badge, I could only investigate half the damn crimes that came in. If it was mob related or tied to one of the big casinos. Forget about it. Shit, we couldn't even go into Binion's place. It was definitely disappointing after growing up believing being a cop was an honorable thing and then realizing that was only in the movies. People look back on the past like it was heavenly. They're just kidding themselves because they don't want to admit what it was really like," Jack said.

Chapter 9

This had to be a waste of time, didn't it?

Glory Days assisted living home was a one-story building that looked like a cross between a motel and a hospital. The woman at the front desk pointed her towards the back where she said Serena was playing cards with her friends. There was only one group playing cards: four women, one of whom was in a wheelchair. The forty-year-old mugshot Maria had seen wasn't much use telling her which one of the women was Serena, so she walked up and asked.

"Hi, I'm detective Maria Varela. Which one of you lovely ladies is Serena Alivari?"

"She's dead." One of the ladies said.

"The aide told me she was back here," Maria said.

"The woman or the man?" the second woman said.

"The woman," Maria said.

"She's always high," the third woman said.

"Serena isn't in any trouble. I just need to speak with her," Maria said.

"Can you not hear?" the third woman said.

"We told you she's dead," the first woman said.

"Gonorrhea," the second woman said.

"In her left eye," the third woman said.

"Terrible way to go," the first woman said.

Maria turned her attention to the one woman who hadn't spoken, the woman in the wheelchair.

"They're just full of it, aren't they, Serena?" Maria said.

"They ain't got much to say, but they sure do love to talk," Serena said.

The women laughed a little too loud, and Maria figured she was the most excitement they'd gotten in a few weeks.

"It's such a nice day. Why don't I take you for a walk?" Maria said.

MARIA WHEELED Serena outside and stopped the wheelchair near a table. She sat down facing Serena and pulled out her notepad. Serena didn't seem surprised by Maria showing up, and Maria wondered if that lack of concern for talking to the police was left over from her youth as a hooker or a sign of some type of cognitive decline that would prevent Serena from being helpful.

"I'm not senile," Serena said.

"I-"

"I see you looking me over like you're trying to figure out if I'm going to hold up a conversation or shit myself right in front of you," Serena said.

"Do people look at you like that a lot?" Maria asked.

"Only the assholes," Serena said.

"You are a pistol, ain't ya?" Maria said.

"So what is it that you want to ask me about?" Serena said.

"I want to talk to you about the Desert Saint."

"Why would you be interested in that? People dying every day. What are you worried about people who've been dead forty years for?" Serena said.

"Humor me. You saw him, didn't you?"

LAS VEGAS *1983*

47

Serena Alivari was pissed.

She didn't want to be stuck outside on a cold ass night like tonight. Weren't no customers cruising Fremont. Weren't no tourists crowding town. Las Vegas was dead, and colder than a witch's tit, but Tommy had told her not to come back home before daylight. And Milena? Where was she at? Serena hadn't seen her all damn night. Tommy probably had her at home, chilling on the couch, feet up, under some blankets, watching a movie. Why did Milena get to be home when Serena had to work? What kind of bullshit was that?

Tommy could smack her around all he wanted. She was going home.

They all needed to go somewhere new. There weren't no money around here anymore. This girl she knew, a Loretta or a Lolita, or some such shit like that had just come from Los Angeles, and she was heading back. Said Vegas was cold and dead, but in LA, some nights you got lucky and ended up in a movie star's car. He might want you to do his whole crew, but he'd pay good and always go first. That's what that girl said, maybe she was full of shit, but better to chase a dream date in LA than freeze her ass off in Vegas.

Serena turned the corner to the house Tommy had them staying at, him, Milena, Serena, and Lonnie. There'd been two other girls, but they'd taken off a couple of weeks ago, said Tommy wasn't worth nothing, said he didn't show them how to hustle, was too busy being sweet on Milena, said sure she was a moneymaker, but they could all be money makers if he'd teach them the way he'd taught Milena.

Serena didn't know if Tommy'd ever really taught Milena anything or if Milena was just prettier than everyone else, but Serena thought those two other girls were partly right, Tommy wasn't worth much as a man. Those other two had run off to a tall brother named Pay Ray, and Serena was wondering if she should go too. She heard Pay Ray's girls ate good. Supposedly, he had them all living in a suite atop the Nugget. Shit, she'd stand outside in the cold as late as he wanted if she was eating and sleeping like a queen.

Half a block from the house, Serena slowed down a bit. Tommy wasn't the type to lay hands for no reason. He always gave fair warning, and if you do this again, you're going to feel it. Serena had tried it out a few times, come in a little earlier than she was supposed to, hid some money, things like that, just testing Tommy out, and he'd always given the warning, the a ver niña, he liked to switch into Spanish when he really wanted her to pay attention, a ver niña, don't play with me like that, he'd say, and he'd come real close to her, pressing her up against the wall like he was going to spread her legs and do her right there with all the other girls watching, but that's what he did when Serena made him happy, when she came home with more money than anyone else, and he'd shower her with kisses and screw her in front of the others and they'd know she was his favorite that day and their faces would screw up with jealousy, but if he was angry he'd switch it up as he drew close and pinned her against the wall with his forearm, pressed just enough she had to gasp for breath, just enough that the first spurt of fear came, and he pressed his face right up against hers and said, the next time, it's going to hurt.

So Serena had tested him by doing it the next time, just to see.

He hadn't been lying.

Tommy doubled her over by punching her right in the stomach, pulled her hair back and held her by the neck against the wall until she was sure she was going to die, and then, just as she thought she'd never draw another breath, he pulled back and looked her in the face, a ver niña, next time maybe I can't get control in time. Then he got sweet, told her how disappointed she'd made him, how he arranged everything so she'd be happy and now here she was, ungrateful for everything he'd done. He wanted to know how she could do that to him after he found this nice house they all lived in and made sure everyone ate well, made sure to get her out of jail when vice swept her up, made sure she was safe and now she was going against him after all the work he'd put in. By the time he was done talking, Serena couldn't decide what felt worse, his disappointment or the bruising on her neck.

She'd never told Tommy that she'd seen her grandfather who'd been dead ten years just before Tommy had stopped squeezing, a hallucination from too little oxygen or the doorway to the other side,

Serena didn't know and didn't want to find out, so she'd been on her best behavior for damn near six months now, but tonight, she'd had enough. Tommy was just going to have to let her come home, and if he didn't, if he forced her to stay outside in this short little skirt on this cold ass night with no customers then she'd just have to go find Pay Ray and see if he treated his girls better.

She used her key to open the front door and walked inside. She heard the television on in the living room, canned laughter from some sitcom.

"Tommy, you home?"

She stepped into the hallway. What she saw next was the kind of thing that never leaves a person. Tommy was on his knees, face to the wall, and a gun was pressed to the back of his head. The gun was small and black, and the person holding the gun had a fedora and a trench-coat and a ski mask and black gloves.

Serena opened her mouth to scream but nothing came out.

The Desert Saint smacked Tommy in the back of the head with the gun and then aimed it down the hallway at Serena. She put her hands up over her face and turned back into the foyer, and she slipped and fell down hard, goddamn stilettos.

Footsteps pounded down the hallway.

Serena scrambled to get to her feet, but she fell again, and a sharp pain ran up her leg. She was breathing so heavy, on the verge of sobs, and she was so scared that she just surrendered, laid there on the floor waiting for the person to come and finish her off. This life had been so hard, her mother dying when she was five, her father behaving in a way a father never should, maybe this person ending it would be ok, maybe this life wasn't worth fighting for anymore. For what? So she could find another man like Tommy who'd beat her when she didn't do what he said when she didn't make enough money, when she said the wrong thing because she was tired.

Was this life really so important to hold on to?

But the Desert Saint never came for her.

And when Serena finally calmed down enough to come back to herself, she realized the Desert Saint was gone, out the back door, and Serena ran out the front, and she saw the police car coming down the street, and she'd never been so happy to see a policeman before or since.

———

"SO HE COULD HAVE SHOT you but chose not to?" Maria said.

"Why would he shoot me? He was after pimps not working girls, and he didn't stop like the press said," Serena said.

"Why do you say that?"

"Because pimps kept disappearing. Hell, Tommy disappeared a few months later. I told the police the Desert Saint got him. Had to be. A couple of years later I ran into one of Pay Ray's girls and she said he disappeared too."

"Couldn't those men have just decided to take off?" Maria said.

"Honey, when a man can take all your money and have sex with you whenever he wants, you really think he going to just up and leave? The man don't exist that just walks away from that."

"Do you remember when Tommy disappeared?"

"Valentine's Day, 1984. Best damn Valentine's Day gift I ever did receive. When Tommy didn't come home, I was free, and I knew it, and I put on my best outfit, and I went out dancing like a regular old girl, not some girl walking the street, just a regular ol girl looking to find herself a real man, and I met my husband, Earl, that night, and I moved in with him not three days later and stayed with him until he died last year. They called that man the Desert Saint for a reason darling, he freed more than a few of us. Maybe a lot of them girls weren't ready for the big change, but I was, and I did."

That date, Valentine's Day 1984, tugged at something in Maria's memory, but she pushed it aside and refocused on Serena. She was having a hard time reconciling the white-haired woman in the wheelchair with the streetwalker in stilettos.

"You have a whole raging river of thoughts crossing behind those eyes, but your face is blanker than a cloud. You should play poker," Serena said.

"You said there was a Milena and a Lonnie who lived with you as well?"

"Milena was a Mexican like Tommy, and Lonnie was a tall blonde from Texas. I haven't seen either of them since I walked out of that house," Serena said.

"Do you know their last names?"

"Nobody had much use for last names back then. Hell, who knows if their first names were their real names. Everybody was always coming and going, and we lived together but you wouldn't exactly call us friends, co-workers I guess, but people in that life have secrets and one of those things you keep secret is your name, and that's how it was. I thought I might a seen Milena years later at a shopping mall, but you know, people change when they get older and I didn't look too close. Could a been her, could a been some other Mexican. Lord knows Vegas is full of Mexicans. Why you so interested in all of this, anyway?" Serena said.

"Every now and then we give important old cases a rerun to see if we can find anything that previous detectives missed."

"Honey, I'm old, not stupid. You wouldn't be re-interviewing witnesses over some redo when you could be testing DNA or something else, god knows what other new technology you all have. No, this must be something serious. The Desert Saint came back, didn't he?" Serena said.

"Would you have noticed if anyone was watching Tommy? Or did Tommy have any visitors in the days leading up to the attack?" Maria asked.

"Tommy wasn't the sociable type," Serena said.

"So how do you think the Desert Saint found Tommy then?"

"What do you mean?" Serena said.

"He had to find your home, right? To do that, he had to follow Tommy or one of you home. Did Tommy ever have customers by the house?" Maria asked.

"Never, just us and him. He told us home was our oasis. All of us knew if we brought a customer by the house, we was going to catch an ass whipping we'd never forget."

Maria leaned back in her chair. Closed up her notebook. On the surface, the interview felt like a waste of time, nothing more than what she could have gotten from the file, but she wouldn't really know until she got further into digging. Sometimes offhand comments came back later on in ways she didn't expect.

"What was your name again?" Serena asked.

"Detective Varela," Maria said.

"Any relation to Dominic Varela, the cop I flagged down?" Serena asked.

"He's my father," Maria said.

"Now there's a gentleman. World needs more men like him."

"Yeah, he's all right," Maria said.

"Better than all right, he took us all to the movies," Serena said.

"To the movies?"

"Yeah, he didn't care what job we had, he treated us all with respect," Serena said.

Chapter 10

Why would her father go to the movies with a hooker?

Maria called her father. He didn't answer, just texted her back: On Fremont Street. Her father didn't like the new Fremont Street with the fancy light show and the canopy that covered the street and the pedestrian walkway. He remembered Fremont Street as being the center of town, neon against a dark sky, Glitter Gulch. But still he felt a pull for the place and went there from time to time to people watch and to think and to remember, and that's what Maria found him doing as he leaned against the wall of the Nugget watching the street.

"What do you see?" Maria asked.

"Disney World," Dominic said.

Maria stood next to him. She saw a line of middle-aged women giggling like school girls as they waited to take pictures with two statuesque rock hard Chippendale's dancers, one a blonde, the other dark-haired. The men were in assless chaps, and a heavyset woman with gray hair squealed as her hands cupped the blonde man's ass for the photo.

On the other side of the street, a young man in torn jeans and a shaved head leaned against the wall. He was looking at his feet. A dark tattoo peaked out from underneath his shirt.

"He could be hawking something," Maria said.

"Nah, he's waiting on his mother. She went inside a few minutes ago."

"I don't know why you come back here when you don't even like this place anymore."

"It's a good place to think," Dominic said.

Through the open doorway of the Nugget, a slot machine whistled and flashed.

"Yeah, that's what I was thinking, a great place to think," Maria said.

"Not everybody thinks the same way. How was Jack?"

"He told me about a kid who was close with the priest. Mentioned a sister that nobody interviewed because they didn't know about her. I'm going to look her up and see if she can tell me anything new."

"What are you expecting to get out of her?"

"Honestly? Nothing, just something to feel like I'm doing something. Serena was more of a pistol than Jack, but I have my doubts about memory. She told me you took her to the movies."

"Not just her," Dominic said.

"Come again?" Maria said.

LAS VEGAS *1980*

The thing was, Dominic Varela did not like Sergeant Morris one bit. He thought the Sergeant was the worst kind of cop, a lazy one who didn't really care about doing the right thing as much as he cared about his pension and demanding respect because he had a badge, but Sergeant Morris was still a sergeant, and Dominic was a nobody patrolman barely out of his probationary period.

"The mayor is tired of looking at all these ratty ass street walkers cruising around. He doesn't want to see them anymore," Sergeant Morris said.

"Great, I'll just wave a wand and they'll all disappear. Just give me the magic wand and off I'll go," Dominic said.

"The magic wand is you. You just don't know it yet. Now, I need you to understand these orders are coming straight from the top, from the mayor to the chief down the line to the unlucky son of a bitch who happened to cross my path at the wrong time," Sergeant Morris said.

"What's with the poetry? You have a few before you came in tonight?"

"Quit talking and start listening. Here's what I need you to do, go and get a paddy wagon and drive around loading that wagon up with hookers-"

"On what grounds?" Dominic said.

"Are you deaf? Grounds? The mayor said so's the grounds," Sergeant Morris said.

"That'll hold up when they get in front of the judge," Dominic said.

"Who said anything about a judge?"

"That's where they go after you arrest 'em," Dominic said.

"Can you let me goddamn finish? Jesus Christ, you're lippy tonight. Now you round up all those hookers, every goddamn one you can find, you cram them in that wagon like sardines, I mean, fill that vehicle to the brim and you drive them out to the state line on I-15 and take them a good half hour/forty-five minutes into California and you dump em. Point toward Los Angeles and tell them to keep on walking," Sergeant Morris said.

"What is this? There's no way-"

"Listen, this is the deal. The mayor doesn't want to see any hookers. The shit has run downhill to you. You can either let the shit keep going or you can get run over by the shit. The choice is yours, but if the mayor sees a hooker out there tonight, it ain't my head that's getting served up."

With that, Sergeant Morris turned around and headed off, leaving Dominic steaming. He hadn't joined the police to leave women stranded on the side of the road. But Dominic also understood the politics of the situation, and if something wasn't done,

Dominic would be out of a job. So how could he get a bunch of street walkers, most of whom have pimps riding herd on them, to stay off the streets for a night?

That's when he thought about the movie theater. One of his grade school buddies had inherited a movie theater when his dad got hit by a school bus a year earlier. The guy, Harvey, was always telling Dominic to go by for a free showing, and Dominic was always promising, but never went. Harvey was also recently divorced, and Dominic had a feeling that a movie theater full of hookers would seem like a gift from god to Harvey. Dominic was right. Harvey was more than willing to babysit hookers all night, so that's where Dominic dumped them, thirty-five in total.

"SOMEHOW WORD GOT AROUND about what I was doing, and the girls, they started lining up on corners like they were waiting for a bus. I think they just wanted a night off. Harvey showed them The Empire Strikes Back. I had hookers chasing me up and down Fremont for a month telling me, Luke, I'm your father," Dominic said.

"You never stop ceasing to amaze me," Maria said.

"Parents. Whattya gonna do?" Dominic said.

"Then maybe I'm dismissing Serena too quickly. She also said that the Desert Saint never stopped. Said pimps kept disappearing."

"If the Desert Saint kept killing pimps, he changed his M.O. which means he was much more cunning and dangerous than we ever gave him credit for," Dominic said.

Maria's cell phone rang, Michael.

"The aristocrat's attorney got the D.A. to not press charges," he said.

"What? Already?" Maria said.

"The wife is saying she never put a GPS on the car. She's saying through their attorney that I forced her to sign under duress," Michael said.

"How is that even possible?" Maria said.

"I screwed up. I forgot to check her signature on the statement. She put someone else's name. At the time, she told me she had the detective's name at home and she'd call me with it, which was obviously part of her plan, so we can't even go through the detective to prove that she's lying because I have no idea what detective she used. I should have seen this coming," Michael said.

"Seen what coming? She must have seen an opportunity to put him over the barrel and took it. God, what a devious bitch. Those two are a perfect match," Maria said.

"Still, I-"

"I, nothing. We are a team. Whatever problems are our problems. We got him the first time. We'll get him again," Maria said.

Michael didn't reply, but Maria knew he appreciated the sentiment, and she also knew that now she wouldn't have to apologize for throwing his other screwup in his face earlier. Wins all around.

"Don't worry. We'll find another way to get after him," Maria said, and then she hung up.

"What happened?" Dominic asked.

"We had a guy dead to rights on murder. He killed an escort and left her in a dumpster, but the D.A. won't go forward with the evidence. Says it won't hold up in court. Now the prick's going back to his high society life," Maria said.

"What makes you more mad, the getting away with it or the returning to high society?"

"Both," Maria said.

"Some old time cops might have had connections with reporters who would run stories for future tips," Dominic said.

"What purpose would that serve other than pissing off Moyer?" Maria asked.

"Well, for one thing, he probably won't get invited to any more fancy events, so he can kiss that high society life goodbye, and that would probably piss him off quite a bit. Might compel him to act again. Was the vic killed in his apartment or where he dumped her?" Dominic said.

"We think he drove her around a while in the trunk of his car and then took her to an abandoned warehouse where he killed her before dumping her," Maria said.

"Cut a deal with the reporter. You give the scoop. They bribe the security guard for a head's up the next time the guy orders a girl to his place. You probably can catch him in the act, and then it won't matter what the D.A. does. You'll have him dead to rights."

"Were you always this devious?" Maria said.

"Only when I thought the risk was worth it," Dominic said.

"And the risk of losing your job for those street walkers, that was worth it?" Maria said.

"Wasn't about losing the job. It was about losing my self-respect. If that's what it took to keep my job, the job wasn't worth it," Dominic said.

Chapter 11

Who would tail a cop?

Maria's father always told her that cops were the easiest people to sneak up on because they viewed themselves as hunters, and hunters don't expect to be hunted, so they never saw anyone coming up from the back, so he'd always taught Maria to look over her shoulder. He drilled it into her, and eventually, looking over her shoulder became a natural part of her walk.

Carla had noticed the habit right away on their first date. They had met at Makers and Finders near downtown. After lunch, they took a walk down Main Street. There wasn't really all that much to see. They were just enjoying each other's company. At least twice a block, Maria casually glanced over her shoulder.

"Looking for someone in particular?" Carla asked.

Maria apologized. Told her it was a habit. Something from work.

"It's ok. I'm glad someone's paying attention because I sure as hell ain't," Carla said.

Maria liked to joke that's when she knew Carla was the woman for her. Like all jokes, there was some truth to it, and Carla's casual acceptance of Maria constantly looking over her shoulder made

Maria feel understood in a way she didn't even know she'd been missing.

So as Maria walked away from her father, she was doing what she normally did, looking over her shoulder at least twice a block. A man was following her. She ducked into the doorway of a restaurant to be sure. A hostess, maybe eighteen, long black hair pulled back in a ponytail and a forced smile plastered on her face came out to tell her about the specials. Maria ignored her and watched the window reflection, waiting for the man to pass.

But he didn't.

Maria smiled an apology at the now annoyed hostess and went back to walking towards her car. The man ducked out of the doorway of a restaurant and resumed following her. He was tall and thin and had wild gray hair that stuck out from underneath his Golden Knights baseball cap. He was definitely over fifty, but was he old enough to be in his sixties? Maria couldn't be sure without seeing him up close. She turned onto Eighth Street and headed for her car. Not wanting to spook the man, she didn't turn around once, but she focused all of her hearing behind her in case he came running up.

She allowed herself to look around when she was at the car. The man wasn't on her block. But on the other side of Fremont, she saw him heading toward a car. Lights flashed as the doors unlocked.

Maria got into her car and dialed Michael.

"Change your mind about yelling at me?" He said.

"I think I'm being followed," she said.

"By who?" Michael said.

"A man who fits our age range," Maria said.

"Hold on and I'll call it in, we'll get a patrol car there," Michael said.

"What if I'm wrong?" Maria said.

"Better safe than-"

"Screw that, I'd rather make sure I'm right first.

.   .   .

61

MICHAEL WAS at a boxing gym off of Spring Mountain and Wynn Road. The gym was at the back end of a strip mall with a narrow parking lot. Maria would lead the man there and if he followed, they could be sure something was up, and they'd be able to block him in before he knew what was going on. Maria told Michael to get ready and started to hang up, but he didn't want her getting off the phone.

"What are you going to do if he rams my car? Push the pound sign?" Maria said.

"At least I'll know what's going on," Michael said.

Maria pulled out and headed away from Fremont. In her rearview, she saw the man pull out and follow her. He was too far away for her to make out the plate, but he was driving a white Honda Civic, and she told Michael as much.

"Great, white guy, gray hair, white Honda Civic. If something happens to you, I'll track him down in like forty years," Michael said.

"Nothing's going to happen to me. I got you on the line, and you're ready to push the pound sign," Maria said.

"Asshole," Michael said.

Maria made her way to I-15. One eye on the road, one eye on the man behind her.

"Do you have any distinguishing features?" Michael said.

"Gray haired white guy in a Knights hat isn't enough?" Maria said.

"Can we be somewhat serious?"

"I got nothing on description and nothing on a plate. He's stayed too far away the whole time. To be honest, when we pull him out of the car, I'm not even going to be sure it's him," Maria said.

"The way we've been running the last few days, we'll end up yanking some Korean guy looking for a massage parlor out of the car," Michael said.

Maria pulled onto the I-15 and stayed in the right lane, so she could watch the entrance in the rearview. The white Honda Civic blew through a red light to get onto the freeway before she got too far ahead, and all the humor went out of Maria. Before she'd been nervous that she was being paranoid. Maybe she was going to end up looking like a fool. But all of that nervousness was gone. Now the adrenaline was starting to kick in.

Was this man the Desert Saint?

Who else would be following her?

"You haven't made a wiseass comment in a solid minute and a half," Michael said.

"He ran a red light to make sure I didn't get out of sight," Maria said.

"All right. I'm already outside and suited up. Bring him to me," Michael said.

Traffic was light, but the sun was already down over the horizon and even if the man had pulled up close, Maria doubted she'd be able to see his license plate. The trip was short anyway. Maria took the Spring Mountain exit and headed west into the garish lights and exotic looking shopping centers of Chinatown.

There was more traffic on Spring Mountain than on the freeway, and the white Civic tried to close the gap between the cars but ended up getting stuck behind a plumbing van. The turnoff onto Wynn was coming, and Maria took her time with the turn, trying to let the van pass so the man could see her, and he did but too late, and he went through the intersection.

"Shit," Maria said.

"What happened?" Michael said.

The white Honda Civic pulled into the gas station and spun around. He was on the other side of the light now, waiting for it to turn.

"He missed the turn, but it's ok. He swung around and is watching me," Maria said.

Maria took her time turning into the parking lot, then sped up when the man couldn't see her anymore. Michael was waiting halfway down the parking lot, a bulletproof vest on over his workout gear. He waved for her to turn into a parking spot behind an F-150 with oversized tires.

"He won't be able to see you parked there. When he passes me,

I'll let you know and we'll both pull out at the same time, you blocking the front and me blocking the back," Michael said.

Maria pulled into the spot. She took a few long breaths, another thing her father had taught her. Cops needed to be calm in the most difficult situations or else innocent people got hurt. Stray bullets. Unnecessary shootings. Training could only prepare for so much. The rest was up to the individual officer. So Maria had learned to control her breathing. Calm herself down.

Then confront the problem.

"He's turning into the parking lot," Michael said.

"Try not to crap yourself," Maria said.

Michael chuckled.

In the rearview, Maria saw a couple with a young boy, maybe five or six, leaving a Chinese restaurant. The boy ran ahead of his parents.

"We have a family heading our way." Maria said.

Michael didn't say anything.

Maria looked for the family again. She was going to have to back out in a hurry, and if that family was there, she wouldn't be able to. She saw the father yell something. Where was the boy?

"Get ready," Michael said.

"Do you see a child running around?" Maria said.

"A child?" Michael said.

Maria turned around in her seat looking for the boy.

"Almost," Michael said.

Where was the boy? She couldn't pull out if she couldn't find him, and then, she saw him, hugging a column and laughing as his father tried to lure him toward the car.

"Now," Michael said.

Maria pulled out fast and then slammed on the brakes. She jumped out of the car and aimed her gun over the hood at the white Civic. Behind, Michael's truck pulled out, a police light flashing red and blue on the dashboard.

The father ran across the lot for his child.

"Turn off the engine and show me your hands and do it now!" Michael said.

Inside the Civic, the man very slowly reached down and turned the car off. The doors on the car clicked, and Michael ripped the door open and pulled the man out. Spun him against the car.

"What the hell? I'm just trying to go shopping," the man said.

"What store?" Michael said.

The man tried to look over his shoulder at a storefront, but Michael kept the pressure on so the man had to face forward.

"He's the right age range, and there's a gun in the car," Maria said. She opened the passenger side door and leaned in. The gun was silver with a black handle. She picked it up and looked at the markings on the barrel. Not a .22.

"This is a .38," Maria said.

"The .22 could be in the trunk. Or maybe he was just scouting you out. Maybe he keeps it at home until he's ready," Michael said.

"Ready for what?" the man said.

"Quit playing dumb. Where's the .22?" Michael said.

"I don't own a .22," he said.

"Cuff him. We'll search the car," Maria said.

"On what grounds? Entering a parking lot?" the man said.

"Stalking a police officer," Michael said.

"Is that even illegal?" the man said.

"We'll figure something out," Maria said.

"I'm a private detective. I was surveilling, not stalking," the man said.

"A private detective?" Maria said.

"My license is in the glove compartment," the man said.

Maria opened the glove compartment and there it was, right underneath the car registration. Milton Winner, private detective.

"Who hired you to follow me?" Maria asked.

"It's a confidential agreement," Milton said.

Michael punched Milton twice, one on each side of the rib cage. Milton doubled over and gasped for air. Michael pulled him back up and pushed him against the car.

"If you can't tell, we're a little tense. There's a homicide investigation we're in the middle of and my partner might be a target, so you are going to tell us who your client is," Michael said.

Milton looked pissed and set in his decision to keep quiet, so Michael reared back to hit him again, but he didn't have to follow through.

"Preston Millicent."

"That prick," Maria said.

Michael stepped back.

"What were your instructions?" Michael asked.

"A basic tail. Get to know her routine. Find out if there's anything disqualifying."

"Disqualifying?" Maria asked.

"He told me you were applying to be his head of security, and he needed to know if you had any bad habits, anything that would make you unsuitable for the position," Milton said.

"And you believed that bullshit?" Michael said.

"Why wouldn't I?" Milton said.

Michael looked at Maria and asked her what she wanted to do.

"Look, I haven't applied for any jobs. You've been hired to stalk a police officer. If I see you again, you'll be arrested for stalking. Am I clear?" Maria said.

AFTER THE PRIVATE investigator had driven away, Maria and Michael sat on the tailgate of his flatbed. The sun was gone, but the parking lot was lit up like day between the lamps and the business signs.

"Can you believe the nerve of that arrogant piece of shit?" Maria said.

"Yes, I absolutely can," Michael said.

"Fucking assholes with money think they can do whatever they want."

"Because they normally can," Michael said.

"I'm going to figure out a way to get him," Maria said.

"We're going to figure out a way," Michael said.

Maria wanted to agree with him because he was right. They were a team, him and her, and she knew he was as angry as she was about Preston getting off and not just because Michael screwed up but also because Michael cared deeply about catching criminals, but he hadn't been the one being followed. The man had been following her. How could that have been anything but a threat? And what if Preston sent someone to follow Carla? Maria could handle herself, she was sure of that, but Carla? Carla was the definition of an easy target.

Michael reached out and grabbed her shoulder. Gave her a little shake.

"Hey, he's just trying to dig up dirt. Investigate the investigators. Find some way to ruin our credibility," Michael said.

"He's a man who preys on women. He wanted my routine. He's planning something."

"He's not that stupid," Michael said.

"No, he just thinks he's smart enough to get away with it," Maria said.

"You really think that?" Michael said.

"Yeah, I do," Maria said.

"Ok, how do you want to handle it?"

"I don't know." In the back of her head, she was rolling over what her father had said about the reporter, but she knew Michael would never go for it. He wasn't the type of guy to go to the press. It's not just that he was a rules follower, which he was, but also he believed in handling things himself, not outsourcing publicly. Normally, Maria would agree with him. But this time was different.

"I see you over there thinking and thinking, but no words are coming out," Michael said.

"I have to go home. It's been a long day."

"Before you go, I did want to ask you something," he said.

"Shoot," Maria said.

"If I find something less than sterling about your brother, do you want to know?"

"What did you find?" Maria said.

"Nothing yet. I'm just asking in case something pops up," Michael said.

The easy answer was of course she wanted to know. Who wouldn't want to know? But if Tommy was selling heroin over the dark web or if he had a bunch of child porn on his computer, did she really need to know? She was tired. She couldn't think through all the possibilities, and while she was sure she'd want to know anything tied to the case no matter how bad, she wasn't sure at all if she'd want to know something not tied to the case, nor did she know where to draw the line.

"Ask me tomorrow after I get some sleep. Right now, I really just don't know," Maria said.

"Wait a sec," Michael said. He jumped down off of the hood and reached into his car. Came back out with a folder. "Here's everything I have so far. It's not much, but you can look it over and see if you see anything I'm missing."

"Moyer would kill you if he found out you gave this to me," Maria said.

"You really think he put me on this case thinking I wouldn't share everything with you?"

ON THE DRIVE HOME, Maria stewed over the private detective. As she pulled into the parking lot of her apartment complex, she decided to call a reporter, Laura Esquivel. It wasn't fear for herself or even anger that caused her to do it, but rather concern for Carla. This man needed to know that if he was going to mess with Maria's personal life, there would be consequences.

"Sorry to bother you so late. I have something that you might be interested in, but I have some conditions," Maria said.

"Conditions, I don't know if I like the sound of that," Laura said.

"Well why don't I lay them out, and we'll see what you think," Maria said.

Chapter 12

Why did he miss this so much?

Dominic sat in his car looking at a low-slung motel. In his mind, he was running over his conversation with Sister Margaret when she had told him a man in an oversized pickup truck had been lurking around the shelter, and Naomi had disappeared shortly afterwards. Sister Margaret would normally just accept Naomi's going as part of the process and wait for her to come back on her own terms. It was just that the girl had really seemed to be opening up, and she wondered if maybe Dominic could take a shot at looking for her.

Dominic had called in a favor and gotten someone from the vice squad to look for Naomi. About twenty minutes earlier, he'd been notified of a young woman fitting Naomi's description entering a motel already under surveillance on suspicion of being used for prostitution. So here Dominic was, his eyes on room 28, two doors left of the stairs, second floor.

The door opened. A man walked out, middle-aged, soft around the middle. Glasses. The man walked quickly, head down, practically ran down the steps and headed for his car, a minivan with a My Child is an Honor Roll Student at Katz Elementary sticker on the bumper. He looked like the type of man who really paid attention at PTA meetings and got too angry at the baseball umpire.

Dominic had spent most of his career trying to get the department to focus on arresting clients rather than prostitutes. The women were just trying to survive. The men were the ones who were the problem, but the reality was a lot more men than anybody wanted to admit frequented hookers, and getting the focus changed meant men in power would have to make their favorite hobby illegal and put themselves at risk. How likely was that to happen, really? So instead, vice kept on going after women just trying to survive. A microcosm of the world if Dominic had ever seen it. Dominic didn't hate clients like he hated pimps though. At least the clients paid for a service rather than stealing the woman's hard earned money. How many times had he had the same conversation over and over inside his head while he sat in a car waiting to make an arrest? He'd missed this moment, the anticipation, the waiting for the action. He was too old for anything serious anymore. God, if he had to scrap with a suspect, he'd probably have a heart attack in the middle. But this moment, this moment was a heavenly thing that could only be understood by someone who'd experienced it.

The door to room 28 opened again and Naomi stepped out. At least a version of Naomi stepped out. Extensions made her hair cascade down her back. Her heels were as long as her skirt was short. Seeing her like that bothered Dominic more than he'd thought it would. It was hard to look at the facade after seeing the actual soul. Naomi came down the stairs a little unsteadily, one hand on the railing and her eyes on the steps, so she didn't see Dominic getting out of the car and making his way across the parking lot. When she did see him though, she took a hard right.

"Hold on a sec, I just want to see how you are," Dominic said.

"Never better, Dom," Naomi said.

"Sisters said you left and didn't come back," Dominic said.

"#hangingwithnuns ain't exactly trending," Naomi said.

"They mentioned a man in a big truck had come looking for you. They wondered if he had scared you," Dominic said.

"Do I look like I scare easy?" Naomi said.

"Yeah, yeah you do," Dominic said.

"OK, Boomer," Naomi said.

"You can always go back," Dominic said.

"Sure thing, be there tomorrow. Now I got business to get to and you ain't exactly a help in that department," Naomi said.

Dominic wanted to push, but he knew it was a waste of time from the tone of her voice. As much as he thought Naomi had a chance at leaving all this behind, something to the set of her face told him she wasn't ready. Not now. Maybe not ever. This moment stung him a bit more than it should, and he knew he'd have to think about that later. About letting people be who they are and not forcing what couldn't be forced.

Then he heard the revving of an engine, a big engine, and a truck turned the corner.

"Fuck. Go Dom. Go now," Naomi said.

High beams blinded Dominic, and he put his forearm up over his eyes. The truck screeched to a halt about twenty feet away, and the driver's side door opened and closed. The high beams stayed on as footsteps made their way towards Dominic and then the lights switched off.

"You looking for a good time, old man?" the pimp said.

Dominic still couldn't see anything, and he blinked his eyes repeatedly.

"Those nuns just wanted him to check on me," Naomi said.

"Get in the truck, bitch," the pimp said.

Dominic could finally see. The pimp was about Dominic's height but slight. He had on jeans ripped in the way that was popular and a t-shirt that was tight enough to show that he had a six-pack. If Dominic didn't know he was a pimp, he would have thought the guy was a gay prostitute.

"He's harmless," Naomi said.

"Did I or did I not tell you to get in the truck, bitch?"

Naomi opened her mouth to say something more, but the pimp smacked her full across the face and sent her sprawling to the ground.

Dominic pulled a baton from his jacket pocket and extended it to its full length.

"So Grandpa thinks he's a superhero," the pimp said.

The passenger side door opened up on the truck and two men got out. One white and one black and both of them much bigger than the pimp. The black guy was muscular, but the white guy was more mass, an offensive lineman type. Either way, Dominic didn't like his chances.

"Guess you only hit women, huh? Figures," Dominic said.

"Fuck up Grandpa while I deal with the bitch," the pimp said.

The two men came at Dominic slowly. Spreading out so they could come at him from different angles. They'd obviously done this before. Dominic took a long slow breath and turned sideways. He shouldn't have put himself in this position, too old, retired, but god the rush was absolutely wonderful. In the back of his head, he was wondering how long before the cops surveilling the motel called this in. Were they watching live or were they taping?

The black man came at him fast, a bull rush, and Dominic got out of the way just in time and clipped him across the back of the head with the baton. The white guy was rushing right behind, but Dominic had moved just enough, so the white guy went by grasping at air. The black man pushed himself off of the ground and pawed at the back of his head, searching for blood. Dominic took advantage of the hesitation to swing for his knee. The baton crunched hard against the bone, and the black man let loose a scream and went down.

"Y'all really getting your asses kicked by grandpa? Fuck this, I'm getting Pepe," the pimp said.

The white guy came forward, more cautiously this time, a wary respect on his face. Dominic circled away. He was breathing much heavier than he should be, and sweat was pouring down his forehead, stinging his eyes. The black man grunted as he got to his feet. He rubbed the side of his knee with his hand. The two of them shared a look and then charged. Dominic took two steps back, but they were about to be on him, and he had nowhere to go.

So he dropped to the ground.

The men tripped over him, their weight and momentum propelling them across Dominic and they both became entangled and fell to the ground in a heap. Dominic reached for his baton which had skittered away. He needed to get to it before the two of them got up.

The clicking of a shotgun stopped him.

The pimp was standing a few feet off, shotgun on his hip pointed at Dominic.

"You don't want to do that. I'm a cop. You pull that trigger; your life is over," Dominic said.

"Like I give a fuck. I'll make sure to take my shells with me and there ain't going to be no witnesses, so fuck-"

Naomi punched the pimp hard in the jaw, and spittle, blood, and teeth flew through the air. The pimp reached for his mouth. Blood poured down his hand. Naomi reared back to punch again, brass knuckles glinting in the headlights, but the pimp jabbed her in the stomach with the butt of his shotgun. Naomi collapsed gasping for air.

No sirens screaming. No flashing lights. Dominic wasn't going to be saved by the cavalry. He reached down and pulled the gun from his ankle holster and shot three times.

A triangle pattern poured blood from the pimp's chest. He collapsed to the ground, slow.

The shotgun clattered against the pavement.

The two other men took off running.

"Where the hell has that gun been?" Naomi asked.

"You can't just shoot someone without a good reason," Dominic said.

"Them you can. Come on. We got to get out of here," Naomi said.

"Relax, I'm a cop, remember," Dominic said.

"Retired cop," Naomi said.

"Some things you never stop being," Dominic said.

Chapter 13

The file contains so little when you know the person in it.

Maria was sitting at the coffee table looking at what Michael had given her. Crime scene reports. Background. Interview notes. All of it so focused on the crime and so empty when compared to the totality of the life. She wanted to remember this later. The miniscule amount of information contained in this folder. She pulled out a photo of Anatov. The only solid motive they could find was the money he'd lost in the virtual currency that flopped, but the evidence said it wasn't him.

Could the evidence be wrong?

Maria was so caught up in her thoughts she didn't notice Carla until she had wrapped her arms around Maria's neck and buried her nose in Maria's hair. The hug surprised her, and her first instinct was to shove Carla off, but Maria caught herself before following through, and instead, leaned her head gently into Carla's arm. The feel of Carla's skin on her own made Maria want to vomit. She wanted to run out the apartment and be alone, but she knew that wasn't Carla's fault nor could she let Carla know how she felt. How long would she feel like this?

"Maybe we could go away for a few days?" Carla said.

"Go away?"

"We could go to that hotel in Half-Moon Bay. Order room service and not leave the room for a few days," Carla said.

"I have too much to do here," Maria said.

"Maybe you should sit this one out," Carla said.

"You can't be serious," Maria said.

"You know, I love being with a cop. I mean, I know the cliche is the job is a disaster for relationships, always gone at odd hours for long days, always dealing with so much nastiness, but I just feel so safe with you. I love that feeling," Carla said. She reached across and grabbed Maria's hand.

"I feel like there's more coming," Maria said.

"And I respect how good you are at your job. I respect the passion you bring to it. I also respect how rational you try to be. So many people running around judging people by what they look like, and I know you really try to see people as they are, not as they appear."

"Here it comes," Maria said.

"You know you can't be rational here," Carla said.

"Did my father put you up to this?" Maria said.

"I'm just worried about you, and you have to let yourself grieve, baby," Carla said.

"Right after we catch the bastard who killed Tommy, you and I can go to Half-Moon Bay for a week, and I'll curl up into a ball, and I'll send you to the store for a box of tissues every three hours because I'm crying so much, but I have to work to do now," Maria said.

Carla nodded and squeezed a little tighter before letting go. She leaned down and touched Anatov's photo.

"What did Anatov do?" Carla said.

"You know him?"

"Not know, know. But I follow him." Carla headed into the bedroom and came back out a few seconds later with her cellphone in her hand. She opened an app and scrolled through until she found Anatov's profile and then flipped the phone around. Showed it to Maria.

Anatov in front of a Ferrari, Anatov skydiving, Anatov with three beautiful women in minidresses. Within five or six rows of photos, Maria decided that she really didn't like Anatov, even if he wasn't even involved with Tommy's murder. Then one picture stopped her short. Anatov, Tommy, and Harold sitting around a table in a cabana. Anatov had his hand on Tommy's shoulder while Tommy was laughing. Harold leaned back in his chair, beer resting on his pot belly.

"That prick, Harold told me that he'd never met an Anatov. Where is this?"

Carla leaned over her shoulder and looked at the photo.

"Two weeks ago at Haven pool party."

"Two weeks ago? Harold told me he hadn't seen Tommy in two months. What the hell?"

Maria looked at the picture more closely. She wondered what Tommy had gotten himself into and why Harold had lied. More importantly, how could this lie fit in with the evidence that they had? Maybe it was just something shady that had nothing to do with Tommy's death. Michael would have to follow up anyway.

Her cell phone rang. Moyer. What could he want calling so late?

DOMINIC LOOKED across the desk at the detective taking his statement. He was a young guy by the name of Javier, a little heavier than he should be, but with a big smile and an easy confidence. The kind of guy you'd be comfortable leaving your kids with at a birthday party. He looked Mexican, but his family could have been from Honduras, maybe El Salvador. Most people just figured anyone from south of the border was Mexican, but Dominic always tried to differentiate. History and culture were important. They shaped us. Those same people who lumped all the Hispanics in one big group would eagerly tell you how different a German was from a Brit. Why couldn't they see the same differences with people from Latin America?

Moyer came in and spied him from across the room. Started over.

"Here comes the boss," Javier said.

"He's going to be mad at me for him getting pulled out of bed over this," Dominic said.

"You broke him in, didn't you?" Javier said.

"Some people are unbreakable," Dominic said.

Moyer looked pissed, and all the cops gave him a wide berth as he made his way across the room. He stopped about five feet away from Dominic. Stood there and stared.

"Please tell me you were not out looking for a gunfight," Moyer said.

"I was not out looking for a gunfight," Dominic said.

"God, sometimes I fucking hate you," Moyer said.

Dominic was trying not to laugh, but couldn't keep the corners of his mouth from curling up.

"Don't even think about smiling," Moyer said.

Dominic pointed a finger at his chest as if to say, who me, of course I'd never smile.

"Detective Quintana, what do we have?" Moyer said.

"Clear case of self defense. All the evidence and witness testimony confirms," Javier said.

"Dom, you and me are going to have a talk tomorrow about what you were doing out there. Hear me?" Moyer said.

"Crystal," Dominic said.

On the far side of the room, a door swung open hard, and Maria burst through.

"Where is he?" she said.

One of the patrol officers pointed across the room at Dominic, and Maria started towards him. She was walking fast and her hands were clenched like she was going to punch someone.

"Oh boy, you're really screwed now," Moyer said.

"At least pretend to look concerned, will ya?" Dominic said.

"Someone has to kick your ass for this bullshit," Moyer said.

"Yeah, and she is definitely an ass kicker. If you'll excuse me,

I'm getting out of the line of fire." Javier stood up, gathered his folders, and headed off.

"Wimp," Dominic called after him.

Maria walked up and looked Dominic over. She took in the scratches on his face and the bandage on his hand.

"Are you hurt?" Maria said.

"No, I'm good," Dominic said.

"Not for long because I'm going to kick your ass," Maria said.

"Come on with that," Dominic said.

"What the hell were you doing out there?" Maria said.

"Not now, ok? Everything's fine," Dominic said.

"Everything's fine? You killed a man," Maria said.

"It was a clean shoot. Self-defense. Some might say civic duty," Moyer said.

"Dad, you're not a cop anymore. You can't be out there cruising the streets like you're on the beat," Maria said.

"It wasn't like that," Dominic said.

"Then what was it like?" Maria said.

"Cut the guy some slack, will ya?" Moyer said.

"Does Mom know about this?" Maria asked.

"I'm heading home to tell her now," Dominic said.

"I'll drive you," Maria said.

"I got my car here."

"Get it tomorrow," Maria said.

"I'm fine. I'll drive myself home," Dominic said.

"Maria, everything's OK. Your Dad's fine. Vegas has one less scumbag pimp and nobody is shedding a tear for that guy, trust me," Moyer said.

Maria took a few deep breaths. Dominic figured she was caught up between wanting to hug him and wanting to slug him, and he wasn't really sure which way she was going to go, but he couldn't handle any more punches today.

"Look, I get it, I messed up. I shouldn't have been out there, but I promise. It was a one-time thing, ok? Let me get home and talk with mom, and I promise tomorrow I'll explain everything to you," Dominic said.

"This conversation is not over," Maria said.

"Mid-sixties," Dominic said.

"Yeah, I know, you're mid-sixties. What does that have to do with anything?" Maria said.

"That's when your kids become your parents. I read it in some article," Dominic said.

"It was mid-forties for me, and the little shit wasn't even fifteen yet," Moyer said.

Maria rolled her eyes and turned to go. She walked slower leaving than she had coming in, but everyone in the room still gave her a wide berth. She didn't seem to notice, and Dominic wondered if she realized everyone in the room was treating her the same way they treated Moyer. He hoped it was respect. His daughter could be difficult to get along with because she was so focused on doing it right. He'd had the same issues when he was mid-career. Eventually, success makes people want to be around you. But those middle years could be lonely. He'd have to ask her about it.

Whenever she got done wanting to punch him.

Chapter 14

Where the hell was he?

Esperanza looked at her phone. The text message from Dominic said: on my way home. He'd sent it over an hour ago. Where the hell was he that coming home took over an hour? She was the mother. She should be the one going crazy and walking the streets at night. But no, here she was, sitting at her kitchen table, waiting for her husband to get home after a night of doing God knows what.

She knew she was exaggerating. He wasn't off doing anything bad, just something stupid. Trying to help the helpless or some such crap like that. Because deep down in his soul, he had to help. He couldn't not help, and Esperanza was grateful for that, who the hell knew where she would have ended up if it wasn't for Dominic. Probably wouldn't still be alive. Sure as hell wouldn't be in a house this nice, but now? Really, now was when he had to be out all night?

The garage door whirred open, and his car pulled in. The slight squeak to the brakes as it stopped. One door opened and closed. Then a second. Dominic saying something low.

Jesus Christ, who the hell was with him?

The door to the garage opened, and Dominic came in. His face bruised. Scratches on his hands. All the blood had been cleaned up, but he'd bled. That was certain. Seriously Dominic? At this age out fighting in the street. How badly had Tommy's death damaged him?

"Save anyone?" Esperanza asked.

"The only person I ever saved was you," Dominic said.

"And the only woman too stupid to not be jealous when her husband hangs out in the street all night is me," she said.

Dominic came across the room and pulled a chair out. Sat down. He had the 'we have a serious conversation we need to have' look on his face. Between that look and the bruises, he could have been in a James Bond movie. Esperanza cursed herself for loving such a complicated man. But she really hadn't ever had a choice. Life gave her Dominic, and she knew, even with his complexity and that shitty job he had loved and the big hole in the middle tied to his parents whom he never talked about, even with all of that, she was lucky that this was what life gave her. But damn, couldn't he wait until a week after Tommy's death before going crazy? Couldn't he just give her time to grieve?

"Did you find whoever you were looking for?" Esperanza asked.

"Maybe we could use someone around the house," Dominic said.

"I vote for a dog. They don't hock your television," Esperanza said.

"That only happened one time," Dominic said.

"And you weren't even mad," Esperanza said.

"She had a good reason," Dominic said.

"I have a feeling I'm not going to like what happens next," Esperanza said.

"We have a visitor," Dominic said.

Dominic walked back to the garage door. Opened it. In the doorway was a girl, a young woman, really. Pretty but too young for the kind of makeup on her face or for those horrible extensions. An oversized police windbreaker hung to her knees, covering up what must have been a micro-mini that would make a porn star think twice, and those stilettos. Esperanza had been fond of heels, still was, but those were stilts, not heels.

"Ay no, no, no," Esperanza said.

"I owe her one," Dominic said.

"Don't even try to make excuses," Esperanza said.

"I don't want to be here either. I was fine, and he screwed everything up," Naomi said.

Esperanza laughed.

"Si, él es así," she said.

"I screw everything up. That's what I do?" Dominic said.

"Mas o menos," Esperanza said, "Ven acá niñita, déjame mirarte."

"I'm not a little girl," Naomi said.

Esperanza laughed and waved with her hand for the girl to come closer. Naomi made a face like she was tasting something bitter, but Esperanza kept waving, and Naomi gave in. Her stilettos clacked against the linoleum floor, and the closer she came, the younger she looked, and Esperanza saw her as she was, not the tramp showing all that skin, but a scared girl trying her best to survive, and looking at her Esperanza understood why Dominic was willing to open his home to her.

This girl reminded him of her.

Chapter 15

What was rattling around her brain?

Maria woke up an hour earlier than she wanted to. She rolled over to go back to sleep, but she couldn't. Something was bothering her, maybe a dream she'd had, maybe something from yesterday. She couldn't remember what it was. She put her arm around Carla, dug her other arm under the pillow. Pressed up against her back. Carla stirred but didn't awaken.

Maria burrowed into her neck and just laid there listening to her breathe.

She was going to have to do something special for Carla when this was all over because Carla had been perfect. Maria knew she was lucky to have a girlfriend who didn't complain about Maria's long hours, who didn't ask a ton of questions about her cases, who let Maria stew when a case was really bad. But Carla had surpassed all of that in these last few days. Maria doubted that she'd have that much patience if things were reversed.

The date.

The date Tommy disappeared.

That's what had woken up Maria. She knew that date.

Shit, she knew that date well.

. . .

AS MARIA DROVE to the station, she thought about tio Tomas or what little she knew about him. tio Tomas's disappearance had been how Dominic and Esperanza had met. She'd called in a missing persons report, and Dominic had been sent to see if there was anything worth looking into, and they'd taken a liking to each other, and almost forty years later, they were still together. When Tommy was younger, Esperanza used to tell Tommy stories about tio Tomas. Simple things. When she wanted Tommy to wear certain clothes or comb his hair a certain way, she'd tell him tio Tomas had been a real lady's man, and he wore jeans like this or he parted his hair like that. Her mother never told Maria much about tio Tomas. Just that he helped get her to Vegas. She used to say if it weren't for tio Tomas, she'd still be in Mexico, and Maria and Tommy wouldn't exist. Of course, Tommy had been named after tio Tomas, but the US spelling, Thomas instead of the Spanish Tomas.

In the conference room, Maria found the file on Tomas Vargas. It was inside the folder with the police report from the night Dominic was shot. She flipped it open. The writing was faded and difficult to read, but then again, there wasn't much of a report made. Tomas Vargas had gone missing on February 15th, 1984. The reporting witness was Esperanza Gomez. As she read, Maria wondered why her uncle had a different last name from her mother. Esperanza didn't talk about her parents much. Maybe she shared a mother with Tomas but not a father. Maria turned the page and saw a mugshot. Tomas had been arrested for pandering, which was just a nice word for pimping.

Maria leaned back in the chair. Her tio Tomas was a pimp?

And he disappeared on the same day as Serena's Tommy.

Tommy, short for Thomas, the English version of Tomas.

What the hell?

This was something she'd need to ask her mother about. But not today. Probably not tomorrow either, but soon. Definitely soon.

. . .

MARIA SETTLED in front of the computer and looked at the names Jack had given her. She ran Steven first, and just as Jack had said, Steven had a rap sheet that went on and on and on. He must have had good attorneys because he rarely did much time, a month here, six months there. Little pit stops in county before going back to the streets.

Then Maria ran Rebeka, the sister. She didn't expect to find anything, but there Rebeka was: two charges for pandering, one for procuring and another for transportation. The charges had eventually been dropped in what must have been a plea bargain, and the contact information was from the late eighties when she'd been arrested. So Maria ran her license and found a current address in East Las Vegas and a phone number. She was about to dial when Michael walked in. She caught him up on what she'd been doing, but Michael seemed to be distracted and as soon as she was done, he asked her if she'd thought over the question he'd asked her last night.

"What question?" Maria said.

"About wanting to know if I found anything strange about your brother," Michael said.

"Shit, what did you find?" Maria said.

"You told me his job was that YouTube channel, right?" Michael said.

"Yeah. I mean, who knows what else he was doing, but he told me he made most of his money from YouTube. Why?" Maria said.

"His YouTube channel wasn't very popular, so he couldn't have been making any money there. He had done well with bitcoin though. Really well, actually," Michael said.

"Tommy told me he got in too late and lost his ass," Maria said.

"I'd love to lose my ass like that," Michael said.

"How much bitcoin did he have?"

MICHAEL TOLD her they'd been lucky. Bitcoin wallets could be nearly impossible to access or find, but Tommy had his wallet in an app on his phone, and once Michael opened the phone, he'd been able to look at everything because the two factor authentication involved typing in a code texted to the phone.

"Who opened the phone?" Maria asked.

"I did. I didn't want some random pressing Tommy's thumb against it," Michael said.

Maria didn't have to tell him she was grateful for that. He understood and just kept talking about the bitcoin so she wouldn't have to say "Thank You." God, he was a good partner.

Michael hadn't even noticed the bitcoin wallet app. Then an email had arrived, notifying Tommy of a deposit to his bitcoin wallet. Michael searched for the app, opened it up, and found over half a million dollars' worth of bitcoin sitting in the wallet. The money had come in increments ranging from $500 to $20000. Michael had gone through everything again, emails, photos, videos, text messages, but nothing seemed to explain the activity in the wallet.

"He was definitely selling something. What do you think it might be?" Michael said.

"I believed him when he told me about the YouTube thing. He was always using these buzzwords I didn't understand and to be honest, I didn't really give a shit about this stuff. I listened because he was my brother. But it was all I could do to keep my eyes from glazing over when he talked."

"Put aside all that we know. Thinking about your brother. Where do you think this money was coming from?" Michael said.

Maria didn't really need to think. Her brother had always been a scammer. Always. Whether it was selling oregano and pretending it was weed in high school or working in high-pressure sales for time shares that may or may not have existed, Tommy had always been after easy money. It was just who he was.

"Harold will know," Maria said.

"You want to take another run at him?"

"Not me, you. He's already lied to me once. I'll watch though, but first I have to go interview the sister, then we'll meet back here after lunch so you can take a nice long run at Harold." She reached for her phone to call Rebeka. Then she saw the look on Michael's face. Like he'd been punched in the stomach.

"What's up?" Maria said.

"I keep messing up. I mean, I messed up with the aristocrat's wife. I didn't even get around to checking your brother's phone until today."

"You checked text messages, didn't you?"

"Yeah, I mean, I made sure the phone was completely unlocked and took off all the security and I checked messages and emails, but this stuff here, it's some shit that might have been useful earlier," Michael said.

"Why? The evidence says the killer is some guy from the 80s. Why would you have been going through Tommy's cryptocurrency accounts? Try to beat yourself up over actual screwups, not imagined ones."

Chapter 16

What were they going to do with the girl?

Esperanza listened to Naomi's footsteps on the stairs. She would be scanning the house. Wondering what she could steal and sell. Her survival instinct in overdrive, driven by her fear of not belonging here. Her fear of not deserving a home that wasn't rented by the hour. The girl turned the corner, saw Esperanza sitting there at the table. The girl was still in the clothes she'd shown up in, a too short skirt, a half shirt. The stomach flat, a black rose tattooed on her hip, horribly.

Esperanza pushed a plastic bag across the table.

"I got you some clothes," Esperanza said.

The girl blinked. Stood there.

"The bag won't bite." Esperanza took a sip from her coffee. Looked out the window.

The girl approached the bag. Looked at it like it was a trap, one of those with big metal jaws waiting to spring shut on her hand. Esperanza kept herself from laughing, barely. She knew the girl wouldn't take the laughing well, but you'd think nobody had ever given her a bag before. The girl looked inside. A three pack of plain white panties, gray sweatpants, a t-shirt, and a sweatshirt with a hood that looked like the head of a panda.

The girl's face scrunched up.

"You expect me to wear that?"

"I don't expect you to do anything, but those clothes are comfortable and will work until we can go out and get something else. Besides, Dom likes to keep the house cold, so you need something to keep you warm."

The girl looked back into the bag. She wanted to say "Thank You" but didn't know how to let go of the fear that somewhere in there was a trick. When was the last time this girl could trust someone? She wasn't one of these modern girls with her own website and her own bank account. No, she was a girl who needed someone to show her how to be a woman. To fill in the details, her parents had never been around to teach her.

"Go take a shower. I'll make you something to eat," Esperanza said.

WHEN THE GIRL came back downstairs, the shower had taken years off of her face, and the new clothes made her look younger than the nineteen Dominic had said she was. Her black hair was pulled back in a ponytail, and she entered the kitchen quicker this time. More carefree.

Esperanza asked her if she wanted milk or orange juice.

"Orange juice," Naomi said. Then a long pause. Then a low, "Please."

Esperanza served her eggs and bacon. The orange juice she put on the counter. Naomi poured her own glass half full. Then stood up and returned the carton to the fridge. Someone had taught her manners, someone had cared for her once.

"I'll go soon. I promise. I know you don't really want me here," Naomi said.

Esperanza smiled. What the girl said had been true when Esperanza saw her standing in the doorway, but now, Esperanza wasn't so sure of what she wanted, and she was beginning to see what Dominic saw in the girl and she was beginning to think maybe a project wouldn't be so bad. Something to think of other than the grief pulsing in her chest.

In the shower this morning, she'd remembered the time her son crashed a bicycle into a car and came home with a bloody nose, and she'd started hyperventilating and had to stumble out of the shower. Anything that could take her mind off of that had to be a blessing.

The garage door opened, and Dominic came in, two shopping bags in each hand. Naomi asked if there were more bags in the trunk, and Dominic nodded. She went to get them.

"What do you think?" Dominic asked after she was in the garage.

"She might stick it out. She might hock our television. Who knows?" Esperanza said.

"We could use a new TV anyway," Dominic said.

Chapter 17

Do people change much more than their addresses?

Maria had thought people didn't change much, but this case was making her wonder as she drove to Rebeka's house on the east side of Vegas in an area full of homes that had been built in the eighties. So much of Vegas was changing, and eventually this area would get bulldozed and made anew as well, but for now, the area was a reminder of what Vegas had looked like before all the developers saw opportunity.

Rebeka had gray hair that hung down to her chin, and wore a long blue skirt and a loose white blouse with long sleeves, and Maria had the same feeling she had looking at Serena. How had this grandmotherly woman standing in the doorway caught solicitation charges?

"I have to admit, I am curious to hear why a police detective would want to speak to me," Rebeka said.

"You can't think of anything I'd want to talk to you about?" Maria said.

"Honey, this is the most excitement I've had in decades, so no, I have no idea," Rebeka said.

"Well, it's decades ago I want to talk about," Maria said.

Rebeka crossed her arms and leaned against the doorway.

"What decade exactly are we talking about? I'm almost seventy. I've seen a few."

"80s. Your brother found a priest-"

"More like a demon. That scumbag priest got what he deserved."

LAS VEGAS *1970s*

Rebeka Brokos hated her mother.

The getting kicked out of the house didn't bother her, who wanted to live with that crazy bitch anyway, but the banning of her brother from speaking with her? What good had that done? If Rebeka had been around, that goddamn priest would never have gotten his hooks into her kid brothers. And look at what happened to them, all because her mother couldn't see the wolf hiding in the vestments.

But her mother would have never listened to Rebeka, anyway. She still believed that Rebeka was a hooker even though Rebeka had told her mother more than a million times, that no, she wasn't a hooker. She worked the phones for an escort agency. Rebeka was a big girl and while there were clients who liked big girls, they generally wanted them to do some weird stuff, like breastfeed while wearing diapers, or some such crap like that, and no way in hell was Rebeka doing any of that gross crap.

But Rebeka had a husky voice, and when the men heard her answer the phone, you could almost hear their hard-ons grow. At least that's what Antoinette, the owner of the agency, said. Rebeka didn't think you could really hear a hard-on grow, but what the hell did she know? She'd never seen Los Angeles much less Paris, whereas Antoinette had not only grown up in Paris but also seen most of the world.

Rebeka worked phones, set up dates, coordinated with the girls, just like any other office job, except this office job paid a whole hell of a lot better, and she didn't have to deal with that office power dynamic that all her friends had to deal with, is my boss going to start wanting blow jobs? Am I going to give him one? Rebeka figured she'd struck gold. Then her mother found a flier for the agency in Rebeka's purse, and what was she doing looking inside the purse anyway, but no way was her mother going to answer that question. Instead, her mother just kicked her out of the house and banned her son, John, from speaking to the fallen daughter. Stephen wasn't but a year old at the time, but playing with him had been Rebeka's favorite thing to do and having that torn away from her branded her soul in a way that only a therapist would be able to explain properly.

So Rebeka pushed her family out of her mind and focused on the life she had and before Rebeka knew it, she was living in a four-bedroom house with a swimming pool and a cleaning lady and more space than Rebeka even knew what to do with. Then gay prostitution became glamorous and Antoinette decided to expand and her brother, John, answered the ad for male models.

Absolutely not, Rebeka told Antoinette.

Would you rather he was out on the streets or have us looking out for him? Antoinette said.

And that's how easy it was for Rebeka to pimp out her brother.

And John was a moneymaker, tall and lean and nineteen. Crystal blue eyes. Rock hard abs. All the clients loved him. Apparently, John was superbly talented. Clients would rave to Rebeka about what John could do with his tongue, and Rebeka hated her mother more and more with every phone call.

But at least John was in her life.

He moved in with her in the big house, and for a time, everything was heavenly. She came in a little later, taking calls on a big block of a cell phone that Antoinette bought her, so Rebeka could make John breakfast and listen to his stories. Rebeka didn't want to hear about the sex, but she did love hearing him describe the penthouse suites he visited and the private house parties behind the gates of mansions, and the life sounded so glamorous, but still, a part of her hated that her brother had to do any of this, and Rebeka started paying attention to her bank accounts, started thinking about the value of her house, started wondering if maybe, him and her could get up and go. Start over some place new.

Somewhere in that time, he told her about the priest.

As soon as John finished the story, Rebeka went to her mother's house. Banged on the door. Her mother answered, Bible clutched to her chest like a shield, but she wouldn't open the screen door. Rebeka had to talk to her through the mesh, so Rebeka told her right there on the stoop. Told her everything that priest had done to John, and she made damn sure that her mother listened to every word, and when Rebeka was done, her mother called her a liar. A Satanist. A demon. And Rebeka punched right through that mesh and pulled her mother against the screen and told her to keep Stephen away from that priest. Stephen was the baby. Stephen had to be protected.

For a brief second, Rebeka thought she had broken through, thought her mother had actually heard her, maybe would consider what she said, but that second wasn't a breakthrough, that second of lightness in her eyes and slackness in her posture was fear, and Rebeka released a hold of her mother's shirt, and her mother pulled back hissing like a scalded cat and slammed the door shut. Rebeka pulled her hand back through the screen half a second before the wood would have slammed her fingers against the decorative metal sheath.

When she returned home, John was sitting on the front steps with a bottle of whiskey and an ashtray full of cigarette butts. He asked her how the visit had gone.

"You knew I'd go?" Rebeka said.

"Who can turn down a chance at redemption?" John said.

And Rebeka knew just by looking at him, he'd already told their mother everything, and she'd chosen the priest and the church over her own son.

"In fairness to Mom, I did hock her television to go to San Francisco, so maybe I'm not the most reliable witness," John said.

"And what about Stephen?" Rebeka said.

"You get used to it," John said. "You can get used to anything."

That's the moment that broke Rebeka in two.

Rebeka didn't have to worry about the priest and Stephen for long though because within a week the priest was dead, his smiling face plastered all over the newspapers, and Rebeka couldn't have been happier. Relieved in a way that is difficult to express in words. Whatever evils this world may hold, that priest was never going to touch Stephen again. She thought maybe things would turn around after the priest died, maybe her and John could do something different, maybe Stephen could be contacted, some kind of forgiveness could be found between her and her mother.

What a bitter pipe dream.

John caught HIV and advanced to full-blown AIDS within months. He was dead, a year after that, a wasted away shriveled version of his beautiful self. A decade later, they found Stephen in a rundown motel, a .45 in his mouth. Rebeka never even got the opportunity to speak to him.

━━

DURING THE WHOLE time Rebeka had unburdened her soul, she'd never looked at Maria. Just kept her eyes looking up in the sky, a heaviness to her voice matched only by the misery of her story.

"Did any of the detectives investigating the Desert Saint ever come to see you?" Maria asked.

"They didn't know I existed until I met Jack at Stephen's funeral," Rebeka said.

"So you don't actually know if the priest was molesting Stephen, do you?"

"Don't see why he wouldn't have. Do pedophiles really stop?" Rebeka said.

"But you never spoke to Stephen yourself, so it's possible-"

"John went to go see him. Told him the priest was bad news, to stay away, and Stephen got defensive, angry, said Father Michael was the only person who really cared about him. Except he didn't call him Father Michael, he called him Mike. That fucking priest was definitely molesting him," Rebeka said.

"You're probably right," Maria said.

"I need a drink. Give me a second, will ya?" Rebecca stood up and went inside her house.

The house was small and on a street with other smaller, older homes. Rebeka's car, a ten-year-old Toyota, sat in the driveway. For all the glamour in her story, Rebeka had ended up in a modest part of town living in modest circumstances. She'd said she worked as a receptionist, and Maria wondered if any money was left over from the glory days.

Maria looked through the living room window. All the furniture looked like it was from Ikea. The house was neat, if a little cramped, not much space between the couch, the coffee table, and the television. Maria would have liked to nose around inside a bit more. See some photos. Check the status of the kitchen. You could tell a lot about someone from their kitchen. But Rebeka hadn't invited her in. With most people that would be a sign of guilt. But with someone like Rebeka who'd worked for an illegal business for so long, it could just be an old habit.

When Rebeka came back out, she had a vodka tonic in one hand and a picture in the other. The picture was of her and John. What'd she said about him being handsome was true. John had a head of shaggy brown hair that hung down to just above big crystal blue eyes. Rebeka had been slightly skinnier than she was now, but not much. Just like John though, she was good looking, a pretty round face, long brown hair.

"Thought you should be able to put faces to the stories. Something more than mugshots anyway," Rebeka said.

"Speaking of mugshots, I saw yours," Maria said.

"Yeah, they finally did end up shutting us down. Antoinette paid for the attorneys and everything got worked out, but that was pretty much the end," Rebeka said.

"I understand the procuring charge. What was the transportation charge for?" Maria said.

"I used the office phone to buy a plane ticket for a girl to go see her mother for Christmas. Can you believe they tried to charge me with that bullshit? No offense, but I found the people working in prostitution to be a hell of a lot more honest and forthcoming than the people in law enforcement. I mean, we weren't hurting anyone. Everybody was an adult. Everybody was taken care of. Antoinette took girls from trailer parks and taught them how to act like a lady. Besides, everybody loves to screw, but we were bad because people were paying for it. Come on," Rebeka said.

"Did you know Anthony Scarvale," Maria said.

Rebeka leaned back her head and laughed.

"Anthony, he had the sexiest voice. That's what I remember about Anthony," Rebeka said.

"So Anthony was a client of your escort service?" Maria said.

"Us, Michelle's, Harry's, shit, everyone's," Rebeka said.

"And you spoke with him often?" Maria said.

"Often? I don't know. Maybe a few times a month. He used to call everyone 'sweetie', he'd call up and say, now listen sweetie, I need me a new live wire, that's what he called the girls that really did their jobs well, live wires," Rebeka said. She smiled as if she was remembering a fond moment.

"Sounds like a favorite customer," Maria said.

"He just had charisma. You could hear it in his voice, and the girls liked to work with him. If you were going to be paid to go to bed, might as well be with a tall, good looking man," Rebeka said.

"There were rumors that he sometimes got a little rough with the girls?" Maria said.

"Honey, they don't pay them to treat them like princesses," Rebeka said.

"So you can confirm Anthony was a little rough from time to time?" Maria said.

Rebeka opened her mouth to say something but then stopped. She scrunched her nose like she was smelling something foul and shook her head.

"Bad memory?" Maria said.

"I just remembered something, something I'd forgotten," Rebeka said.

"Well, don't keep me in suspense," Maria said.

"We had a girl, Ruby, hit him with a lamp," Rebeka said.

"A lamp?" Maria said.

"One of the long-standing ones. She knocked him on his ass and gave him a couple more shots to make sure he didn't follow her and headed out of the house," Rebeka said.

"Was there a reason for her hitting him with the lamp?" Maria said.

"Something about him smacking her in the face after she told him not to," Rebeka said.

"Sounds like a good reason to hit someone with a lamp," Maria said.

"Maybe. She claimed he was choking her as well, but I asked around, and none of the other girls said that Anthony was a choker."

"So Ruby clocks Anthony and says he was choking her. Then what happened?" Maria said.

"Antoinette fired her, of course," Rebeka said.

"Fired her for defending herself?" Maria said.

"All the girls had drivers. All she had to do was go outside and the driver would have taken care of everything," Rebeka said.

"And if Anthony wouldn't let her go?" Maria said.

"Well, if she could hit him with a lamp, she probably could have gotten outside," Rebeka said.

"So it didn't bother you, the whole situation?" Maria said.

"Bother me? Those women knew what they were signing up for and they made more money than most attorneys. The women who worked for Antoinette weren't there because they had to be. They made a choice. They weren't like those poor girls out on the streets being herded like cattle by pimps. Most of the time, the girls were worshiped and showered with money, and almost all of them ended up marrying clients. Probably seventy percent of them. So no, I wasn't bothered by what happened between Ruby and Anthony, if anything, I felt bad for Ruby. She threw away the chance to really make something of herself just because of one bad date. How many shitty dates do most women go through before they find the one who puts a ring on their finger? So Anthony was a little rough. All she had to do was ride it out and tell Antoinette to never book her with Anthony again," Rebeka said.

"So there was a process in place if a girl didn't like a particular customer," Maria said.

"Of course, they weren't slaves," Rebeka said.

"Which means that there had been issues with customers. Any serious issues?" Maria said.

Rebeka frowned. Maria leaned forward. Touched her on the arm.

"Believe me, I've learned more in the last twenty minutes than people have learned in decades. Whatever else you can tell me will be very helpful," Maria said.

"I came along a few years after this incident, but one of the girls got beaten up bad. Miracle she was alive. The man had followed her home after a date, so there was no driver, no witnesses, but she was able to fight her way free," Rebeka said.

"What did the police do?" Maria said.

"Police? In 1970s Vegas? The man who attacked her was connected to the mob. He was untouchable. I heard Antoinette bought her a one-way plane ticket to New York as soon as she was released from the hospital." Rebeka frowned. Looked at her feet.

"What is it you don't want to tell me?" Maria said.

"It's just rumor and innuendo. You know. I shouldn't be talking bad about Antoinette. She gave me an amazing life," Rebeka said.

"I promise I won't follow up on anything that isn't solid. I'm looking for answers, not to hound people," Maria said.

"I was mugged one night walking out of the office. Antoinette gave me the cutest little .22. Told me I'd have to shoot a man in the face or in the balls because a .22 doesn't have much stopping power. I showed it to one of the girls a few weeks later, a girl, Miranda, who'd been with the agency a long time. She told me to be careful. Said Antoinette might have shot Big Al with that gun. Apparently someone killed the man who followed that girl home and attacked her. Shot him in the head in the street. Police never found the killer. Miranda thought it was Antoinette defending her girls in the only way she could," Rebeka said.

"Do you still have that gun?" Maria said.

"No, I threw it away years ago."

"Do you remember when Ruby had the issue with Anthony?"

"Hard to be sure. I don't remember booking him much after that date with Ruby though," Rebeka said.

"And when did Antoinette give you the gun?" Maria said.

"A year or two later," Rebeka said.

"Whatever happened to Antoinette?" Maria asked.

"She moved back to France after our case got dismissed. I tried to keep the business going after she went, but it didn't work out. The girls, they looked up to Antoinette, she was sophisticated and elegant, all the things they wanted to be. Me, I was just this dowdy woman from dusty ol Nevada. Last I heard Antoinette died of cancer a few years back," Rebeka said.

Chapter 18

How did you figure out what to focus on when nothing made sense?

Maria filled Michael in on what Rebeka had told her. He was standing by the whiteboard in the conference room looking at a photo of Father Michael McGuire in full priestly regalia.

"How did they miss that during the original investigation?" Michael said.

"It was a long time ago," Maria said.

"But still, the detectives should have heard rumors."

"They heard the rumors but thought they were just that, rumors," Maria said.

"What else did you get from the woman?"

Maria laid out everything Rebeka had said about working for the agency. Then she told him about the gun Antoinette gave her and the rumor of it being used before. Maria pulled up a website on her phone devoted to unsolved mob killings and scrolled down to Big Al's murder. No witnesses. Two .22s to the head.

"Could be the first Desert Saint shooting. Matches the telltale signs," she said.

A patrolman stuck his head in the conference room and told

them that Harold was waiting for them in the interrogation room. Michael thanked him.

"Should we head over?" Michael said.

"Nah, let him stew a bit. It'll piss him off."

"Ok, back to your theory, you like a woman for this. The madam. I don't know," Michael said.

"And all this time I had you for a closet feminist," Maria said.

"Female serial killers, not exactly common. Call me sexist if you want, but I'm just talking about what we've seen. Not just not common. Downright rare," Michael said.

"Rare doesn't mean never," Maria said. "Besides, if it's the madam, we're not really talking about a serial killer anymore. She would have selected her victims for what they did, not who they were."

"A vigilante killer? Don't they only exist in movies?" Michael said.

"Admittedly, it's an unlikely scenario, but what else have we got?" Maria said.

"Where does the priest fit in? You're figuring this woman told her boss and the boss lady went to exact vengeance," Michael said.

"Yeah," Maria said.

"And the nurse?"

"There were doubts about whether the woman was actually killed by the Desert Saint. The M.O. changed," Maria said.

"But the husband was a definite," Michael said.

"So imagine you're the Desert Saint and some husband kills his wife and blames it on you," Maria said.

"Yeah, that guy would make the list," Michael said.

"The other victims were people who abused women and if the Desert Saint was someone who saw herself as protecting vulnerable people then there must have been a reason why the vics drew attention, and seeing how she had an escort agency, maybe these pimps were trying to recruit her girls, or maybe she was taking in girls who were leaving the pimps," Maria said.

"From street walker to high-class hooker? Really?" Michael said.

"Rebeka talked about her old boss, Antoinette, like she was

some kind of savant in turning women around. She taught the women how to act classy, taught them how to dress, turned them into women who could pass as respectable, a woman like that might do her own recruiting on the streets, maybe she'd see girls walking around and see potential," Maria said.

"And the pimps probably wouldn't like that. A lot of them might try to get those girls back. This is all really thin. It's hypothetically hypothetical-"

"You been smoking weed and reading philosophy books on me?" Maria said.

"I'm just saying that it requires quite a few leaps and you know as well as I do, usually figuring out who the bad guy is doesn't take so many leaps," Michael said.

"Usually we're not chasing serial killers who started killing again after almost forty years," Maria said.

"And now we come to the real issue. Was she in Vegas a few days ago?" Michael said.

"Rebeka says she died of cancer," Maria said.

"There goes that lead."

"Maybe she left the gun to someone. I'm going to follow up and see if she has family here."

"But first, let's see what Harold has to say."

Chapter 19

The observation room felt colder.

Maria looked through the glass. Harold looked different sitting at the interrogation room table. Maria tried to figure out what it was, his hair, his clothes, the way he sat, but after looking him over and trying to compare the present Harold to the Harold she'd known her whole life, Maria realized, what was different wasn't Harold, it was her. She suspected Harold of something and she was looking at him how she looked at any other perp, and what she saw was a man in his late thirties who looked like he was pushing fifty. Pasty white skin, pot belly, flabby arms, and an unshaven face. He looked pathetic, but Maria wondered what that pathetic outside was hiding. Harold had always been Tommy's tag along. Not good looking, not outgoing or athletic, but deeply loyal to Tommy. Would he open up about any secrets that Tommy might have had?

Or would he take those secrets with him?

"How do you think I should go at him?" Michael asked.

"Like you're his best buddy. If you get too aggressive, his back will get up, but he wants to be liked. So if you act like you guys are buddies, he'll go along," Maria said.

Michael headed next door, and Maria leaned against the glass.

Felt the coolness against her cheek. She was exhausted, the emotion, a sleepless night, the stress. She needed to focus, but all she wanted to do was melt into this wall. How was she going to figure this out if she couldn't even think straight? She stepped back from the glass and smacked herself on the cheek.

Michael entered the room on the other side.

"What the hell, man? You brought me in here and leave me waiting forever? What's that about?" Harold said.

"I'm sorry. I had to go and find my files and somebody moved them. Can you believe that? I mean, who messes with a man's desk, am I right?" Michael placed the folders on the table and flashed a smile at Harold.

Maria knew Michael was good at this, but normally she was standing next to him. She rarely got to view him from a distance, and she found herself even more impressed than she expected to be. That posture. That smile. It screamed, easygoing. She knew Michael was as tense and tired as she was, but that smile was so genuine, Michael shouldn't have been a cop, he should be playing a cop on television. Very few people could pretend that well.

Harold wanted to be angry, aggrieved, but couldn't be. Not facing that likeability. He leaned back in the chair, waved at Michael with his hand as if to say, they were good, no big deal. His hand had a bandage covering the thumb and pointer finger.

Michael asked what happened.

"Phone rang when I was hanging a photo of me and Tommy. Like a dumbass, I let myself get distracted and bam. I nailed them both good." Harold turned the hand around and looked down at it. Shook his head as if remembering the pain.

"Hope it was at least an important phone call," Michael said.

"Telemarketer trying to sell me home cameras," Harold said.

Michael sat down and gathered his folders together, took his time selecting the one that he was looking for and opened it up. He ran his finger down a list and then stopped halfway. Tapped at it and looked up at Harold.

"You and Tommy were tight, huh?" Michael said.

"Best friends since first grade."

"No shit, a friendship lasts that long, that means something, something a lot of people can't even begin to understand," Michael said.

"You ain't kidding. You know we never fought, not over girls, not over bullshit, not over nothing. I'd a died for him," Harold said.

"And I'm sure he would have for you too," Michael said.

"Damn right," Harold said.

"Look, I'm not going to sugarcoat things for you. We don't have much to go on with this murder. That's not to say we got nothing. But we don't have much, and we're really looking for some help to get us over the top," Michael said.

"Anything you need, anything I can do, I'm ready," Harold said.

Maria pulled up a chair and sat in it. Put her feet up against the wall. Michael had Harold roped in now. The trick was in setting up the question in such a way that the target couldn't say no. By starting with friendship, Michael had put Harold in a corner. Of course Harold would express his devotion, and since he was so devoted, he had to be willing to help because a devoted friend would help, of course he would, unless... Unless that friend had something to hide, and no target whether hiding something or not would admit to being constrained. So Harold had to be willing to answer questions and now Michael could bring that up every time Harold balked. "What do you mean you don't want to get into this? I thought you wanted to help." And that's exactly what Michael did as he walked Harold through the whole file starting with where Harold was when Tommy was killed.

"What do you mean by asking me that? I thought you needed help," Harold said.

"Just ruling you out. Standard procedure. Don't you watch cop shows?" Michael said. Another great line, everyone watched cop shows, everyone "knew" what a cop could and couldn't do, what standard procedure was, how hard it was to solve a crime after forty-eight hours. Believing that you knew made people arrogant, and arrogant people were easily tricked.

Harold didn't have an alibi, not a real one at least, but he was online, so the internet provider could provide evidence, not foolproof evidence but still, proof that someone was at his home at the time of the murder.

"You and him used to frame houses together, didn't you?"

"Sure, but I moved into remodeling, fixing up living rooms, making cabinets. It's harder work, but it pays better, and you don't have to be outside in 110 degree heat," Harold said.

"Tommy though, he had hit it big with that YouTube channel, right?"

"Yeah man, he's got a great face for the camera, you know? I mean, I didn't see all that YouTube stuff blowing up or anything, but he did. He was smart, smarter than he looked, I used to tell him. Not smart like his sister, she was always smarter than the two of us combined, but he could figure people out, that's a different kind of smart. He saw what people were interested in and then used that to make money," Harold said.

"He knew how to hit people's sweet spots, didn't he?" Michael said.

"Yeah, he did. Most non-political guy I ever met. He never voted, not once. Didn't even read the papers, but he heard some old guy ranting about immigrants one day, and he did his research and figured out that a character, an anti-immigration Mexican-American would really take off. He told me he'd have to keep it virtual. He couldn't imagine going to conventions and all that crap, but yeah, he wanted to draw people in with the act and then hit them up for other things," Harold said.

"What other things?" Michael said.

Harold had been leaning forward, arms resting on the table, and now he sat back, visibly uncomfortable. He crossed his arms across his chest. Made a face like he was chewing on something bitter. Michael was approaching something Harold wasn't sure about telling.

"Look, I'm a homicide detective. If it ain't related to a dead body, I don't give a shit, so if Tommy was involved in some kind of scam, not my concern, but I might be able to trace that scam to the guy that killed him, and you want us to find that guy, don't you?" Michael said.

Harold turned over what Michael was saying.

Maria leaned forward in her chair and focused on Harold's face. She saw dark circles around his eyes and stubble lining his chin. He looked like a man about to break from the stresses of life, and just for a second, Maria felt for him. Losing Tommy must have been devastating, but he had to own up to his responsibility as a friend to help find the killer. If he didn't, she might go in there and start ramming him into the walls.

"I don't think the YouTube channel was the real thing Tommy was focused on," Harold said.

"Really? I mean, I saw those videos. They were slick. He put time and effort into them," Michael said.

"Yeah, he did, but I think those videos were just an attempt to find people."

"I'm confused. How does a video help you find people?" Michael said.

"Look, I'm just a guy who installs cabinets. I'll make your bathroom look nice. I can build a hell of a bookshelf, not that anybody reads anymore, but the stuff Tommy was into, the things he talked about, it was a little bit over my head," Harold said.

"But you guys were tight. He must have explained it to you," Michael said.

"Yeah, yeah he did. The thing is, I barely understood what he was saying, so I might give you bad info if I try to remember, and besides, I mean, I don't even know if this is related at all to anything. I could be wasting your time," Harold said.

"Trust me, I got nothing else to go on, so everything helps," Michael said.

"And you're not going to go telling this stuff to his folks. I don't want them hearing things about him after he died, you know?" Harold said.

"I'm only interested in finding his killer, Harold. Nothing else matters to me."

Michael hadn't answered Harold's question, another trick, make a statement unrelated to the question but with a tone of voice that implies agreement and the target will hear the tone of voice and not the words. People believe what they want to believe.

Harold leaned forward again. The tension went out of his shoulders, and he told Michael that Tommy wasn't really interested in YouTube views, the medium was too competitive, a few big names and everybody else fighting for scraps, but he was interested in the ecosystem of people who watched YouTube videos. He had created an Instagram account and a twitter account for his anti-immigrant Mexican-American persona, and he searched for people who subscribed or followed him and then tried to map out all of their friends, searching for connections that he could use.

"Use for what?" Michael said.

PACS, Harold said. PACS for whatever political purpose was near and dear to that person's heart, and Tommy would bombard those people with emails asking for donations to PACS that didn't even exist, but he had a guy, Anatov, who had a payment processing company, and him and Tommy had a deal. Anatov let him use the payment processing even though Tommy didn't have the proper paperwork, companies, PAC registration, whatever, and Tommy gave Anatov a cut of the profits.

"How much money are we talking about?" Michael asked.

Harold didn't know. But Tommy figured the world was messed up, everybody was angry, and people were so used to spending money online and nobody gave a crap about twenty dollars here or fifty dollars there. People just wanted to feel like they were supporting something, like they were doing something more than just shaking their fist at the television, but Tommy's genius, Tommy's real contribution was in researching social media for targets. There were companies that would sell you that information but Tommy didn't want any evidence tying him back to the emails, so he did it all himself and nobody could say he was doing anything other than building a social media presence.

"But they could have traced the money back to him," Michael said.

"Anatov's company was in Russia which was where the

payments went, and he rerouted the money to Tommy in bitcoin, totally untraceable," Harold said.

"Now this, this is very helpful," Michael said.

But was it, Maria wondered. All the Saint's previous victims were tied in some way to victimizing others. A personal, usually sexual victimization. This was a different kind of victimization. How would this have brought the attention of the Desert Saint?

Something was wrong.

WHILE MICHAEL SAW HAROLD OUT, Maria ran Antionette, but all the information she found was old and unusable, and Antoinette did not have nor had she ever had a Nevada Driver's license. A Google search of Antoinette's name found a bunch of archived articles that had been uploaded to the internet, and one newer article by a national magazine. A reporter had written a retrospective on Vegas in the 80s, and Antoinette's agency and her arrest were major parts of the story. Maria emailed the reporter her contact information and asked her to call, but she wasn't holding her breath on receiving any help.

Going back into the old case files, Maria was able to find the name of Antoinette's attorney, Morris Iverson. She found a number for his law office and reached Morris's daughter who had taken over the business while Morris mostly golfed and sunned himself. The daughter, Felicia, had no knowledge of Antoinette, but Maria impressed on her the importance of this case, and Felicia agreed to get in touch with her father. Five minutes later, Morris was on the phone. He sounded like he was outside and annoyed to be bothered, but when Maria explained she was investigating a homicide, he gave her all of his attention.

"And you suspect Antoinette of a homicide? That's absurd," he said.

"Some information points to her. We'd like to give her a chance to rule herself out."

"What information exactly?"

"I just want to interview her," Maria said.

"If you don't give me more information, I'm not sure if she'd be willing to talk," Morris said.

"So she's alive?"

A long pause as Morris reviewed his options.

"Look, this isn't solicitation, this isn't something that's going to go away. The best thing we can do is all get on the phone-"

"Fine, hold on," Morris said.

The line went silent as Morris put her on hold and then the tinny sound of a phone ringing and a woman's voice, old but firm. Morris told Antoinette that a homicide detective was on the line who had some questions for her.

"Homicide?" Antoinette said.

"I know, it's absurd. Best to just answer the questions," Morris said.

A long sigh came through the receiver and then a pause that seemed to last a week.

"I believed I was done with the police. If they don't have their hand out, they're chasing after you for some other nonsense," Antoinette said.

"Maybe-" Morris started to say.

"Morris, I'm eighty-two. At this point, none of it matters," Antoinette said.

"You sound about twenty years younger," Maria said.

"Buttering me up to start? Not likely to work. What the hell do you want?" Antoinette said.

"I'd like to start with a man named Big Al," Maria said.

"Big Al? Al Deltoro? You're investigating his death? Why? To give the person a medal?" Antoinette said.

"My client does not mean to diminish the seriousness-"

"Morris, do be quiet, please. I'm talking with the detective. I know you're trying to do your job, but I don't have anything to hide, so you don't have anything to worry about," Antoinette said.

"So you did know Al Deltoro?" Maria said.

"Yes, I knew him and apart from his mother, I can't think of anyone who would shed a tear over the death of such a horrid man," Antoinette said.

"Yeah, I heard he had a thing for attacking women," Maria said.

"Attacking? I think he killed at least two of my girls. Maybe three," Antoinette said.

"One girl got away, right?"

"Veronica. Poor thing. She was in the hospital for a month, but she survived," Antoinette said.

"That must have bothered you," Maria said.

"That's a stupid statement," Antoinette said.

"Stupid?"

"It's obvious it bothered me. Are people really this dense when you interview them? I wish I had killed Al Deltoro, but I didn't. Can I hang up the phone now?" Antoinette said.

"We understand you used to own a handgun," Maria said.

"A what?" Antoinette said.

"A handgun. A .22," Maria said.

Antoinette laughed. A relieved laugh. A laugh at the ridiculousness of what Maria said, but the laugh petered out halfway through as Antoinette realized something. When she spoke again, her mood had gone from aggrievement to rage.

"You talked to that crazy bitch Rebeka and like a fool, you believed her," Antoinette said.

"Why do you think I was talking to someone named Rebeka?" Maria said.

"Because she's the only person I ever knew who owned a .22, and she's damned crazy and likely to have done something she would need to blame on someone she thinks is dead," Antoinette said.

The rest of the conversation took maybe five minutes, but the details left Maria thinking she was a fool. Rebeka had started working for Antoinette before Al Deltoro's death, and Antoinette had never given her a .22. Antoinette despised guns, but Rebeka had used her first pay from the agency to buy a small .22 that fit snugly in her purse. Also, Rebeka had been obsessed with Anthony Scarvale. When Anthony called in to set up a date, Rebeka would need to be pushed off the phone because she was so busy flirting with him, and her brother hadn't come in due to an ad. He came in because Rebeka dragged him in. Antoinette hadn't wanted to hire him. It was obvious the young man had a problem with drugs, but Rebeka had pleaded. The whole thing had been a fiasco since her brother had ended up attacking a client. Sure, eventually Rebeka's quirks grew on Antoinette and she always showed up for work and never spoke about business to anyone not working for Antoinette, but when everything came to an end and Antoinette moved to New York, Rebeka lied to the girls. She said Antoinette was still running the agency just under the radar, and this was after Antoinette had agreed in her plea deal to not be a part of any aspect of a business involved in prostitution. After Morris sent her a cease and desist letter, Rebeka showed up at Antoinette's doorstep in New York.

"She was raving about how I had to return. How I needed to come back to Vegas and start over. I told her absolutely not and to not use my name, and that crazy bitch showed me her .22 and threatened me. Said she used it before and she'd use it again. I had literally just left the doctor's office where I found out I had cancer and there she was, waiting outside my building. What a miserable day," Antoinette said.

"We, of course, filed a police report, but Rebeka returned to Las Vegas before the NYPD even got around to investigating. I waited a few months and then I had a funeral notice printed up and sent it to Rebeka and a few others," Morris said.

"You faked her death?" Maria said.

"Seemed like the best option. I didn't want someone thinking Antoinette would eventually spill her secrets. A lot of powerful people were clients of her service, so I thought if maybe word got around she had passed, people would breathe easier and no one would have any stupid fears, and since the chemo made her lose her hair and weight, we had a convincing photo to share," Morris said.

"Can you prove any of this?" Maria said.

"I can send over a copy of the cease and desist letter, the restraining order, and the forged funeral notice," Morris said.

"I kept some phone bills from back then as evidence. She called me two hundred and eighty times in one month," Antoinette said.

"So she thinks you're dead, huh?" Maria said.

"And we'd like to keep it that way," Morris said.

"Unless you telling her otherwise will achieve something," Antoinette said.

"I'm not sure-" Morris said.

"Oh Morris, like she can do anything to me now that wouldn't be a relief," Antoinette said.

MARIA HUNG up and tossed her cellphone onto her desk.

"Sounded like a hell of a call," Michael said.

"I'm an asshole," Maria said.

"Normally this is the part of the conversation where I list the reasons why you're an asshole," Michael said.

"I didn't even think to question Rebeka's story. I just accepted everything she said. How could I be so blind?"

"And what did the madam say?" Michael said.

Maria laid out all the parts that Michael couldn't figure out from listening to her talk. As she went through everything, he made notes and when she was done, he stared at his notes in silence for a bit before circling words and drawing lines. Maria got up from her chair and walked around to look over his shoulder, but she couldn't read Michael's handwriting. It looked like a cross between Japanese and Egyptian hieroglyphics. He did that on purpose, in case his notes were ever subpoenaed. He didn't like the idea of anyone getting inside his brain.

"Are you thinking this woman, Rebeka, could be the Desert Saint?" Michael said.

"You got anyone else better in mind?" Maria said.

"We've been wondering what the connection to Tommy was, right?"

"We're not in a Sherlock Holmes movie. Get to the point," Maria said.

Michael leaned back in his chair. Put the tip of his pen in his mouth and looked thoughtfully up at the ceiling.

"I'm getting my taser," Maria said.

"I think I know how we can find the connection," Michael said.

Chapter 20

Reality was there, if searched for properly.

Michael had been talking about social media. Rebeka had no Instagram or Twitter. Maybe she had a Snapchat, but Michael doubted it, not right for her demographic, but Rebeka did have a Facebook account, and Rebeka, for all of her calm grandmotherly exterior, was a very angry woman.

She railed against the drug companies, against health insurers, against politicians. Sometimes she complained about immigrants, but she trained most of her anger at people who were more power-ful, not less powerful, but what was most interesting as Michael and Maria scrolled through her feed was how Rebeka had gone from supporting Obama to Trump to Andrew Yang.

"And they said swing voters don't exist," Michael said.

"How is that possible, though? To swing from those candidates to the other?" Maria said.

"What do all of them have in common?" Michael said.

"Dicks," Maria said.

"Other than that," Michael said.

"Nothing."

"Not nothing, they're all outsiders. Or at least have successfully portrayed themselves that way. This is a woman deeply disillusioned and disappointed with life, and why wouldn't she be? Her parents betrayed her. Both of her kid brothers were abused by a priest. Both of them died. She's screaming at the world because the world has let her down," Michael said.

"The PACs. You think maybe Tommy ripped her off, and she figured it out," Maria said.

"That would be the direct link we're missing, wouldn't it?" Michael said.

"But we don't even know if she made any donations to a PAC."

"Then let's find out," Michael said.

"What are we going to do? Call her up and ask her?"

"We'll get a warrant for her bank records and look for any payments to PACs and then see if those payments went to Anatov's payment processing company," Michael said.

"Yeah, and then I'll walk on water. Who's going to give us a warrant with this flimsy ass case?"

"I went out with an assistant D.A. last week. I'll call her," Michael said.

"Sure, because going out on a date with you is going to make her help us," Maria said.

"We had a great time," Michael said.

"You tried to get her to split the bill, didn't you?"

"It was obvious that we weren't going any further than that dinner. We both knew it halfway through," Michael said.

"You didn't even pay for dinner and now you think she's going to help us out."

"She's a reasonable woman," Michael said.

THE ASSISTANT D.A. wasn't going to help. Michael didn't even get the chance to ask, since she hung up on him when he mentioned he was looking for help with a case. Nor was Moyer who found the whole scenario laughable. They thought the Desert Saint was a woman who happened to be a former escort service receptionist.

"Not fucking likely" was Moyer's reply before kicking them out of his office.

"Go do some real police work," Moyer said.

Whatever the hell that meant.

They had one move left. Bring in Anatov and bullshit him.

ANATOV HAD a much different look from the pool party photos: a light gray suit, no tie, royal blue button-down shirt and wire-rimmed glasses. Most importantly though, he didn't come to the station alone. He came with his attorneys, Wilfred and Wendy Pritchard. As soon as Maria saw them entering the interrogation room with Anatov, she knew they were toast.

A year earlier, Maria and Michael had busted an attorney for killing his wife. Settling on the husband hadn't taken long because they'd found out within a few hours the wife was having an affair, but proving the husband was guilty had been much harder and was only made possible when they tracked down a Nevada Power and Light lineman who'd seen the husband leaving the house about the time of the murder. When the trial happened though, the lineman wasn't so sure. He claimed that maybe the guy he saw had dirty blonde hair, whereas the husband had black hair.

Maria had been in court watching the testimony, and she was sure someone had gotten to the lineman, so she'd run a check on him. No big deposits in his accounts, no new purchases. If he'd gotten paid off, he'd been smart. But then Maria had run a background check on his family. The lineman's son had an assault charge and a pending trial. One of Wilfred and Wendy's associates defended the son and got everything dismissed. Being a lineman was a good job, but Wilfred and Wendy's firm was the best, and a lot of their associates worked "pro bono" cases supposedly building up experience, but Maria suspected those cases weren't randomly selected. Good luck proving that one though.

"Why is our client here?" Wilfred asked.

"We need his assistance in solving a murder," Michael said.

"My client has no knowledge about any murders," Wilfred said.

"I haven't even told you who I'm talking about," Michael said.

"You don't need to. We spoke with our client on the way over, and we know that there's nothing that he could possibly help you with," Wendy said.

"Can I at least get a question or two out before you two decide what he can and can not help with?" Michael said.

"So our client isn't suspected of being a part of anything?" Wilfred asked.

"We have a dead male, Thomas Manuel Varela, who had business ties to your client. We are curious if those business ties could have been a factor in his murder," Michael said.

Anatov scrunched up his nose and looked at Wilfred. Shook his head.

"Our client doesn't know any Thomas Manuel Varela. Your information is wrong. He had no business ties with this person," Wilfred said.

"He went by Tommy," Michael said as he pulled out a blown-up photo of the post that showed Tommy and Anatov sitting at the pool cabana.

"A social media post? This is what you are presenting as evidence that our client had a business relationship. Spare me the nonsense, please. Anatov is a well-known promoter who has his photo taken hundreds if not thousands of times a week," Wendy said.

"This is Dominic Varela's son, isn't it? Which would make it your partner's brother. Is she involved in this case?" Wilfred said.

"No," Michael said.

"I would sure hope not because it would hopelessly taint the whole investigation, and we would hate for you all to not be able to solve a crime because of doubts about the veracity of the investigators." Wilfred leaned back and looked at the one-way mirror.

Maria knew he couldn't see her, but he was smart enough to know that she was there, and him looking her way made her uncomfortable enough that she wanted to leave the room. God, she hated Wilfred and Wendy.

"We have a witness who ties Anatov and his payment processing business to our vic," Michael said.

"And who is this witness? Another nutjob spreading conspiracies about Russians?" Wilfred asked.

"What?" Michael said.

"Our client has suffered enough with the anti-Russian sentiment in this country. It's open season on blaming Russians for whatever the police or FBI can't solve. To be honest, I'm a little disappointed, detective. I had you pegged as an honest cop," Wendy said.

"You'd think an African-American man like yourself would be sensitive to false accusations and unfair treatment," Wilfred said.

"This has nothing to do with him being Russian. That's absurd. We don't even currently suspect Anatov of being personally involved in the crime, but we'd like to know more about his business relationship with the deceased," Michael said.

"Well if he's not suspected of being involved in anything, we'll be going, and Detective, the next time you want to go on a fishing expedition, may I suggest the White River in Arkansas." Wendy stood up and turned to open the door.

"You going to let those two talk for you all day?" Michael said.

Anatov smiled.

"Me English not so good. Better they talk, yes?"

Michael waited for Anatov and the attorneys to be well away before he came into the observation room. He looked upset, and Maria realized he had been hopeful about the chance to get something out of Anatov. She had been hopeful too until she saw Wilfred and Wendy flanking him.

"I messed that up. I never should have said that we didn't suspect him of being involved. That gave them an opportunity to walk," Michael said.

"They were walking regardless. The only thing you did was save time."

"Could you believe that crap about Russiaphobia? I was so damn surprised it totally threw me off," Michael said.

"Yeah, they're amazing. The assholes."

"Now what do we do?" Michael asked.

"We take another run at Rebeka. But tomorrow. I have a wake to go to," Maria said.

"Shit, I forgot."

"You don't have to go. You didn't even know Tommy," Maria said.

"You think I'm going to make you sit through all those people and their sincere demonstrations of empathy by yourself?" Michael said.

Chapter 21

How could a life so lived end up so empty?

Maria opened the sliding glass door to Tommy's backyard and walked outside. She needed a break. When her father told her that the wake would be at Tommy's house, she'd thought that was more appropriate than some generic funeral home, but standing in the living room surrounded by Tommy's things, she'd wished they were somewhere generic with carefully chosen photos of Tommy staring at her from a stand.

Here, everything was just too real.

The wake was mostly full of cops, men who had worked with her father and now came to pay their respects. Harold had showed up for a little bit, mumbled something to Esperanza, and left. Other than that, Tommy didn't seem to have any mourners who were there for him. Tommy was a life of the party kind of guy, but party friends, they tended not to show up when the booze and drugs run out.

But cops, cops showed up in spades.

The devotion of her coworkers really drove up the emptiness of her brother's life in a way that just thinking it couldn't. She'd thought it many times, how Tommy never kept a girlfriend for long, how Tommy mostly trusted Harold and no one else, how Tommy spent most of his time on his computer or drunk at a nightclub, how Tommy had a closet full of nice clothes but barely enough furniture to fill his house, but she'd always told herself that's just Tommy, but now she wondered.

Was he miserable in this life?

Had she ever really asked him?

Was there something she could have done so the ending wasn't like this?

The glass door slid open, and her mother walked out.

"I want to go home," her mother said.

"We have to stay," Maria said.

"I know. It's bullshit. My son's dead. I should get to do whatever I want," she said.

Maria looked through the window. Her father was standing in the living room. Moyer was on one side of him. Jack was standing on the other. Jack had a flask in his hand and was telling a story. Moyer and Dominic were hanging on every word.

"I never wanted him to retire. He was always happiest surrounded by cops. I wanted him to stay there, work until he died, surrounded by people who could understand him," Esperanza said.

"That's probably the best part of the job, the interactions with other cops, the camaraderie, replacing that is definitely impossible," Maria said.

"I thought it would be different for you," Esperanza said.

"Because I'm gay?"

"No, because you're a woman," Esperanza said.

The sliding door opened and Carla leaned out. She looked nervous. Maria smiled at her and motioned for her to come outside, but Carla was focused on her mother.

"¿Le gustaría tomar una copa de vino?" Carla said.

"Yo si quiero una," Esperanza said.

Maria shook her head.

Carla turned and went for the wine.

"I didn't know she spoke Spanish," Esperanza said.

"She's been studying with a tutor, trying to find a way to get you to open up. She probably practiced that phrase for ten minutes in the bathroom before she came out here," Maria said.

"I know, I'm a terrible mother," Esperanza said.

"I had you more in the mediocre bin," Maria said.

Esperanza didn't notice the attempt at a joke. She was staring at the ground. Maria reached out and put a hand on her shoulder.

"Didn't he have any friends? He was always surrounded by people but nobody's here but cops. How did I not know his life was so empty?" Esperanza said.

"I was thinking the same thing," Maria said.

"Tommy, he wasn't like you or your father. He had too much of me in him, too much troublemaker, too much wanting to push the boundaries-"

"You were a troublemaker?" Maria said.

"Ay amor, tu no sabes y tampoco te voy a decir," Esperanza said.

"Wait-"

"Just let me talk for once, will you? Jesus. Isn't that what detectives do? Listen, but you can't listen to me?"

Esperanza looked over at her daughter, and Maria saw the anger and the shame in her eyes. She could understand the rage, but why did her mother feel guilty? She couldn't think this was her fault, could she?

"Your father always wanted to be stricter with Tommy, always wanted to give him a lot of attention and direction. Begged me to convince him to join the army. But I wouldn't let him. I doted on him. He was such a handsome young man, and he always knew how to reward me, how to hug me, how to show me love. The relationship between a mother and her son is different. There's no competition like with a daughter. The resentments don't come as easy. The expectations are different."

"If this is a long way of telling me that Tommy was your favorite, I've known that since I was five," Maria said.

"No todo es lo que parece," Esperanza said.

Before Maria could dig into what her mother had said, the glass door slid open and Carla walked outside with Esperanza's wine.

Esperanza forced a smile at Carla and took the glass and turned away. Walked off to look across the pool at the sky.

Carla looked at Maria as if to say, not perfect, but something.

Maria looked back inside and saw her father watching the three of them through the window.

AFTER EVERYONE HAD FINALLY LEFT, Maria found her father sitting in a chair in the back office where they'd found Tommy. The room itself was empty. All the furniture had been removed, and the rug pulled up. The walls, cleaned and repainted. Dominic had grabbed a folding chair and pulled it into the room and was just sitting there. Looking at where the desk had been.

"Don't do that to yourself," Maria said.

"Do what?" Dominic asked.

"Stare at it."

"There's nothing there."

"We both know what you're seeing," Maria said.

Dominic looked up at his daughter. Forced a smile across his face. He looked exhausted, dark circles around his eyes. The lines in his face deeper, more severe. His exhaustion had turned his face into a pit of shadows.

"How's the case coming?" Dominic asked.

"I don't know. We've found some shady things tied to Tommy," Maria said.

"Unfortunately, I'm not surprised by that."

"I also met a woman who had ties to the Desert Saint victims."

"A woman? Ties? What would that have to do with anything?"

"Jack pointed me in her direction," Maria said.

"Yeah, he told me you went by to see him. Said I was lucky you look like your mother and not me," Dominic said.

"He's an enjoyable guy to be around," Maria said.

"Not for much longer he ain't. Pancreatic cancer. He's got another four or five months," Dominic said.

"Shit," Maria said.

"Yeah, the hits just keep on rolling in, don't they?" Dominic said.

"He thought the Desert Saint might be a woman. Between the gun and the victims. He just thought it was more likely that the perp was female."

"So you found a suspect?"

"She worked at a high-end escort service, one patronized by Anthony Scarvale, and her brother was sexually abused by the priest who was killed," Maria said.

"How did nobody find her earlier?" Dominic said.

"Her mother had kicked her out of the house. Who would really have been looking for a woman, anyway?" Maria said.

"So you think this woman started with people she knew and what? Branched out? Got a feel for it and kept going?" Dominic said.

"We haven't figured that part out yet. What do you remember of that night outside the house? Can you tell me anything about the height of the Desert Saint? Could it have been a woman?"

"It was dark and all I remember seeing is the gun and a dark coat and a hat. So, who knows? Your guess is as good as mine on that one. But being tied to the first two victims really isn't enough, and what would that have to do with Tommy?"

Maria told her father about the scam with the PACs and how Rebeka was a disgruntled political junkie who'd lost everyone she'd ever cared about. She told her father the theory about Rebeka figuring out that Tommy had ripped her off.

"So that's going to get her to start killing again after decades? I have my doubts."

"So do I, but we're going to pull on the thread and see where it heads."

Her father nodded. It had been the first lesson he'd ever given her about detective work. You grab the thread and follow it wherever it goes until it runs out. Sometimes it's the wrong thread, and the end is a big fat nothing, but you follow that thread like it's the only thread that matters and then when you realize it's nothing, you look for the next thread. Perseverance. Dedication. Rationality. It was all there in the thread metaphor.

Dominic shook his head and went back to looking at the spot where Tommy had been shot.

"Tommy dies. The only people at his wake are cops and friends of your mother. Jesus Christ, something really went wrong in that guy's life," Dominic said.

"Mom said the same thing. I was thinking it, but-" Maria said.

"I failed your brother," Dominic said.

"Don't start with that crap. You and Mom both trying to look at what you did wrong. You guys did nothing wrong. Tommy was killed by a serial killer, and nothing you two did in raising him caused that," Maria said.

Dominic opened his mouth to say something but the words couldn't come out and tears started to stream down his face, and Maria couldn't believe it. Her father was the most stoic man she'd ever met. She'd never seen him cry. Hardly ever seen him raise his voice. Just an even keeled man whose emotions consisted of slight frowns or a steely stare.

But once the first sob came out, he crumbled.

Chapter 22

Desert scrubland whipped past.

Michael was driving fast up 95. Vegas's sprawl falling away behind them, the vast emptiness of the rest of Nevada in front of them. Amazing how quick all that development disappeared into miles of nothing.

"Going to tell me where we're going?" Maria asked.

"You got something you want to tell me first?" Michael said.

"Why do I feel like we're dating and you've been going through my phone? Michael I'm gay. We're not lovers. If you have something to say, just say it," Maria said.

"I got a call from a reporter wanting to ask me about that asshole that got off," Michael said. His voice had an edge to it.

"You know those reporters. They got ears everywhere," Maria said.

"She sure seemed to know a lot about that case," Michael said.

"Some of them are just amazing at their jobs," Maria said.

"Look, I don't have a famous father. If shit runs downhill, it's going to run right over me."

"I'd never let you take the fall."

"So you did talk to her," Michael said.

"Do you really want to have this conversation?" Maria said.

"Seriously? We could have found another way to get that guy, and now Moyer isn't going to let us go anywhere near him. That wasn't your smartest move."

Maria didn't respond. She figured that Michael needed to vent and truth be told, she understood why he was mad. It hadn't been a smart move, but the move was made now. There was no undoing it and besides, fuck Preston, fuck anyone that threatened Carla.

"I get you got a lot on your plate right now, but can you just run shit by me before you go off half-cocked?" Michael said.

"Where are we going?" Maria said.

Michael waited long enough before answering to let her know he was pissed and changing the topic wasn't going to make him any less pissed. Maria let him have his moment. She knew he was right, but he also didn't want to go any further with this conversation, and they both knew it.

"Tommy's DNA matched a corpse from a cold case. Some guy was opening a whorehouse in a ghost town and when he built the building, they found bones."

"A buried body?" Maria said.

"Not one, seven," Michael said.

"Wait a minute. Where are we going?" Maria said.

"To the scene," Michael said.

"We're going to a whorehouse?" Maria said.

"Just bear with me, will ya?" Michael said.

THE SIGN for Big Louie's Gentlemen's Club was large and perched on top of a hill that blocked the club itself from being seen from the road. Big Louie was spelled out in oversized purple light bulbs. A woman's crossed legs sat on top of the B.

"Please tell me that's not it," Maria said.

Michael didn't say anything.

He slowed down as they approached the turnoff and pulled into the winding drive that turned right and then came around left behind the hill. Big Louie's club consisted of an oversized parking lot, a pool, a single story squat building with an old-fashioned horse hitching post out front, and two buildings that looked like a motel. The parking lot had two tractor trailers, and in front of the hitching post was a big purple F-150 with oversized tires and one of those exhausts that belched black smoke.

"Fifty bucks says that truck belongs to Big Louie," Maria said.

"That's a bet only a fool would take," Michael said.

"So you're taking the bet?" Maria said.

THEY FOUND Big Louie inside the bar portion of his brothel. The bar itself was empty except for a bartender and a woman sitting in the corner. The woman had looked up at them when they'd walked in and immediately ruled them out as customers and gone back to her phone. Big Louie, who had a smile as big as his truck and a belly that was bigger, was standing next to a pool table looking up at a television. When they identified themselves, he motioned for them to sit down and asked what he could do for them. Michael asked him about the bones.

"Got to tell ya, I thought we'd discovered some Indian burial site. Figured shit, I'm done for. No way in hell I can build," Big Louie said.

"The state wouldn't have let you?" Michael said.

"State? I could a hid those bones and nobody a been the wiser. I wasn't going to be messing with some shaman's remains, though. End up having ghosts haunt the girls and who wants to party with a girl who's convinced a ghost is in the room? How's a fella supposed to have any fun like that?"

"Could you show us where you found the bones, sir?" Maria asked.

"Shit, you're standing on where we found 'em," Big Louie said. He tapped his purple cowboy boot on the floor.

"Was there anything about their placement you can remember?" Michael asked.

"They was in a row," Big Louie said.

"A row?" Maria said.

"Yup, all lined up a few feet apart. Kind of weird, ain't it? At first, I thought it was some mass grave, something the mob did, but I heard later that them bodies were dumped at different times." Big Louie leaned across the table and lowered his voice. "I don't give out that information much. Girls might freak out if they knew we're built on top of a serial killer dumping ground."

"Never know, might actually be a boon to business. This country sure does love their serial killers," Michael said.

"Not in the bedroom they don't," Big Louie said.

BACK OUTSIDE, Michael and Maria looked around. They imagined the place as desert and hill and nothing else, and they saw a place that a serial killer would love.

"Great spot to dump bodies. Nice little hill to block the view from the road," Michael said.

"Easy access from Vegas," Maria said.

"Or Reno," Michael said.

"Nearest thing is a ghost town," Maria said.

"If Louie hadn't decided to put a cathouse here, probably never a been found," Michael said.

"So who dumps seven bodies in a spot like that?" Maria said.

"How does this fit with Rebeka? Would she be strong enough to get those men here and to bury them?" Michael said.

"I don't know. She didn't seem like the fitness type, but if she had help..."

"You're thinking her brother was involved," Michael said.

"Why not? Then again, my father told me that there was only one person when he was shot by the Desert Saint."

"He only saw one person. Maybe Rebeka was waiting in a nearby car. Maybe that's how the perp got away so easily," Michael said.

What Michael said could make sense. They'd assumed there was one killer, but two killers was just as possible as one. Still, it was a complication, and generally complications didn't lead to good theories. Usually, the simple answer was right.

"Ok, maybe, maybe there was a driver," Maria said.

"But..."

"Or maybe Rebeka is wrong for this," Maria said.

"It's currently just as likely the bodies could be something unrelated. We have to find out how they were killed," Michael said.

"Serena told me that the Saint didn't stop like the press said. She said pimps kept disappearing. So it's highly unlikely the bodies aren't connected. Besides, those bones could be my tio Tomas."

"tio Tomas?" Michael said.

"Tomas Vargas, my mother's brother, was the one that my father interrupted. Then he disappeared a few weeks later. It's how my parents met," Maria said.

"Aw shit, don't tell me that," Michael said.

"Why?"

Michael just stood there, looking at the ground.

A truck driver walked out of one of the rooms behind the bar and headed for his truck. He was heavyset and bearded and looked freshly showered. He gave the two of them a quick glance and hurried his steps. Maria wondered what he was carrying and why he was worried about seeing two cops outside a brothel when brothels were legal. She focused her attention back on Michael, who looked like he'd eaten something bad and wanted to throw up.

"Spit it out," Maria said.

"There was an issue with the DNA," Michael said.

"Someone contaminated the scene?" Maria said.

"Remember how we took some of your DNA to have something to compare specimens to? Also to rule you out?" Michael said.

"No, I totally don't remember that thing that happened two days ago," Maria said.

"Brothers and sisters should have around 50% of the same DNA. It ranges, but that's ballpark."

"Are you really mansplaining DNA to me? Didn't I teach you this when you slept through the conference presentation?" Maria said.

"You and Tommy only share 23%," Michael said.

"So you're trying to tell me-"

"You and Tommy share one parent, not two."

"Something must be messed up with the tests," Maria said.

"There were some unwashed glasses in the sink. Your mother and father had been over his house that afternoon. One glass matched you and Tommy fifty percent," Michael said.

"My mother."

"One glass matched you fifty percent but nothing to Tommy," Michael said.

"Shit."

"It gets worse. Your brother was a fifty percent match to the skeleton."

"So you're saying..." Maria didn't finish the statement. They both knew what Michael was saying.

"I mean, what do I even do with that information? Do you have any idea how much of a legend your father is?" Michael said.

"No, no idea. I've never heard people say that my whole life," Maria said.

"Now, I'm supposed to be the one who tells him that his son wasn't his? I don't think so."

"I'll deal with it," Maria said.

"I was hoping you'd say that," Michael said.

ON THE RIDE BACK, they didn't talk much. Maria turning over what Michael had told her, and Michael giving her quiet and time to process. Maria found herself feeling no different about Tommy or her father. Tommy was still her brother, regardless. Same with her father, but her mother. Her mother was someone who had taken on a different shape. Maria saw the constant lectures on how to be ladylike, how to dress appropriately, how to behave as one long string of hypocrisy from a woman who had hidden the true parentage of her son from her husband and her daughter.

And her father, her poor father, lied to for all this time.

How was she going to tell him?

She wasn't one to shirk responsibility. She'd sit down face to face with him and give him the news, but she wasn't looking forward to it, and a part of her wondered if maybe she should give her mother the chance to own up. She could tell her mother she knew and give her mother time to come clean. Maria saw her father collapsing off of the chair to the floor the night before in Tommy's office. Now was probably not the time to bring this up. Maybe there was never a good time for this kind of information, but with everything going on, Tommy dying, his friend Jack getting cancer. What else could go wrong?

Cancer.

Maria saw Jack complaining about cops having to look the other way.

The bitterness in his eyes at not being able to do his job right.

The anger still there all those years later.

"I might have another suspect," Maria said.

"Who?" Michael said.

"You're not going to like it," Maria said.

Chapter 23

How did you catch someone who wasn't hiding?

If Maria was being honest, the whole series of killings screamed disillusioned cop, and Maria and Michael both knew that any cop who had a strong sense of integrity would have been disillusioned working in Vegas in the 60s, 70s, and 80s. And if Jack was still bitter after all of these years, how bitter must he have been when he was in the middle of it?

So liking him for the killing of a bunch of degenerates was easy.

Liking him for killing Tommy was much harder and Michael pointed out as much.

"Yeah, but that was the original theory, right? Revenge on my father. But think it through even further. What did my father become?" Maria said.

"A fucking legend," Michael said.

"That could eat at someone, couldn't it? A person has to have a serious hero complex to do this as it is, and now here Jack is, the end is near, and he never received the respect and adulation that he believes he deserved. Might be time to settle some scores," Maria said.

Michael rolled it over silently for a bit and then let out a low groan.

"I hope it's Rebeka," Michael said.

"Me too, but let's be honest, it's probably not likely that Rebeka dumped these bodies."

"There's no way Moyer is going to let us dig in on Jack unless we come up with something ironclad," Michael said.

"I have an idea. It's a little unorthodox, but it might work," Maria said.

MARIA'S IDEA was a double interrogation, sort of. She wanted to play off of the idea that she couldn't really work Tommy's case, so since they suspected Rebeka of being involved, Michael would have to question her, but Maria could sit in the observation room and invite Jack to watch with her. She'd tell Jack that she wanted his opinion since he was around at that time and he knew all the background information, but really what Maria wanted to do was observe Jack and if the chance came, break him.

"And if he's guilty of your brother's murder?" Michael said.

"I wasn't working my brother's case. I was asking a retired police officer for his expertise and happened to be fortunate in the result," Maria said.

"And then also no one could accuse us of going after a cop because-"

"Because we're just asking for help," Maria said.

"You are devious sometimes," Michael said.

"Do you think it'll work?" Maria said.

"No. But it ain't like we got much else to work with," Michael said.

"Thanks for the vote of confidence, dickhead," Maria said.

"We're doing it, aren't we?"

"You just want to be able to say I told you so if it doesn't work," Maria said.

"More or less," Michael said.

"And you wonder why you can't hold on to a girlfriend," Maria said.

"Ha fucking ha. And we're getting permission from Moyer," Michael said.

"Are you high? There's no way he'll let us pull Jack in," Maria said.

"Let's give him a chance to surprise us," Michael said.

"You're serious," Maria said.

"As a mother with a switch in her hand," Michael said.

Maria couldn't see any way of presenting this where Moyer agreed, but she hadn't cleared the reporter with Michael, and she was going to have to go with him on this one, and he knew it. But she was the manipulative one.

Yeah, right.

MOYER DIDN'T KICK them out of his office immediately.

"We're not planning on accusing him of anything," Maria said.

"He won't actually be a target of the interrogation," Michael said.

"Basically, you want to drag a man dying of cancer in so you can try to trick him into admitting something that you have no evidence or reason to believe that he did," Moyer said.

"That was the first trigger we listed, wasn't it?" Maria said.

"Jesus Christ-" Moyer said.

"We're just saying, cops back then, had to jump through a lot of hoops, obey a lot of hidden rules and lines, but Jack, everybody says Jack was a straight shooter," Michael said.

"Must have been hard and super frustrating," Maria said. She was about to go on, but Michael put his hand on her shoulder, and she realized Moyer wasn't really listening to them. He was looking straight up at the ceiling and mouthing words as if speaking to himself.

"What's up?" Michael said.

Moyer shook his head.

"My uncle. My uncle was on the task force. Said Jack didn't take being pushed aside lightly and was always hitting him up for information. How was the investigation going? What new leads did they have? Were they getting anywhere?" Moyer said.

"Jack told me he didn't mind getting pushed aside. Said the Desert Saint investigation killed a lot of careers but not his because he was in and out quick," Maria said.

"My uncle didn't remember him taking it easy. Thought maybe Jack was obsessed with the whole case. When I became a detective, he told me this whole story as a means of warning me about getting attached. Everyone knew Jack had developed a friendship with the boy who found the priest and that friendship took Jack through the ringer. Poor guy was in here every other month bailing that kid out of jail," Moyer said.

"Bailing him out? Jack told me he just came in to talk with the kid," Maria said.

"People couldn't decide if Jack was in the closet and involved with the kid or if he just couldn't let the case go, and my uncle didn't want any of that happening to me. Said you had to let a case go. You ain't going to solve all of them," Moyer said.

"And now you're wondering if all of this was a little more complex," Michael said.

"Who else knows about this idea?" Moyer asked.

"No one," Michael said.

"We want to pitch it like we need his expertise because he knows Rebekah, and he's the one who told me that the killer might be a woman anyway, so I think it'll fly," Maria said.

"Not a word of this to anyone else. If anybody asks, you're giving a dying detective one last taste of the chase," Moyer said.

WHEN MARIA and Michael got back to the conference room, Michael sat down, put his feet up on the table, and leaned back with his hands clasping the back of his head. Maria tried to ignore him, but the smile plastered on his face was impossible to ignore. That and the lingering guilt she felt over the shitstorm that was coming for the news article about the aristocrat.

"You were right," Maria said.

"Come again? Sorry, didn't hear you," Michael said.

"I said go fuck yourself," Maria said.

Michael laughed. He took his feet off the table and reached for one of the folders.

"Maybe you should call Jack and see what time he can come by, and then I'll arrange to have Rebeka here at that time," Michael said.

"Wow, two good ideas in one day. You're on a roll," Maria said.

Maria's phone buzzed. A message from her father.

"What's up?" Michael said.

"My father wants me to go see him," Maria said.

"Well, isn't that serendipitous," Michael said.

"I can't tell him today. I'm going to wait a bit. It's too soon with Tommy and all."

"You know him better than I do," Michael said.

"I'll call Jack on my way to see my dad and give you a time," Maria said.

Chapter 24

Why would he be here?

Maria found Dominic sitting inside Our Holy Father Catholic Church. The church was empty, no mass or confession going on, just Dominic and the stained glass windows. He didn't even look back as she walked down the aisle towards him.

"When'd you decide to start going to church?" Maria asked.

Dominic looked up at her and smiled.

"I don't go to mass. Just come here every now and then to sit. I like the quiet, you know?"

Maria sat down in the same pew but across the aisle from her father. The pew was all wood, no cushions. She tried to make herself comfortable but couldn't. Maybe that was the point. Seemed like a dumb point though.

Her parents hadn't raised her in a church, and she wondered what it would have been like to come here every Sunday. Would she have liked it? Tommy would have loved it if their mother was here. He adored being wherever their mother was because she doted on him so much.

They sat there in silence for a bit. Dominic looking up at the stained glass window behind the altar, a depiction of Jesus's birth in the manger. Maria wondering why he had asked her to come visit. He never interrupted her during the day, which was why she had dropped everything and come. Whatever he wanted to talk to her about, it must be important, but he was having a hard time getting started. Something rare for him, which meant whatever he wanted to say would be something she didn't want to hear. Which could really only mean one thing.

"I'm not giving up on this case," Maria said.

"Who said anything about giving up the case?" Dominic said.

"You were about to and don't try to deny it," Maria said.

Dominic grimaced.

"That's why you asked me to come here, isn't it? You want me to stop working the case."

"Your mother and I are worried about how this is going to affect you," Dominic said.

"You and mom talked about this?" Maria said.

"You know, she's never been one to complain about the job. All those years I was in and out at the worst hours, overtired, ornery-"

"Ornery? I never remember you being ill-tempered," Maria said.

"Your mother used to tell me all the time, you take it out on me. You be sweet for the kids, and if you have to be short-tempered or nasty, you save it for me. And from time to time, I was, and she just let it go right by. Amazing the things she could tolerate. That woman is so tough. I wish I could be as tough as her," Dominic said.

"And you're telling me how tough mom is because..." Maria said.

"Because she's not a complainer, and if she's telling me she's worried about you, it's for a reason. Not something she's made up."

"There's no way in hell-"

"Just hear me out, will you?"

"Can you imagine the guilt I'll have if I don't pursue every avenue available?" Maria said.

"Can you imagine the guilt you'll have if you don't catch whoever did this?" Dominic said.

Maria was stunned. The thought of not catching Tommy's killer hadn't even crossed her mind. Did her father think she couldn't do it?

"Don't look at me like that. I'm not doubting your ability. You're already a hell of a better detective than I ever was," Dominic said.

"But you don't think I can catch this killer," Maria said.

"You have zero physical evidence, zero witnesses, and zero suspects with ties to the victim. Your only suspect is a woman on the wrong side of seventy. How are you going to solve this case with that set of circumstances?" Dominic said.

"So you just want me to give up?" Maria said.

"No, I want you to be honest with yourself about the toll this case is going to take on you. It's just not healthy," Dominic said.

"Healthy? You think I'm worried about my health?" Maria said.

"No, no, I don't at all. But your mother and I are," Dominic said.

"I'm not stopping," Maria said.

Dominic didn't say anything.

"Michael is in charge of the investigation, anyway. I'm just helping out," Maria said.

Dominic laughed.

"Everyone knows who wears the pants in that partnership," he said.

"I appreciate your concern. But I'm not stopping," Maria said.

"I heard you the first time, and I knew what you were going to say anyway," Dominic said.

"So why are we here?"

"Your mother wanted me to talk to you."

"And it couldn't wait until tonight?" Maria said.

"Your mother wants to invite you and Carla for dinner tonight," Dominic said.

"What?"

"Yeah, I was just as surprised as you. But I don't think we should make a big deal about it."

"She invited Carla into her house for dinner?"

"People are just full of surprises, aren't they?" Dominic said.

Maria's phone buzzed, a text message from Harold asking her if she could meet him, maybe he'd found something out and he wanted to run it by her. He was at the Wynn. She stood up and told her father she had to go.

"Something come up?" Dominic said.

"Not really. Harold wants to run something by me. He's at the Wynn, so he's probably broke and wants to borrow money."

"He hit you up for money often?" Her father said.

"No, I was kidding, but he seems to think he's found something out about Tommy. He probably just wants to talk. Tommy was his best friend after all."

Maria turned to go but stopped. There was one last thing she wanted her father's opinion on. She knew Moyer didn't want her telling anyone about suspecting Jack, and her father was friends with Jack, so he would be totally biased, but still...

"What do you think about the Desert Saint being a cop?"

"What's the rationale?" Dominic said.

"You always told me that things were different back then. Casinos cops couldn't go into. Mob influence everywhere, and all of these crime scenes were totally clean, right? They never found anything. Even Tommy's house, nothing. Who could be that clean besides a cop?" Maria said.

"You know as well as I do that serial killers study. They study procedure. They study crime scene technology. They perfect their craft," Dominic said.

"Yeah. Serial killers do all that. But was all of that information publicly accessible all those years ago? And serial killers are often publicity hungry, and there's usually a sexual aspect to the crime. There's none of that here. Just someone offing people who were not solid citizens."

"Are you saying your brother wasn't a solid citizen?" Dominic asked.

"I don't know. I can't see him being involved in anything more than scamming people out of money, but maybe, maybe there is something to the fact that he's your son."

Dominic raised his eyebrow.

"Fair enough. The theory is weak when it comes to Tommy, but what do you think about the rest of it?" Maria said.

"It's fine as a theory because the idea is so general. Sure, it could have been a cop, but then again, it could have been a priest or a janitor or the President of the USA because we have no physical evidence to look at," Dominic said.

"What about Jack?" Maria said.

"Come on with that," Dominic said.

"The cancer. How long does he have? When did he find out?" Maria said.

"You can't be serious," Dominic said.

"That was the first thing we said in that meeting. What makes a killer start again? We said a terminal diagnosis. We have a cop who was around at the time all of these started, a cop who we all know was devoted to catching bad guys and from all reports largely disgusted with the corruption he saw all around him. The dates fit. He was a big guy. He could have easily moved bodies and dug holes."

"You're not going to ruin a cop's reputation while he's dying," Dominic said.

"I'm just going to pull on the thread. That's all. And I promise, I'll do it quietly," Maria said.

Dominic looked her right in the face and held her gaze for a long second. She could tell that he was angry, but she could also tell that he knew her theory was logical, and his devotion to Jack was crashing up against his devotion to rationality.

"Very quietly," he said.

MARIA PARKED in the self-parking at the Wynn and headed inside. Maria wasn't a particular fan of either the Wynn or the Encore. She thought the color schemes and design were more fitting for watching a carnival while high on acid than for a luxury casino. Still, this was where Harold wanted to meet, so here she was. Like most casinos, the actual gaming floor was shrinking as more and more space was given to stores and restaurants and nightclubs, so it didn't take long for Maria to spot Harold sitting in front of a slot machine, a lit cigarette poking out of an ashtray, a half full drink in his left hand. The right hand pushing buttons on the screen.

"Meeting at a casino? Your house wouldn't have been quicker?" Maria said.

"Put some money in the machine," Harold said.

"I'm not looking for free drinks," Maria said.

"Please," Harold said.

Something in Harold's tone put Maria on edge, and she looked him over closely. He had a Raiders hat pulled low, and a long-sleeved shirt and pants, clothes that he never seemed to wear, but useful for hiding the tattoos that ran up and down his arms and legs. He looked like a random man playing slots, but from Maria's perspective, Harold looked like he was trying to disguise himself.

What the hell was going on?

Maria relented. She sat down and put a twenty in the machine. She started pushing buttons, but didn't even know if she was winning or losing. The game seemed ridiculously complicated for three rows of spinning symbols.

"I need an excuse. In case we're seen together. I think they're watching me," Harold said.

"Who is?"

"Anatov," Harold said.

"The man you lied to me about knowing? Why would he be watching you?" Maria said.

"I think he's the one who killed Tommy," Harold said.

"We matched the ballistics to previous cases. There was no connection to Anatov as far as we can tell," Maria said.

"Are you positive about that? 100% sure?" Harold said.

"Pretty close to 100%," Maria said.

"Then why are they following me?" Harold said.

"Who's following you?" Maria said.

Harold's eye's strayed over Maria's shoulder and he turned away from her. Focused on the machine in front of him. He looked tenser than she'd ever seen him.

Maria looked over her shoulder and saw two men, tall and lean, close cropped blonde hair. One man was looking down the row towards them. Not at them, just in the general direction. The other was typing a message into his phone. They both wore loose fitting short-sleeved button-down shirts and jeans, and they both had the tightly corded muscles built up by hauling rucksacks and pulling themselves up ropes.

"I should go," Harold said.

"Harold, what's going on?"

"I'll call you. Just don't follow me. Please. It's better for us both."

Harold pulled his player's card out of the slot machine and tossed back what was left of his drink. He shot a glance over Maria's shoulder at the men and then stood and turned and walked away. Maria looked over her shoulder, but the two men were already gone. When she turned back around, Harold was gone too.

Chapter 25

How could people contain so many contradictions?

By the time Maria made it back to the station, Jack and Rebeka were already there. Jack in the observation room, and Rebeka sitting at the table on the other side of the window. Jack was perched on the edge of the chair, hands resting on his cane, eyes fixed on Rebeka. Jack looked up and smiled at Maria when she walked in but then returned his attention to Rebeka.

"I don't see it," he said.

"See what?" Maria said.

"The way she's sitting. Something's not right. She looks upset, like she's keeping it together barely, and our killer would be more controlled than that," Jack said.

"Rebeka has ties to the first two victims," Maria said.

"Thousands upon thousands of people have ties to the first two victims," Jack said.

"Yes, but she's the only one we can unearth who had a motive to kill," Maria said.

"So your theory is that the opening victims weren't random. They were personal. Then you think the killer switched up and started picking vics at random?" Jack said.

"I guess we're going to have to see what she says," Maria said.

"So why am I here, exactly?"

"I wanted your background knowledge. You were there during this whole time. You knew her brother. If she starts being evasive, maybe you'll have a better idea of things we can ask her or confront her with. Rebeka presents as very calm, but I think she's really angry. I want to get that anger out. I think you might be able to help me prod her," Maria said.

"Did your father put you up to this? One last thrill before I kick the bucket?"

The comment was delivered with Jack's signature bluntness and devil may care tone, but he didn't look at her as he said it. He could play off dying all he wanted but the reality of it was daunting, and Maria could sense the competing desires between wanting to be useful and not wanting to be pitied. Being as perceptive as Jack couldn't be easy. Those who can delude themselves go through life with much less inner turmoil.

Could a killer fake that so easily?

Then Michael entered the room with Rebeka and flashed that genuine smile.

Yes, a human was capable of amazing acts of deception.

So was Jack being honest?

Or was he a killer?

MICHAEL DIDN'T EVEN GET the chance to sit down before Rebeka started talking.

"Who was it?" Rebeka said.

"I'm sorry. I don't understand," Michael said.

"Stephen's killer. They called it a suicide, but I always suspected there was something more. Sure, his life was fucked up, but all that time going to church had to have made suicide just an unbearable thought, so who was it? Was it the Desert Saint that killed him? That had to be why that woman came around asking me questions," Rebeka said.

"We don't have any new information on your brother. As far as we know, he killed himself," Michael said.

Rebeka's face changed. Up until now, she'd been anxious, and then when asking the question, the agony had been clear in the tone of her voice, but all that emotion was gone. Now she just looked pissed.

"So why am I here?" Rebeka said.

"We wanted your help with some more background on the Desert Saint killings," Michael said.

Rebeka leaned back in her chair. Cocked her head.

"Background? I told that other detective everything I knew," Rebeka said.

"You might be surprised what you can remember once I start asking questions," Michael said.

"If you say so," Rebeka said.

Michael settled into his chair. Organized his folders. Only one of them had anything to do with the case, but he liked having multiple folders. He thought all those folders made the suspect nervous, and he was probably right, but Maria preferred one folder, as if everything they needed to know was in that one folder and they knew so much they didn't even need a bunch of material. Both ways seemed to work, and maybe the folders didn't even matter. Maybe being in a room across a table from a detective was what really caused people to lose it.

Not Rebeka though. She didn't look nervous at all.

Just pissed.

MARIA ASKED Jack about how angry Rebeka looked.

"Could be she's just upset to be bothered. But she also just might not be that bright," he said.

"You think she believes Michael when he says he just wants background?"

"You said she worked for Antoinette?" Jack said.

"You knew her?" Maria said.

"Hell, everyone knew Antoinette. That woman knew how to run

a business. Nobody could touch her for years. She got her hooks into anybody she thought would become a mayor. Just about every new election, didn't matter who won, it was going to be good for Antoinette," Jack said.

"I spoke with her yesterday," Maria said.

"She's still kicking? Good for her. What was she like?"

"Blunt and dismissive," Maria said.

"Yup, that's Antoinette," Jack said.

"You think working for Antoinette could have rubbed off on Rebeka?" Maria said.

"That'd be a hell of a rubbing if it's still good all these years later," Jack said.

"Antoinette said Rebeka has a temper and is obsessive," Maria said.

"Well, I think we're about to find out if Antoinette was telling the truth," Jack said.

MICHAEL SELECTED a folder and pulled it toward him. He flipped it open and ran a finger down the page. For the first time, Rebeka showed a shred of nervousness. Her body leaned forward as she tried to get a look at what Michael was reading. But he leaned back as well, folder coming up off the table and out of Rebeka's line of sight. His face scrunched up like he couldn't believe what he was seeing. Like something just wasn't right.

"So you worked for Antoinette for a long time, huh?" Michael said.

"Fifteen years, thereabout," Rebeka said.

"Must have been boring stuck in a strip mall answering phones all night," Michael said.

"I wasn't stuck there. Girls were in and out all night long. Antoinette was always around. Sometimes customers who wanted to set up something really special would come by and work things out with Antoinette. So I wouldn't say I was stuck there," Rebeka said.

Michael continued on like that for a while. Talking about Rebeka's time working at the agency. Asking about the people that worked there. Asking what Antoinette was like. All the questions were free flowing and easy, and Rebeka more or less told him the same thing she had told Maria, everything was great. Antoinette was amazing, and their relationship had been solid. Michael acted very interested in all of Rebeka's responses, but it was all a setup for what was coming.

A patrol officer opened the door to the interrogation room and stuck his head in.

"That file you requested from New York arrived," the officer said.

Michael glared at the officer like he'd done something terribly wrong, and the officer's eyes shot from Michael to Rebeka and back to Michael.

"Shit," the officer said.

"What file?" Rebeka said.

"It's nothing," Michael said. He shooed the officer out the door with his hands and stood up. He grabbed the dummy folders but left the one with the crime scene photos from the priest's killing on the table. Michael told Rebeka he'd be right back and headed out the door.

"New York?" Rebeka said.

Michael didn't respond. Just went out the door.

JACK LEANED FORWARD in his chair and peered more intently through the glass at Rebeka who was becoming more and more fidgety. The folder on the table was calling to her, and she was doing everything she could to resist the pull of opening it. But the compulsion was getting stronger and stronger and the exertion of resisting was showing on her face.

"The folders always seem to work, don't they?" Jack said.

"I could never decide if it's really the folders or if it's just all of it. The room. The badge. The lack of information," Maria said.

The door opened and Michael came in.

"How's she holding up?" Michael asked.

"Looks like she's about to have a heart attack if she don't touch it. What's in it?" Jack said.

"Father McGuire's crime scene photos," Maria said.

"You want to see how she reacts to 'em," Jack said.

"We were hoping she would have grabbed them by now," Michael said.

"What's up with New York?" Jack said.

"Antoinette moved there. Apparently, Rebeka didn't want Antoinette to close up the agency," Maria said.

"She took it bad, did she?" Jack said.

"That would be putting it lightly," Michael said.

Jack's eyebrows arched, and he returned his attention to Rebeka who had settled herself and was now looking up in the corner of the room. Her lips were moving as if she was talking to herself, but nothing was audible over the speakers.

"How long you think we should leave her waiting?" Maria said.

"She's ready to jump out of her skin right now. I'd give her a good five minutes to make sure," Jack said.

"Just enough time for me to hit the little boy's room."

Michael walked out of the room.

"He's good at this," Jack said.

"Yeah, he's a real natural with suspects."

"Another thing in this life I was wrong about," Jack said.

"Michael being good at interrogation?"

"Nah, whether blacks could be good cops. I was against integration. Against working with blacks. Wouldn't partner with a black for years. But your father's partner was a black guy by the name of Russell. I didn't want Russell around, but your father wouldn't come out on an arrest without Russell. Said he knew he could depend on him. And well, I needed your dad because the people we were arresting were not afraid to shoot a cop, and your dad was damn good at shooting back. I was always more of a thinker than a shooter, but your dad wasn't going without Russell, and sure enough, Russell was everything your father said he was, smart, brave, dependable. A couple of months later, I ended up volunteering to partner with a black guy nobody wanted to partner with.

Me and Charlie were partners til I retired. One of the best friends I ever had. When I found out about the pancreatic cancer, first person I called was Charlie."

Jack paused for a moment. Looked over Maria's way.

"The thing about old dogs is they can learn new tricks, they just don't like to be taught, they got to learn them on their own," Jack said.

ON THE OTHER side of the glass, Rebeka was struggling to maintain control. She was focusing on her breathing, in and out, at an even pace. She placed her hands on the table, palms down, and closed her eyes. Kept breathing. She didn't open them again until the door opened.

Michael smiled his genuine, friendly, sweet smile. In his hand was a single thin folder.

"What's that?" Rebeka asked.

"This?" Michael held the folder up.

"Yes, that," Rebeka said.

Michael didn't answer right away. Instead, he sat down. Put the folder on the table. Adjusted it, so it was directly in front of him, neatly lined up. Then he sat there looking at Rebeka for a solid ten seconds. Normally, that ten second wait, the combination of the file, the stare, the silence, was enough to crack a suspect. Especially one who'd never been really through the system. Rebeka had been arrested, but Antoinette's fancy lawyers had handled everything. This was her first real interrogation. She should have been jumping out of her skin, but the whole buildup seemed to have the opposite effect. She grew calmer and calmer and instead of nervously demanding answers, she quietly stared back at Michael. Maria knew her reaction had to shake Michael, but he kept his expression neutral.

"What do you think is in that file?" Michael asked.

"How would I know? I haven't seen it," Rebeka said.

"You know it's from New York."

"Why would I know that?" Rebeka asked.

Michael ignored her question and instead asked what New York would have to say about her.

"I don't know. Is New York some person? One of those new gender free names? What bathroom does New York use?" Her voice was even, but the rage was palpable in the clipped manner with which she spoke.

"It's a restraining order. From New York," Michael said.

Rebeka didn't say anything. Just sat there looking at Michael.

"You do remember the restraining order, don't you?" Michael said.

"Nope, I don't. Why don't you remind me," Rebeka said.

"You don't remember going to New York, stalking Antoinette, threatening her outside of her brownstone," Michael said.

"Stalking Antoinette? Is that what talking to people is called these days?" Rebeka said.

"It's stalking when you're told multiple times to not contact a person, and instead of leaving them alone, you show up to talk to them with a gun," Michael said.

"If you were in New York City in the 1980s, you'd a carried a gun too. That city was full of animals, some of whom may have been related to you," Rebeka said.

"She claims you threatened her," Michael said.

"Antoinette overreacted. We talked afterwards and patched it all up. Just a big misunderstanding. If she was alive, she'd tell you the same thing," Rebeka said.

"She is alive, actually, and we spoke to her, and she has a different recollection than you."

"Antoinette died from cancer almost twenty years ago," Rebeka said.

"No. That was something her attorney concocted to keep her safe," Michael said.

"Safe?" Rebeka said.

"Can you think of someone she would be afraid of?" Michael said.

"Well, since she's alive, why don't you ask her?" Rebeka said. "Why am I here exactly?"

"Do you still have that gun?" Michael said.

Rebeka's eyes narrowed.

"You think I killed someone," Rebeka said.

"I didn't say that. I just asked if you still had the gun," Michael said.

"The woman who came by the house was a homicide detective. You are too, huh? Who is it that you think I killed?" Rebeka said.

"The gun was a .22, wasn't it?"

"You know it was. I told that female detective it was, and no, I don't have it. I threw it away a long time ago. Women who work in dental offices don't tend to need guns," Rebeka said.

"You threw it away? How?" Michael said.

"Took it apart and threw it in the trash. Now is when you tell me why I'm here."

"Do you remember where you were on the night Father McGuire died?" Michael asked.

"Yes, yes I do," Rebeka said.

Michael waited for Rebeka to tell him where, but she didn't answer. Just sat there quietly.

JACK CHUCKLED.

"She's a lot more complex than she seems, ain't she?" he said.

"Have you ever seen anyone react like that?" Maria said.

"The icy rage? The casual disgust?" Jack said.

"Yeah, I mean, suspects react in strange ways, but it's like she's a different person right now."

Jack stood up and walked to the glass. He walked with a slow shuffle, one of his legs stiffer than it should be. He put his hand on the glass and stood there watching Rebeka.

"The only people I ever seen be like that were guilty people, but still I can't see her being your perp," Jack said.

"Why?"

"Don't know. Something in my gut is screaming no," Jack said.

Maria didn't think much of decisions made by one's "gut" but now wasn't the time for a philosophical argument. Mostly, she was wondering about him and not Rebeka. Why had Jack shared with her the story about his conversion from being a racist to having a best friend who was black? Was he trying to shape the way she saw him? And why was he pushing back on Rebeka being involved in these killings? She had all the main signifiers, means, motive, and opportunity, and she was a liar. He should be noticing and latching onto all the same things that she was. But then again, the real Desert Saint wouldn't want the credit to go to anyone else.

"Regardless, you're just spinning wheels now. If you don't have anything concrete to bust her apart with, you ain't going to get anywhere," Jack said.

REBEKA'S grandmotherly exterior was completely gone. She looked flatly at Michael as if he wasn't worth her time or her respect.

"So where were you the night Father McGuire died?" Michael said.

"He didn't die at night. He died in the afternoon, and I was where I always was. At work."

"What about three days ago? Right about this time, we'll say, 3pm. Where were you three days ago at three pm?" Michael asked.

"Don't remember," Rebeka said.

"You remember where you were thirty-eight years ago, but you don't remember where you were three days ago?" Michael said.

"Was I speaking a different language? Should I put it into a rap lyric so you can understand? I don't fucking remember, yo yo dawg, you feel me yo," Rebeka said.

"You're big into politics, huh?" Michael said.

"Jesus Christ, does any of this have any fucking rhyme or reason?"

"Have you donated to any PACs lately?" Michael said.

"Why are you asking me any of this?"

"Yes or no, have you donated to any PACs lately?" Michael said.

"Define lately," Rebeka said.

"Within the last year," Michael said.

"I don't remember," Rebeka said.

"Ok, have you ever donated to any PACs?" Michael said.

"I don't remember," Rebeka said.

"How can you not remember if you've ever donated money to a PAC?" Michael said.

"Your kind can always forget who the daddy is, but I'm supposed to remember if I pushed a button one time. Seriously?"

Michael laughed out loud.

"Well, I never pimped out my own brother, that's for sure," Michael said.

"He applied. I didn't want to. Antoinette talked me into it," Rebeka said.

"That's not what Antoinette said. She said you forced her to take on your brother."

"She's a lying cunt," Rebeka said.

"Maybe. Maybe the liar is you. But I tell you one thing. You got a whole lot of rage pouring out of you. You hide it well. But it's there. Chilling underneath," Michael said.

"Are you going to charge me for this session, or is this free therapy?" Rebeka said.

"I don't blame you, you know? Mom kicked you out. Both your brothers are dead. Being angry. Who wouldn't be?" Michael said.

"At least I'm not a nigger," Rebeka said.

"You are definitely not that, but what I don't understand is why Antoinette seems to think you were always angry. She says life didn't make you pissed. You just were always pissed," Michael said.

"Ask her. She's the one who knows everything apparently," Rebeka said.

"You see what I think is-"

"Let me stop you right there. I could give a shit what you think. Now why am I here?"

"Where were you three days ago about three pm?" Michael said.

"I want to see an attorney," Rebeka said.

"You're not under arrest," Michael said.

"And I'm not some idiot from the hood. I don't have to be under arrest to speak to a lawyer. Now I'm not answering any more questions. So piss off," Rebeka said.

Michael gathered his folders and left the room.

JACK LOOKED up at Maria and smiled.

"That was fun," he said.

"We didn't get anywhere though, did we?" Maria said.

"She clammed up when he went back at her asking where she was. There might be something there. We couldn't trace cell phone locations back in the 80s. Maybe you all can find something more concrete," Jack said.

"So you're coming around on her being a suspect," Maria said.

"Nah, not really. Then again, I'm not sure you really suspect her anyway," Jack said.

"Come again?" Maria said.

"I thought it was a cop, too. The clean crime scenes. The targets. I thought it was someone cleaning up messes they couldn't clean up otherwise," Jack said.

"Rebeka isn't a cop," Maria said.

"But accusing a cop of a crime, well, that doesn't make anyone popular around the precinct, but if someone were to bring that cop in to watch an interrogation with them, while asking them questions, and if something were to slip, well, then that would be just lucky, wouldn't it?" Jack said.

Maria opened her mouth to object, but Jack cut her off.

"I'm old, but I'm not stupid. And I appreciate how you went about it. If you were wrong, which you were, nobody's the wiser and nobody can think that you're doing anything other than giving a dying old man one last thrill. No suspicion cast, no reputations slandered, and everybody gets to lay eyes on the old detective before cancer finishes him off," Jack said.

"Guess I'm not as smart as I think I am," Maria said.

"Shit, you're smarter. I'd a never thought to do this, and I had some cases when I wish I could have. You told me you wanted me to help you draw out the anger, but you never once asked me for any help with that. Besides you already had all the information you needed, so either you were just doing me a favor, giving me one last thrill, or you wanted to see if I was your guy, and since you were paying more attention to me than you were to Rebeka, well..." Jack said.

"You must have been a hell of a detective," Maria said.

"I had some good days," Jack said.

"So you probably had a list of cops you suspected. Care to share that list with me?"

"They're all dead but one. And he couldn't a done it. He was on duty at the time of one of the murders and on the other side of town on a call when it happened, and then he was later shot by the Desert Saint," Jack said.

"You had my dad down as a suspect?" Maria said.

"I had everybody down as a suspect, but your dad, he was more interested in the case than most, and he was an intense guy. Having you mellowed him out, but he didn't like the gray area of being a cop in Vegas in the 80s. He was a black and white kind of guy," Jack said.

"Why don't you give me that list of names? Maybe the Desert Saint is dead but the gun lives on," Maria said.

Chapter 26

What if being rational didn't lead anywhere?

After Rebeka and Jack were gone, Michael and Maria met with Moyer. He looked at them across his desk and said, "Give me the bad news."

Michael told him about Rebeka's evasive answers and lawyering up. He didn't bring up her racist comments. Michael had told Maria when a perp started making racial comments, he knew he was making progress because racial taunts were the weapons of the weak, but Maria knew it still bothered him because whenever she checked on him a few hours after dealing with a racist perp, he was always in the boxing gym and sounding more out of breath than normal, so Maria told Moyer about all the racist taunts that Michael hadn't brought up. Moyer's face scrunched up as she repeated verbatim what Rebeka had said.

"Well, I think we can all agree we hope it's her, but do we have anything more than the fact she's a racist asshole?" Moyer said.

Michael looked at Maria. He always let her speak first, not that she needed much incentive to put her two cents in, but she had always appreciated this little detail. Today though, since he'd done the interview, she said he should answer the question.

"There's something off with her, but I don't think she's our perp. Mostly because of the dumping ground," Michael said.

"We don't even know if that's connected," Maria said.

"Seems a bit too much to be coincidental, doesn't it? Also, if she was guilty, I doubt she'd have popped out with racist comments. She wouldn't have been aggressive towards me, she would have wanted to be helpful. As soon as she realized we weren't there to talk about her brother, she was a volcano of anger," Michael said.

"But why would she get so evasive?" Maria said.

"Could be a lot of reasons," Michael said.

"She's definitely hiding something," Maria said.

"That doesn't mean it's tied to this case," Michael said.

"I think it's tied to the brother," Maria said.

"Which one?" Moyer said.

"The older one. The one who lived with her. He was abused by the priest, and he worked with her at the escort agency. Antoinette ended up firing him for attacking a client," Maria said.

"So you think the brother might have been the original killer but with her gun," Michael said.

"I guarantee you she still has that .22. She was lying about tossing it," Maria said.

"I didn't get that impression," Michael said.

"Seriously? We caught her in so many lies, can we really expect her to be telling the truth about the gun?" Maria said.

"The line about working in a dental office. There was a bitterness to it. She loved working for Antoinette. Life was exciting. Everything after that was boring, mundane. I think she's telling the truth about the gun," Michael said.

"We should still search her house. The gun might be there," Maria said.

"I couldn't get a judge to give us a warrant for this if the judge was my brother. And Jack?" Moyer said.

"I felt like he was trying to manipulate me. He was telling me stories that cast him in a flawed but improving light, and he should have been interested in Rebeka as the perp, all the elements are there, but he kept almost defending her," Maria said.

"And so you think..." Moyer said.

"The problem is, I screwed up. I was too obvious. I paid too much attention to him, and I didn't ask the right questions, so he saw through the whole charade," Maria said.

"Was he mad?" Moyer said.

"No. He said he thought it was a cop too, and he gave me a list of cops he'd suspected. They're all dead, but maybe one of their kids has the gun and is connected to Tommy somehow," Maria said.

"Wouldn't that be a bitch? Us chasing after a long dead ghost when we should be looking at their kids. I'm going to be so pissed off I didn't come up with that theory if it turns out to be true," Moyer said.

"We'll tell everybody it was your idea," Michael said.

"So you're sure it's not Jack?" Moyer said.

"I'm not sure of anything right now. The thing is, if those skeletons are tied to this case, Jack is a lot more likely suspect than Rebeka for all the reasons that Michael said, and his mannerisms and reactions fit more with the profile we expect," Maria said.

"I feel like there's a but coming," Moyer said.

"It's also possible that her brother was the original Desert Saint, and Rebecca killed Tommy over PAC money," Maria said.

"To be honest, I don't like either of them for it. It feels like we're trying to fit the crime just because they're the only two we can kind of come up with a reason for. I like the idea of the gun outliving the original owner better," Michael said.

"Focus your efforts on figuring out where the both of them were three days ago. See if we can eliminate them from that killing. Traffic cameras, friends, whatever it takes to figure it out. But with Jack, make sure you do it quietly," Moyer said.

MICHAEL WALKED out to the parking lot with Maria. He had that we should have a talk look on his face, but Maria wasn't in the mood for a serious conversation, and she was trying to get to her car before he could start.

"Hold up a sec," he said.

"I already had one person give me a lecture today, so if that's where you're heading-"

"Lecture?" Michael said.

Maria turned to look at him. He was standing a few feet off, the low desert sun blurring his features, but what she couldn't see in his face, she could hear in his voice. Confusion. He didn't understand why Maria thought he was about to lecture her.

"My father gave me the whole I'm too close, don't work the case, not healthy, blah blah blah speech earlier today, and I just don't want to hear it again."

"Oh, I mean, shit, I agree with him. This case is probably tearing apart your soul, but not any worse than not working the case would do to you," Michael said.

Maria could feel the tension go out of her shoulders. It was a relief to hear someone express exactly how she felt if only so she could know what she felt was normal.

"I just wanted to thank you for telling Moyer the shit that woman said. I... I wouldn't feel right bringing it up myself. I wouldn't want him to think I was complaining."

"She was a raging bitch, huh?" Maria said.

"That woman is so bitter that even when she was calling me a nigger I almost felt bad for her. Almost," Michael said.

Chapter 27

How long can someone hold on to a rage so cold?

Maria spent the ride home thinking about Rebeka's icy rage. As the low slung strip malls and tan colored homes passed, she became more and more convinced that Rebeka was the Desert Saint and her perceived weakness as a woman was preventing everyone from seeing it because the only thing keeping her out of the crosshairs was the bodies under the whorehouse, and why couldn't that have been Rebeka? A woman couldn't dig a ditch? She could have dug it early in preparation and then shown up later with her victims. Or she could have made her victims dig the ditch themselves. Or her brother was the original and she was the copycat.

Maria was so caught up in her thoughts that she was already pulling into her parking lot before she remembered the dinner invitation. The day had been so busy, she'd forgotten about it the minute she'd left the church and still hadn't told Carla.

Maria found her girlfriend on the couch watching a documentary on a cocaine shipment, and Carla didn't have her hair done or makeup on, so she wasn't working that night unless she was working an overnight shift. Maria could never remember when Carla was working and when she wasn't, which had caused Carla on more than one occasion to accuse Maria of being selfish. But Maria knew enough to know, no makeup at this hour meant Carla would be available for dinner. Which meant Maria would have to sit across from her mother, knowing her mother had cheated on her father. She didn't know if she was up to that. No, she was sure she wasn't up to it. No way in hell she could do dinner.

Maria sat down on the couch. Stared at the screen.

Carla reached over. Touched her arm.

Maria forced a half smile across her face.

"If you're going to be miserable, could you at least rub my feet?" Carla said.

Carla put her feet on Maria's lap, and Maria grabbed one of them with one hand and half-heartedly pushed her thumb in circles against the sole.

Carla was scrolling through some app. She turned the phone around so Maria could see. A video of a bunch of baby goats playing on a seesaw.

"How adorable, no?" Carla said.

Maria nodded.

Carla pulled her feet back so her legs were at a V, and she grabbed Maria's hand and placed it on top of her knee and then settled her chin on top of Maria's hand. She sat there, big blue eyes looking right at Maria.

"Don't look at me like that," Maria said.

Carla cocked her head. Smiled. Kissed Maria's hand softly and went back to watching her.

"How long are you going to sit there staring at me?" Maria said.

"As long as it takes," Carla said.

"Not fair. You know I love it when you do that," Maria said.

"Spill it, baby. You'll feel better when it's out," Carla said.

"DNA results matched Tommy to a skeleton. Apparently, Tommy and I share a mother but not a father," Maria said.

"I didn't know the old broad had it in her. Very impressive," Carla said.

Maria yanked her hand back.

"She carries herself all proper, but the woman's got a history. First reason I've had to like her in months," Carla said.

"I can't believe you're making light of this," Maria said.

"I'm not making light of it. I'm putting it in its proper place," Carla said.

"I was sitting with him, and I wanted to tell him, but I just couldn't get it out," Maria said.

"Who?" Carla said.

"My father," Maria said.

"You think he doesn't know?" Carla said.

"I know my father. He'd have never stayed with her if he knew," Maria said.

"Nobody knows their parents. They just know what their parents choose to show," Carla said.

"Not all of us had truck stop hooker parents," Maria said.

"We're going to let that one slide because your brother just died, and I know you're going through it right now, but believe you me, we will come back to that comment at a later date. And as for my mother, who worked as a stripper, I always had food and clothes. She bought me a car when I was sixteen and did a hell of a lot more for me than most of my friend's parents ever did for them."

Carla pulled her legs back underneath her and went back to her phone. Her mother had died before she moved to Vegas, and while Carla didn't talk about her mother much, when she did, she talked about her in an open way that amazed Maria. Carla's mother had been a woman of great appetites, sex, drugs, concerts. Her mother loved them all, and when Maria listened to Carla talk about her mother, Maria envied her ability to be honest. If her own mother had been so scandalous, Maria would have never been able to admit it so openly, and sitting on the couch, Maria wondered if Carla rarely talked about her mother not because she was ashamed of her mother's shameless lifestyle as much as she knew Maria wouldn't really approve and they'd end up where they were now. Maria criticizing a dead woman for no reason.

Who was the flawed one, really, the mothers or Maria?

"I'm sorry. I didn't mean that," Maria said.

"Yes, you did. But I'm used to it. People judged my mother her whole life. But she was who she appeared to be. Judging her says a hell of a lot more about those people than it does about her."

"I'm a total asshole," Maria said.

"I always thought it was one of your better qualities," Carla said.

"There's something else," Maria said.

Carla put her phone down and looked over at Maria.

"My mother invited us to dinner," Maria said.

"Us? Your mother invited me into her house?"

Carla leapt off of the couch and started running around the room in circles, hands making pistols shooting up in the air.

"How can we go with me learning all of this today? How can I sit there at the table?"

"It took you a year to admit that we weren't just friends. We are not missing this," Carla said.

"How can you not see how difficult this is going to be?"

"Seriously? You interrogate murderers for a living. Put on the big girl panties. We're going to that dinner," Carla said.

Chapter 28

Dominic slammed the car door shut with his foot and headed for the house.

His arms were full with the takeout order from Casa Don Juan. Esperanza wasn't a fan of their mole, but Carla was, and Esperanza picking Casa Don Juan for the meal was a preemptive peace offering. Dominic felt hopeful that perhaps his wife was finally accepting that Maria was who she was, which meant accepting Carla.

When Maria had come out as gay, Esperanza had gone through all the stages of trying to convince her daughter what she felt wasn't real. Esperanza did the 'it's a stage' talk. Then the 'did someone abuse you, trauma, we'll find a therapist' thing. Then she tried the 'how could you do this to your mother' routine. Maria knew how her mother was, so she hadn't necessarily been surprised, but the disappointment on her face had angered Dominic, and he'd finally told Esperanza to shut up. To this day, that night was the only time Dominic had said those words to his wife. The next day, Esperanza had accused him of being overjoyed about Maria being a lesbian, and Dominic had done a poor job of denying it, but he knew how shitty men could be to women. Did he really want his daughter dating in that pool?

Being a lesbian seemed like a better option to him.

That conversation was almost fifteen years ago, but tonight was the first time Esperanza had invited one of Maria's girlfriends into the house for dinner. Dominic could make excuses, tell himself better late than never, but Jesus Christ, this shouldn't have taken this long, and in a way, the duration was his fault. He should have pushed for this sooner. They'd all be in a better place if he'd been more forceful about Esperanza accepting reality. Then again, getting Esperanza to do something she didn't want to do, well, the phrase stubborn as a mule should be changed to stubborn as an Esperanza.

Naomi was waiting at the door for him, a cellphone in one hand and the screen door pushed open with the other. She'd slid into suburban anonymity fairly well. The tattoos, they weren't going anywhere, but then again, who didn't have tattoos anymore? But without extensions or ridiculous acrylic nails, Naomi looked like any other nineteen-year-old girl. Dominic figured they'd been lucky, Naomi was just a girl without parents to guide her, but she wasn't a junkie. Her pimp had kept her well fed and off drugs because he wanted her productive, and her record could be wiped totally clean if she stayed out of trouble for another year. Dominic was giving her better than fifty percent odds of turning it around. On an optimistic day, he might put it up to seventy-five percent.

He dumped one of the bags into Naomi's arms, and she grunted. Feigned annoyance. But Dominic could see the smile as she turned away. Like anyone else, she just wanted to be a part of something. That a client attacking her might end up being the best thing that happened to her. Funny how life was like that, the person you think is killing you might be saving you, and the one who looks like a savior might just be waiting for you to turn around so he can pull a trigger.

Esperanza came out of the kitchen with a glass of red wine in her hand. She was still in a bathrobe. That combined with the wine could be a bad sign. Then Dominic saw that she had on makeup. She was just waiting to get dressed last, perhaps scared that she'd spill some wine on her dress. A good sign. Esperanza was trying to make this night special.

"You want everything on the table?" Naomi asked.

"Take it to the kitchen. We'll put it on plates in there," Esperanza said.

"I should know that," Naomi said. She put her phone in her pocket and reached for the other bag, taking it from Dominic and heading for the kitchen.

Dominic moved next to Esperanza and leaned into her.

"If this is a disaster, it's your fault," Esperanza said.

"Your daughter is coming over for dinner. What could be disastrous about that?"

Esperanza rolled her eyes and turned away from Dominic. Headed for the kitchen.

"How much wine have you had?" Dominic asked.

"Not enough," Esperanza said.

"That thing we talked about. How are you planning on bringing it up?" Dominic asked.

Esperanza turned to him and reached out with her free hand. Touched him on the chest. A mischievous look crossed her face. She got like this when she knew something was important to Dominic, and he was leaving control of it to her.

"Are you afraid that I'll handle it wrong?" Esperanza said. A fake shocked look crossed her face. "Pero mi amor, you know I always say everything right and at the right time."

Dominic let out a laugh. He hadn't realized it until it escaped his mouth, but he'd been horribly tense, and his wife had just popped all of that tension. It was a scene they'd played hundreds of times in their decades together. Dominic nervous about what Esperanza was going to say. Esperanza pretending to be shocked about Dominic's nervousness. She always said whatever needed to be said in the wrong way at the wrong time. Esperanza considered it part of her charm. Dominic didn't know how charming this particular trait was, but this woman was his wife, the only woman he'd ever truly loved, and if he had to clean up messes from time to time because she'd pissed someone off, well, then that's just the way it was.

169

The doorbell rang.

Esperanza looked at her watch.

"Shit, my daughter is always early." She went running off to the bedroom to finish dressing, almost knocking over Naomi who was coming out of the kitchen.

"Good thing she's not in heels. She'd fall flat on her ass on that rug," Naomi said.

Dominic turned for the door. Dominic wasn't worried about how Maria would handle this dinner. His daughter was all smooth iron. But Carla, Carla was his concern. Carla and Esperanza had eaten together at a restaurant once, and they'd been in the same car a handful of times, but tonight being the first time Carla was in their home was going to make this difficult. Dominic had spent much of the day trying to figure out how to make her feel at ease. How to take the edge off so she could relax. He hadn't really come up with a good plan. None of his worrying mattered anyway. Carla looked more at ease than he'd ever seen her. She was wearing a paisley dress with flats and was still almost as tall as Dominic, and her hair was pulled back in a ponytail. Maria was in jeans, nicer jeans than normal, but jeans all the same and a black t-shirt.

"You need to stop dressing like Jessica Jones," Esperanza told her daughter when she came out of her room.

"así me gusta," Carla said. *I like her like that.*

So natural, so calm, something had definitely changed, and Dominic didn't know what, but he was just happy that she could be herself finally around Esperanza. This was the Carla that he knew. Confident, beautiful, and completely in love with his daughter.

What more could a father really hope for?

Esperanza could sense the change as well. Being dismissive of someone was much more difficult when they couldn't care less what you thought, and Dominic could see his wife thinking everything over, and when she took Carla's arm and led her on a tour of the house, Dominic felt sure that the night would go well. At least as well as it could.

"Talk in your office?" Maria said.

A joke, Dominic didn't have an office; she meant the backyard.

. . .

DOMINIC LOVED Las Vegas at night. No matter how brilliant the sun burned in the day, the desert night air was always cool. He walked halfway out his backyard and looked up at the night sky. Maria pulled a couple of chairs away from the house and sat in one.

"Carla's different," Dominic said.

"Seems the same to me," Maria said.

"She's more relaxed," Dominic said.

"Maybe I finally convinced her to stop caring about what my mother thinks," Maria said.

"Sure it's not something else?"

"What else could it be?" Maria said.

Dominic noticed the evasion right away. All those years a cop, his sense for when someone was lying wasn't going to disappear in this lifetime, but Maria didn't give him a chance to follow up.

"We caught that woman I told you about in a bunch of lies today," Maria said.

"Lies about what?"

"About pretty much everything, and she lawyered up when Michael pressed her on where she was during Tommy's killing, and she admitted to owning a .22 but claims she threw it away years ago," Maria said.

"She worked for an escort service for how long?"

"Fifteen years," Maria said.

"Lawyering up doesn't mean as much for her as it would for a solid citizen," Dominic said.

"Asking about her whereabouts really triggered something. She's hiding something big, and let's be honest, what else could it really be?" Maria said.

"I'm just having a hard time believing a woman was responsible for these killings."

"Getting sexist in our old age?"

"Most of the women I arrested were crimes of passion or protection. We almost always caught them at the scene. Usually covered in blood," Dominic said.

"Protection?"

"Protecting their kids or themselves," Dominic said.

"Just because female serial killers are rare doesn't mean they don't exist," Maria said.

"Agreed, but your theory points to anger. An obsession with Anthony. Hatred toward the priest. Where's the anger in those killings? They were cold-blooded executions," Dominic said.

"I will concede that point, but you also weren't in there watching her. When we started confronting her with her lies, she changed. That woman is angry, but her anger is cold. She almost freezes with it," Maria said.

"A freezing anger? That's your evidence?" Dominic said.

"Admitted. We got no evidence. But we have a lying suspect who clammed up the minute we started pushing buttons. I don't know how I'm going to break her because it's a confession or nothing, but I'm going to figure out a way," Maria said.

Dominic looked over at his daughter. She might as well have been describing herself. Her anger was cold too, and she was roiling with it. A freezing cauldron of focus, and he wondered how far she would go to overturn this woman's life all the time believing she was being driven by logic but really just trying to deal with the grief of her brother's death. How could he help her through this?

"At least you're off Jack as a suspect," Dominic said.

"I like her better, but that doesn't mean I'm not considering Jack. He saw me coming a mile away with that double interrogation trick," Maria said.

"Double interrogation?" Dominic said.

"I brought him in under the guise of watching the Rebeka interview. Told him I wanted his background knowledge since he was so tight with her kid brother."

"You brought Jack in for questioning? I thought you told me-"

"I brought Jack in to help us with an investigation. He accused you of putting me up to it to give him one last thrill."

"I would have if I'd thought of it," Dominic said.

"Something was off there, too. He was too open," Maria said.

"You're complaining he was too compliant?"

"It was like he was diverting me, opening up about his now corrected flaws, so I'd like him and not look too closely," Maria said.

"Maybe he's just an old guy facing death and getting it all out before he goes," Dominic said.

"Maybe but it seemed like a weird place for a life talk, and since he had me figured out on the whole double interrogation angle, perhaps that was his way of brushing me off," Maria said.

"How do you know he had you figured?"

"He thanked me for my discretion. Told me he'd always thought it might be a cop, too. Said once upon a time, he'd wondered if it was you," Maria said.

"Me?"

"Yeah, said you were too interested in the case," Maria said.

Dominic laughed.

"Everybody was interested. Whoever solved that case was going to get a chance to write their own ticket. They'd a been able to work whatever department they wanted."

Maria's phone buzzed, a message from the reporter. Preston had told his apartment security he would be expecting a guest around 11:30.

"You might have been right about the Aristocrat. He ordered a girl for tonight," Maria said.

"I doubt he'd be stupid enough to do anything this close to the last one, but he might be trying to see if anyone is surveilling him, so he can prepare for the next," Dominic said.

"I'll be sure to be invisible then," Maria said.

Naomi slid the door open and stuck her head out into the back-yard to tell them that dinner was ready. Then she slid the door back shut and walked off into the dining room.

"And her? Where did she come from again?" Maria asked.

"Ask me later. Time to eat now," Dominic said.

Chapter 29

Could an honest effort be too late to matter?

Maria knew right away when she saw the food that her mother was really trying, but Maria couldn't quite shake the anger at how this had taken so long. Maria and Carla had been together almost four years already, and this was the first time they were both invited to the house for dinner? Tommy needed to die for Maria's girlfriend to get an invite? And now, knowing what she knew about Tommy's parentage, keeping the edge out of her voice when responding to her mother was hard. Maria was keeping everything under wraps, not for her mother's sake, but for Carla's. Maria didn't want this night to turn into a disaster, but soon, her and her mother were going to sit down and have a real conversation without Dominic hovering over her shoulder to protect her.

Maria was going to get some answers.

And the girl. What to make of her. The outfit, a bright pink sweatsuit, softened her roughness but didn't erase it. Her mannerisms were of a teenager, but the wear was there. Lines in her face that shouldn't show up for years yet. The tattoos that peeked out at the neck. A decade of coverup work was ahead of her and hopefully by an artist that didn't learn how to tattoo in prison.

But what was she doing here?

Maria realized her mother was watching her watch the girl, and she put her eyes to her plate. She felt a brief flash of shame. Had she been that obvious? Then that anger flared up again. Why should Maria feel bad? Maria wasn't the one with secrets.

"This mole is kind of watery," Naomi said.

"That's what I always say, but she likes it," Esperanza said.

"I like it too," Dominic said.

"Yeah, but you're like the whitest guy I know," Naomi said.

"How did she end up here again?" Maria asked.

"Did she really talk about me in front of me like I wasn't here?" Naomi asked.

"She didn't mean anything by it," Dominic said.

"Who does that?" Naomi asked.

"I tried to teach her manners. I wanted her to have some more grace," Esperanza said.

"Maybe it's a lesbian thing," Naomi said.

"That's probably it, a lesbian thing," Maria said.

"I mean, Carla, is def the woman in that relationship," Naomi said.

"We're both women. That's how the lesbian thing works. Two women," Maria said.

"You're a woman, but she's a WOMAN," Naomi said.

"Does this make any sense to anyone but you?" Maria said.

"I get what she's trying to say," Dominic said.

"Oh, do you?" Maria said.

"It's a shame you two can't have kids, though. They'd be super hot," Naomi said.

"They could do the sperm donor thing," Dominic said.

"Yeah, but it ain't them, ya know. I wonder what color hair the baby would have," Naomi said.

Carla reached out and grabbed a Darth Vader shaped pepper shaker.

"I love Star Wars. Especially the Empire Strikes Back," Carla said.

"It was her favorite," Dominic motioned toward his wife, but

Esperanza didn't seem to be paying attention to anything that was going on at the table anymore. She had a wineglass in her hand, poised a few inches from her cheek, and she was looking down, deep in thought.

"That scene when you find out that Luke didn't really know who his father was, so powerful," Carla said.

Maria turned her head to look at Carla, but Carla wouldn't return the gaze. A mischievous smile was on her face, but no one else seemed to notice.

"Yeah, then he lost his hand. Maybe he was better off not knowing," Dominic said.

"I always wanted to be a showgirl," Esperanza said.

From the tone of her mother's voice, Maria knew the night was about to go to shit, and from the look on her father's face, he knew it, too.

"Everybody worshiped those women. But I never had legs like you. That's real blonde hair too, isn't it? Either that or the most amazing stylist. They didn't have short, dark-haired show girls," Esperanza said.

Dominic shot a look his wife's way. Not angry, but not pleased, either.

"Don't look at me like that. The girl is lovely. I'm complimenting her," Esperanza said.

Maria opened her mouth to interrupt, but her mother started up again before Maria could start to speak.

"You can barely tell it now, but I was quite the looker myself. Before having Tommy at least," Esperanza said.

"You can still see it," Carla said.

Esperanza smiled. Batted her eyes at Carla.

"Do tell me more," Esperanza said.

"You're as beautiful as ever to me," Dominic said.

Esperanza's smile faded. She took another sip of her wine. What worried Maria the most was that Esperanza had stopped looking at anyone as if looking at the people here would prevent her from saying what was to come.

Maria reached under the table and grabbed Carla's hand.

"I don't like it, you know? The fact that you two do what you do. I just always wanted to see my baby get married in a white dress, and I wanted to be so proud, and now-" Esperanza said.

"We can still get married," Carla said.

"Not in a church. Not like it's supposed to be," Esperanza said.

"Who gets married in a church anymore?" Naomi said.

"You promised me," Dominic said.

Maria stood up and motioned for Carla to follow. Until now, Maria hadn't been angry, but the disappointment on Carla's face was enough to make Maria want to scream. How could anyone shit all over someone so sweet? Especially when they had their own secrets.

"Thanks for the food. I'll check in on you guys in a few days," Maria said.

"Am I supposed to pretend to not think what I think? Would that be better?" Esperanza said.

"Yes, yes it would," Maria said.

Maria headed for the door with Carla right behind. She had Carla's hand in her own just in case Carla was tempted to stay and try to talk it out.

"Hold on a sec," Dominic said.

"I'll talk to you tomorrow," Maria said.

Dominic caught up to them at the door. He looked as devastated as Maria was angry. He gave Carla a hug, said something low in Carla's ear. Maria couldn't make it out, but it made Carla smile.

"I wasn't done," Esperanza said.

"Nobody wants to listen," Maria said.

Esperanza came halfway down the hall. The wine goblet still in her hand but clearly forgotten, and Maria wondered if she was about to drop it.

"How many of those did you have before they got here?" Dominic asked.

"If the two of you are going to continue this relationship-" Esperanza said.

"I'm leaving," Maria cut her off.

"déjame hablar, por favor," Esperanza said.

Maria turned and faced her mother. Her mother only ever switched into Spanish when she really wanted Maria to pay attention, when she wanted Maria to know that what she was about to say was incredibly important, but Maria fixed her eyes right on her mother's face because she wanted her mother to clearly understand how important the next moments were going to be for their relationship.

"If the two of you are going to continue this relationship, I think you two should have a child," Esperanza said.

"What did you just say?" Maria said.

"Have a child. Please. With Tommy gone, how the hell else am I going to have a grandchild?" Esperanza said.

"How drunk are you exactly?" Maria said.

"That's a fantastic idea," Carla said.

"Did you know she was going to say this?" Maria asked her father.

"I had hoped it was going to come out better," Dominic said.

"And you willingly invited me here to get mugged with this?" Maria said.

"You know, you ain't getting any younger. I'm not saying it's now or never but-" Dominic said.

"What's that supposed to mean?" Maria said.

"Seemed pretty clear to me," Naomi said.

"Crystal," Carla said.

"How can I hate all of you at the same time? That shouldn't be possible," Maria said.

CARLA SETTLED on the couch and started scrolling through her phone. She hadn't said much on the way home, but Maria could tell she'd been pleased with how the night ended whereas Maria felt like she'd been in a boxing ring with Michael for a good ten minutes. She was still trying to figure out how before dinner her mother had been the bad guy and after dinner her mother and her girlfriend were aligned. Not necessarily aligned with Maria but definitely in a short-term alliance. Who knew how fucked up things would get after the baby arrived, but for now the two of them were going to be working in concert. Did she just admit to herself that she wanted a baby?

Carla showed Maria an ad for a baby stroller with oversized gold rimmed wheels.

"You want our baby to be a cholo?" Maria said.

"So you're in," Carla said.

"I haven't agreed to anything," Maria said.

"You just said, 'our baby'," Carla said.

"I wasn't agreeing to anything," Maria said.

"It was a subconscious slip. But it was there," Carla said.

"I can't deal with this right now," Maria said.

"You'll have to carry the baby," Carla said.

"I'm a detective. I can't work the streets if I'm pregnant," Maria said.

Carla stood up and walked over in front of a mirror. She turned one way and the other. Looked at herself over her shoulder.

"I depend on my frame to make money," Carla said.

"You want me to get off the streets, so you can keep walking around in heels and a short skirt while men leer at you," Maria said.

"I have a limited time to use these legs. You can work your job well into your fifties," Carla said.

"I'm not carrying a baby. If you want a baby, you have to carry," Maria said.

"Shit," Carla said.

"Called your bluff, huh?" Maria said.

"So you're saying, yes," Carla said.

"I'm saying, we can consider it," Maria said.

Chapter 30

In the abstract, this idea hadn't seemed like a disaster. But now...

Maria parked her car half a block down from the entrance to Preston's apartment. She had a clear view of the front door and behind her, visible in her rear-view mirror, was the entrance to the building's parking garage. Leaning the seat back, she checked the time on her phone: 11:15PM. The appointment was for 11:30. Through the front window, she saw the security guard, a tall African-American man, leaning against a wall looking up at something, probably a television.

Maria reran the dinner over in her mind. The way her father interacted with Naomi stuck out. There was a patience there, a kindness, an empathy. She wondered why she was so surprised. Her father was famous for his empathy for the people who lived and worked in the streets. More than a few older cops had told her that her father had made so many busts because he was comfortable with criminals. He talked to them like normal people, treated them like good citizens, and because of that, they always opened up to him. Nobody wanted to be judged even when they knew what they were doing deserved judgment. But Maria had thought that treatment was limited to the streets, something learned and used on the job, not demonstrated in his home.

And a child?

Did she really want one?

Probably. Yes. But now? Was now really a good time to bring that up?

Right after Tommy?

God, her mother just couldn't not make it about her.

A white car pulled onto the street. The headlights flashed across Maria's windshield, and she scooted down to remain hidden. Preston wasn't looking at parked cars, though. He was looking at the entrance to see if anyone was awaiting him, but the front door was empty except for the security guard watching television.

In the rearview mirror: WLTHY.

Preston pulled into the parking garage.

Maria sat all the way up. Tonight was probably going to be a waste. Preston couldn't be so stupid that he'd murder another woman right after the article being posted, but maybe, maybe what her father said about him viewing it as a challenge was right. Maybe, she could catch him in the act, and if she did that, Moyer would be so happy about the bust that he'd be willing to overlook the less than appropriate way in which the bust happened.

Another car pulled onto the street and stopped.

The backdoor opened, and a woman stepped out.

Tall, blonde, high heels, short skirt, top covered by a blazer. The woman made her way to the front door and smiled through the window. She checked her phone as the security guard opened the door and stepped aside to let her in.

Maria saw a tall hooker on her way to meet a date, but she wondered what her father would see. What was it that gave him such empathy, and could she develop it? Would it make her a better cop? She really focused on the woman in the lobby, picked up the binoculars on the passenger seat and looked through them. All the woman's attention was focused on her phone. She answered the guard's questions but barely looked at him. Her jacket, black like her skirt, was zipped up tight probably hiding a low cut top. Or maybe nothing. Maybe just a bra. She reached down and tugged the hem of her skirt lower and then looked out the window to the street.

The woman looked nervous.

What must that feel like, waiting to go have sex with a man you'd never met? Did she feel a rush, did she enjoy being wanted and desired, men being willing to pay money just to sleep with her, or did she feel trapped, no other options, stuck spreading her legs for men she could barely stand much less want to sleep with? Maybe both. Maybe neither. Was it possible she could feel powerful and powerless all at the same time? Maybe she'd started off feeling one way and now had shifted to the other. Maria wondered if the woman would even give her a straight answer if Maria asked. Did the woman really understand herself? The thought of doing the woman's job made Maria's stomach turn, but was that because of the job or because the thought of sex with a man was so revolting?

Maria refocused her attention on the woman in the lobby. Something was wrong. She should have already been let in, but the woman looked annoyed, and the security guard was shrugging his shoulders like there was nothing he could do. The woman said something, and the security guard picked up the phone and held it to his ear. He punched some numbers on the dial and waited. But nothing. He put the phone back down and said something, but the woman was already wheeling around on her heels and heading out the door.

In the rearview, the flash of headlights as a car pulled out of the parking lot.

The car turned right and headed away from Maria, but she saw the license plate clearly in the rearview: WLTHY. Preston was leaving, but why? And why was he going the opposite direction of his home? He'd looked eagerly at the front door when he arrived, but now he was leaving while the woman he had ordered was here. Something wasn't right.

Maria pulled her car out and followed Preston.

Chapter 31

You don't know this man, but you know the type.

Elegant, expensive clothes draped over a black soul. You've never been one to envy wealth but neither have you been blinded by it. You hear his muffled yelling from the trunk, rage overcoming fear. He kicks against the seats. They buck inward.

You brake suddenly, just for a second, just a brief jolt to let him know that you are in control.

You're not here to give him pain. Just to end the carnage.

But control. Control is everything.

You look in the rearview and see the same headlights that spun around and followed from the apartment. A small thing to deal with. A minor annoyance.

You put your eyes back on the road, black asphalt rushing under the headlights.

The man in the trunk moans. Starts to cry. It's something all of them do. Those who think themselves powerful are always the weakest. And after that realization hits, the tears and the sobs start, and then eventually the muttered self-pity when they realize the hopelessness of their situation.

Pathetic, really.

Chapter 32

Something was terribly wrong.

Maria's eyes stayed pegged on Preston's car, and she was starting to wonder from the way he was driving if he was trying to see if he was being followed. He drove for a solid twenty minutes, first going south on the 515 before looping back around on the 215. Could he have noticed her in the car? She didn't think so, but she also couldn't be totally sure, so she stayed back. So far back that she almost missed him exiting, but she caught sight of him pulling to a stop at a light at the top of the ramp just in time to pull over into the exit without it being ridiculously obvious.

He was turning right and was a good two blocks away before she even hit the light.

Something was definitely wrong. This whole drive was a mess of conflicting signals. She had known before that she should have looped in Michael, but now she really felt the need for backup, or at least someone to talk this through with.

Up ahead, Preston was turning left into a neighborhood. She sped up afraid that if he turned in and got around a bend, she'd lose him totally, but when she hit the entrance, Preston's car was straight ahead going over a rise, deeper into the community.

Maria followed.

Most of the houses she passed were dark. Some with cars parked out front but others just looked empty.

Preston's car was turning right up ahead.

Maria slowed. All the streets she had passed so far were dead ends. She doubted that the one Preston was turning onto would be any different, and she was beginning to wonder. Was Preston luring her here? He had sent a detective to follow her, so she was definitely in his sights, and he hadn't gone inside to the waiting escort. Instead, he'd driven here, to this half-deserted housing development.

Was she the one hunting or the one being hunted?

She parked her car at the head of the street Preston had turned onto. Just like all the other side streets, a dead end with a cul-de-sac. Three houses lined each side of the street and the cul-de-sac had three houses ringing it. Most of the houses were dark. Lights flicked on the second floor of one. Another house had a black jeep with oversized tires parked in the driveway.

But Preston's car was gone.

Into one of the garages, probably.

But which one?

Maria stepped out of the car. The air was cold, and the wind stung her cheek. She checked her gun and her flashlight and started walking down the street. She looked left and right as she went. Only the two houses seemed to be occupied. Every other house was dark with empty porches and windows. She made it a third of the way down the street before she heard the two gunshots. They had come from one of the houses in the cul-de-sac. She couldn't be sure which one because she hadn't seen any muzzle flashes through the windows. Just the cracks carrying through glass and up the street. And the cracks had been faint. A small caliber weapon. So small she might have missed the sound entirely if only one shot had been fired except for two.

Two shots. Small caliber.

She pulled her gun out.

Why was Preston here?

He hadn't shot Eva. He'd strangled her.

Another possibility dawned on Maria.

This street was a good place to kill someone. The kind of place someone who planned would pick. Not many people who would hear the gunshots. No traffic cameras out front of the entrance. No guard. One way in and one way out wasn't great. But if you were going to kill someone, this would be the type of place to do it. The type of place someone who knew how to plan would use.

Maria realized she was standing in the middle of the street like a fool and made for the Jeep. She crouched against the bumper and looked down the street. Everything was quiet. But a killer was no more than two houses away, and she needed to close fast.

Fast but smart.

She made for the house and ran along the front. Eyes fixed down the street, gun out but down low. She paused at the corner of the next house. Nothing was moving in front of her. No lights on anywhere. No more gunshots. No more sound.

Just her and the quiet street.

She made the first house on the cul-de-sac and checked the garage window.

Empty.

She eyed the house in the middle.

All the windows were dark. Not a hint of life anywhere.

She sprinted across the yard and pulled up against the wall. Her heart was pounding so hard that she couldn't hear, and she took three long breaths to calm herself down. Hearing was everything right now. She inched up to the garage window and looked through.

Preston's car. Trunk still open.

Maria made her way around the front of the house. Stopped next to a window. Not a sound came from inside. Maria put her face against the house and inched forward until she could look through the window. She saw a perfectly staged living room, oversized sofa with a coffee table. Picture book centered at an angle. Everything inside looked like the perfect vacation rental, except for the Italian leather shoes attached to the foot sticking out of what must have been a hallway. The rest of the person was hidden behind a wall, but the foot was pointed down and at an odd angle that would be uncomfortable for anyone alive. And the foot wasn't moving.

Maria went for the front door. Closed but unlocked.

She went in slowly, gun up.

She heard nothing but her own breathing.

When she turned the corner, she saw Preston face down on the floor. Two shells next to his corpse and a printout of the newspaper article linking him to Eva's murder on top of his left hand. Maria had led the Desert Saint right to Preston.

A slight breeze came through an open sliding glass door.

Maria headed for the backyard.

A car engine started one street over. The car started to pull down the street, headlights flashing against the wall of a house. Maria had to decide. Stay here and search the house or chase the car. She was sure the killer was gone. Why go to all this trouble to pick a location and then stay there? If Preston's car wasn't being used to escape, then another vehicle was being used, and parking it a street away, a simple jump over a fence and jog through a yard away made sense. The only weakness in the plan was Maria, who shouldn't be here, but the Desert Saint couldn't know that. She still had a chance, but she had to make it to her car so she could block the exit.

Maria exploded into a run and headed up the street pumping her legs all out. The cold air hit her lungs like a brick, but she pushed on. She was wheezing horribly halfway up the block, but she forced herself to keep moving. She was so close. She couldn't stop.

Maria could hear the other car but couldn't see it. Then there it was turning onto the street. She'd been lucky. The other street curved away instead of running directly parallel which had bought her some time, but Jesus, she needed to work on her cardio.

Maria reached her car just as the other car was picking up speed. She slung the door open and jumped in. She reached down into the passenger seat for the flashing police light to stick on her dashboard, but the light slipped and fell to the floor. She looked up through the windshield.

The car was almost to her.

Maria bent over again. This time, she was able to grab the light and slam it onto the dash. The car was crossing the intersection, a gray Mazda. Tinted windows. Maria flipped on the light and pulled out across the street. She'd forgotten to put on her seatbelt. She wasn't sure of much, but she didn't think the Desert Saint would surrender easily. She just hoped he wouldn't slam his car into hers.

The Mazda pulled to a stop.

Maria jumped out of her car and pulled her gun. Aimed it over the hood at the windshield of the Mazda. The tint was too dark. She couldn't see anything. Just shadows inside. Maybe one shadow. Maybe two. She couldn't be sure.

"Hands out the window where I can see them," Maria yelled.

The engine growled.

Red and blue flashed across the dark windshield.

"I said, hands out the window, NOW!"

The driver's side window whirred as it lowered. The passenger side window did the same. Why were two windows going down? Maria started to have a sinking feeling. The car hadn't tried to escape. Two passengers, not one. Then the driver stuck her hands out of the window.

Small hands whose nails were painted pink.

Maria approached, gun still out but not pointed at the car anymore. She closed the gap quickly and found a girl, about seventeen, behind the wheel. The girl looked to be about to cry.

"Don't shoot, I didn't do anything," the girl said.

In the passenger seat was a boy, maybe fourteen or fifteen. He had his cellphone up and pointed at Maria. A light about the camera glowed. He was filming.

"We're live y'all. Hands up, don't shoot," the boy said.

Chapter 33

The string was a dead end.

Michael wanted to meet Maria on the scene, but she told him not to bother. She was sure they weren't going to find anything. At daybreak, she'd seen the bicycle tracks leading off to a wash. The Desert Saint had led her into the house and had a bicycle waiting and taken off on it. She'd followed the tracks, and on the other side, a new shopping center, still under construction. No cameras. No security guards. No bicycle.

A clean getaway while she was off chasing a car of teenagers.

Maria wanted to tell herself that knowing how the Desert Saint escaped would be helpful. Another layer to the pie. But she knew she was kidding herself. All it told her was that she didn't know shit. Jack had a bum knee and wasn't getting on any bicycles, and she doubted Rebeka could maneuver a bicycle through that wash in the dark at her age. All this killing told her was that her two main suspects were innocent. She had another dead body but was still grasping at smoke. That's what she was thinking as she made her way down the hall and entered the conference room where Michael was waiting.

"You look like shit," Michael said.

"I feel worse," Maria said.

"Wait til Moyer sees that video which is already all over social media," Michael said.

"My actions were totally reasonable," Maria said.

"Not sure people care about reasonable and unreasonable anymore," Michael said.

Maria walked over to the wall. A bunch of new photos were up. Almost all mugshots.

"At least you didn't shoot anyone," Michael said.

"He was right there and I let him get away," Maria said.

"Guess we can rule out Jack?" Michael said.

"We can rule them both out," Maria said.

Michael pointed at the tacked up photos.

"I ran the DNA from the skeletons through every database I could find. I was able to put names to most of them. Luckily for us, most of their kids are in the system. The missing persons reports give us a timeline. I tracked down the ME report from when they were found. They all died from double taps to the head," Michael said.

"Besides my tio Tomas, anyone interesting?" Maria said.

"Mostly pimps. One guy collected for the mob," Michael said.

Maria walked up to the wall and looked the photos over. A grim collection of men scowling at a camera. White, black, Mexican. Some in their twenties, others in their thirties. Men who'd been aged more than their years by a life spent in the streets. She was getting nowhere looking at these photos, and she knew it.

"When did the last vic disappear?" Maria asked.

Michael looked down at some folders and pawed through them looking for the right one.

"Victor Spinella, last seen in late February 1985," Michael said.

"When did the M.O. shift again?" Maria asked.

"Tomas Vargas disappeared in December of '82," Michael said.

"So we got seven vics in three years," Maria said.

"Two years, really," Michael said.

"He was busy. We need to be searching for someone who left town in '85 and came back recently," Maria said.

"What about that list of suspects Jack gave you? Weren't you going to look into the kids?" Michael said.

"Shit, I forgot about that."

The door opened and Moyer leaned in. He looked as tired as Maria felt.

"I need to speak with you," Moyer said.

"I know that video looks bad but I had every reason-"

"It's not about the video," Moyer said.

Something in Moyer's face made a chill go up Maria's spine.

"Did something happen to my dad?" Maria asked.

"No, he's fine. Just come on. We have to talk," Moyer said.

MOYER LED MARIA down the hall towards interrogation. He opened the door to the viewing room and motioned for Maria to go inside. Through the one-way glass, Maria saw Carla sitting at the table. Her eyes were puffy and red from crying, and while she had a jacket around her shoulders, her cocktail waitress uniform was still on, a short minidress with an exaggerated slit to the hip. Carla's legs, even crossed, were too long to comfortably fit under the table, so she was sitting with them sticking out to the side rather than underneath.

"What the hell?" Maria said.

"Vice pulled her in. She verbally confirmed and took a chip from what she thought was a customer soliciting sex," Moyer said.

Maria walked up to the glass. Carla was trembling.

"Security has been suspicious of her for a while. That's how vice got involved," Moyer said.

"A while?" Maria said.

"Look, I don't know what happened. I'm getting everything secondhand, and she did not mention your name one time to anyone. She came in here and didn't once try to pull you into it. I just happened to be walking by when they pulled her in and I recognized her," Moyer said.

"How much was the chip?" Maria asked.

"The Vice lieutenant went to the academy with me. I talked

with him and they lost the recording and the statements. It's all going away," Moyer said.

"I'm not asking-"

"I made the call. I did it. It's done, and I did not explain to him why," Moyer said.

Maria knew she should be thanking Moyer, but she didn't want to. She wanted to go into the room on the other side of the glass and scream. How could Carla do this?

"Look, it's best for everyone if you took a vacation," Moyer said.

"I can't take a vacation now. I mean, Jesus, I almost got him last night. Granted, I fucked up, and he got away, but still-"

"Maria, worst case, those bullets don't match the others and people accuse you of murdering that guy and trying to blame it on the Desert Saint," Moyer said.

"Come on with that, someone drove him down there," Maria said.

"The only witness who saw that was you," Moyer said.

"Then how did my car get down there if I was driving the vic," Maria said.

"You could have left the car down there and gone back up to the apartment. Kidnapped the vic and framed him," Moyer said.

"Do you really believe that?" Maria said.

"No, I'm just pointing out how bad all this looks," Moyer said.

"The traffic cameras will prove that I arrived behind the vic's car," Maria said.

"If we get a decent shot," Moyer said. "But that's the worst-case scenario. The best-case scenario is you were staking out a suspect from another crime who just happened to have had his case file information leaked to the press. Some people might say that whoever did that, and I'm not asking who it was, but some people might say that person was trying to catch that asshole in the act but because that person was working by herself, another dead body made it into the papers. That's not a fuckup. That's a disaster. The press is going to be all over this, and somebody might find it useful to leak this info about your girlfriend. Do you really want all that publicity?"

"I don't care what the press says. I just want to catch the guy who killed my brother."

"What about the rest of us? You want me to lose my job because you're out of control? You need to take some time to deal with all of it. After a break, you can come back fresh and everything will have blown over and we start new," Moyer said.

"You're going to send me home like this? Home is the last place I want to be," Maria said.

"The last place we want to be is usually the place we need to be," Moyer said.

"Oh, Jesus Christ, did someone post that to your Facebook wall?" Maria said.

"Home. Now. Two weeks," Moyer said.

Chapter 34

How could a life go completely to shit so fast?

Maria sat in her car and looked through the windshield at Tommy's house. Her parents were inside packing up, but Maria didn't know if she was up for facing them right now. She didn't want to go home. She couldn't go back to work. She didn't know what to do, and that frustrated her more than anything. Mostly, she just wanted to cry. But when she tried to relax enough to let the tears out, nothing came.

Her phone buzzed, a text message from Michael wanting to know how she was doing.

How the hell did he think she was doing?

She ignored it.

Maria thought back to the night Tommy died, Carla coming home later than normal, with the thousand-dollar chip. She searched her memory for other instances of missing time. A few, here and there spread out. Times Carla went to the bar after work with friends. Times she stopped at the store to buy something when the shopping took a half hour longer than it should have.

How long does it take to go to a hotel room, have sex, and leave?

Could Carla really have been doing this the whole time?

Her phone rang, Carla. Maria sent it to voicemail and turned the phone off. She stepped out of the car and headed for Tommy's house. Helping her parents clean out her murdered brother's house was easier than facing that call.

ESPERANZA LOOKED up at Maria as she walked in and smiled. Told Maria she was happy she'd had time to come and help out. Maria searched her face for some sign of knowing about the disastrous trip to Henderson or about Carla but nothing. Maria sat at the kitchen table.

God, she was exhausted.

"I was thinking Maria Isabela if it's a girl or Antonio Miguel if it's a boy," Esperanza said.

"What are you talking about?"

"What you and Carla can name your child," Esperanza said.

"You wouldn't look at her for the last four years and now you're coming up with baby names?"

"You'd think you'd be happy I've come around."

"Can we not talk about this right now?" Maria said.

Dominic came into the kitchen and placed a coffee mug on the kitchen counter.

"Are you going to tell your daughter?" Esperanza said.

"Tell me what?" Maria said.

"It's nothing," Dominic said.

"He's got a profile coming out in The Atlantic," Esperanza said.

"No shit?"

"He's been corresponding with the journalist for a few weeks and the photographer came by yesterday," Esperanza said.

"It's no big deal," Dominic said.

"The journalist said, it was his honor to profile such a trailblazer. An honor, he said," Esperanza said.

Dominic leaned against the dishwasher and looked his daughter over. He didn't seem to like what he saw, and Maria could tell that he'd already spoken with Moyer. She couldn't decide whether she was relieved or disappointed she wasn't going to have to be the one to tell him the whole story.

"You look like shit," Dominic said.

"Job hazard," Maria said.

"Quit now, get some cush casino security job before you end up a grizzled mess like me."

"You're handsomer and handsomer every year," Esperanza said.

"I told you that Lasik surgery wouldn't work, but you just had to have it," Dominic said.

Esperanza grabbed a dish towel and spun it into a whip and flicked it at Dominic's thigh. She came up a full foot short, but Dominic hopped around on one leg, pretending to be wounded. Maria laughed. The laugh surprised her, and she cut it short. The relief made her feel guilty, but damn, her father always knew how to make her feel better. She was thirty-four years old, and all she wanted to do was climb into his lap and let him rock her to sleep.

God, she was a mess.

"What needs doing?" Maria asked.

"You can help me pack boxes in the living room," Dominic said.

THE LIVING ROOM looked mostly packed up. Dominic had been putting all the books from the bookshelf into boxes, and the boxes were stacked in the corner. One half-empty box sat open a foot from the shelf. Dominic squatted and looked down into the box and then eyed the remaining books. Even now, putting books into a box, he had to have a system, an order to it.

"Getting famous in retirement, huh?" Maria said.

"It's a load of horseshit. Most cops were like me. They just wanted to catch the bad guy. They didn't care who the vic was. Why should I get the photo spread?"

"You were probably the only one willing to risk his job for women he didn't even know though," Maria said.

"I was probably the only one with a friend who had a movie theater," Dominic said.

"Still, I thought that part of your life was over. You turning your home into a runaway shelter now? The Valera Home for Wayward Women?"

Dominic looked up at Maria like he didn't understand what she was saying.

"What's up with the girl?"

"What's it matter?" Dominic said.

"What's it matter? You have a street walker living in your house," Maria said.

Dominic focused his attention back on the books he was packing.

"Why did he have all of these books? He didn't even like to read," Dominic said.

"Dad, what's up with the girl?"

"The girl came into the shelter a couple of weeks ago. She'd been beaten up pretty bad by a client. I took an interest in her. Then she disappeared from the shelter. The nuns thought her pimp more or less kidnapped her back to the streets, so I went to go check on her. The pimp didn't like that. The rest is, as they say, history," Dominic said.

"And now you got her living at home with you? What did she do to win the lottery?"

"It's just for a little while. Give her some time to figure out what's next," Dominic said.

"You sure that's all there is to this?"

Dominic finished packing one box and shoved it aside.

"Dad?"

"How many times you going to ask me the same question? Am I a perp now?" Dominic said.

Maria sat down and leaned her elbows on her knees. Looked right at her father. She wanted him to know she wasn't letting this go so easy. But her father switched things up on her.

"Moyer called me. Let me know what happened with Carla," Dominic said.

"Does Mom know?"

"She's got a list of baby names at home longer than my arm. I haven't seen her so excited about something in years. You think I want to screw that up?"

Maria leaned back into the chair and closed her eyes. Pushed the tips of two fingers into the bridge of her nose. She wanted to stay sitting like that for a bit, but she knew if she didn't open her eyes soon, she'd be asleep right there in the chair.

When she opened her eyes, she saw a scrapbook on the end table. Oversized and red, the scrapbook had rounded edges from years of use. She'd never seen it before. She picked it up and pawed through. The whole thing was newspaper clippings about her father and his years as a cop: the time he caught a serial rapist who worked in a daycare facility, the time he found four kidnapped teenagers from Kansas in a motel on Western Ave, his retirement photo with all of his medals. Maria remembered her mother threatening to divorce her father if he didn't put the medals on for the photo. Dominic had been adamant he wasn't doing it, but Esperanza had yelled and screamed until he'd relented. The argument had taken half the afternoon and seemed like a microcosm of their marriage. Dominic never wanting to talk about the job or his accomplishments, Esperanza wanting to make movies about him.

"Have you seen this? Apparently, the magazine writer isn't the only one who sees you as a hero," Maria said.

Dominic grunted. He was focused on filling what looked like the last of the books into a box. He might not be the type of man to care about what the press said about him, but his murdered son with a scrapbook. That must have both stung and filled him with pride at the same time.

The DNA tests.

With everything going on, Maria had forgotten about the family secret that had been so important just yesterday. Now it seemed meaningless. Maria still hadn't brought it up with him, and she wondered if she ever would. Maybe that was a secret she should take to the grave. Too many decisions in too short a time.

"When's the last time you slept?" Dominic said.

"I can't go home and sleep. Not right now," Maria said.

"Don't go home then. Crash in the guest room. I'll come wake you in a few hours, and we'll go have a cup of coffee. Talk shit through," Dominic said.

"I should help out," Maria said.

"Help everyone out by getting some sleep. It's a little unsettling to see you like this."

Chapter 35

Dominic put the last of the boxes in the garage.

He turned to return to the house and saw his wife standing in the doorway. She had her arms crossed and looked pissed. Dominic did a mental review of the last few hours to see if there was something he'd said or done to anger her, but he couldn't come up with anything. All he'd been doing was working.

"What's up with Maria?" Esperanza said.

"Just work stuff. It'll be fine. She just had a rough night and Moyer wants her to take a few weeks off. He feels like everything is too raw with Tommy's death and all," Dominic said.

Esperanza narrowed her eyes at Dominic. She knew he was lying, but she also knew to let it alone. She turned and went back inside the house. His wife was going to let this slide for now, but if in a few days, Maria was still in the crapper, and Dominic hadn't helped her through, Esperanza would be all over him, and he wouldn't be able to keep her from finding out what happened.

This week had been brutal for all of them.

But especially for Maria.

Dominic wondered what stung more: Carla's arrest or the suspension. Most people would think the relationship problem would be the bigger issue, but Maria's whole life, whole identity was being a detective. When Dominic looked at her, that's what he saw, a dogged, determined homicide detective. Would she be able to recover from her failure in this case?

Perhaps the problems with Carla would be a blessing, a little perspective.

The person we spent our lives with was more important than our jobs.

At least she should be.

MARIA LOOKED BETTER after her nap. Dark circles around her eyes, sure, but her face wasn't as wan. She looked up at him as he arrived at the table with the coffee mugs, and she smiled. Dominic felt that bittersweet struggle inside his chest between pride and anger. Pride in his daughter being so strong willed and determined and anger at this life for putting her in a situation to feel so much pain. He could be all philosophical about people needing to go through their own problems in order to build up their identities, but one thing happened to his adult daughter, and he wanted to take a blowtorch to the world.

He sat down and let Maria start the conversation when she was ready. It didn't take long for her to get going, and as he listened, he wondered if he'd lost his instincts in his retirement because he just couldn't see Carla doing what vice said she had. The more he sat there thinking about it though, the more sure he was.

"Did she go to the room?" Dominic asked.

"She took a chip and verbally consented," Maria said.

"Maybe she was just taking the money without intending to follow through."

"Would that make it better?" Maria said.

"You know how high rollers are. They act like everything belongs to them. If she ran a little game now and then, can you blame her?" Dominic said.

"Does anybody have any morals anymore?"

"The only angels in Vegas are Hell's Angels," Dominic said.

Maria rolled her eyes and let loose a short breath, but Dominic could tell she was desperate to believe what Dominic was saying about Carla. Nobody wanted to believe the worst about someone they loved and not just for the betrayal, but also for what it said about their own foolishness.

"What are you going to do?" Dominic said.

"Kick her the hell out of my house," Maria said.

"You sure that's right?" Dominic said.

"She showed up the night Tommy died a little later than normal with a thousand dollar chip. Can I really be sure that she wasn't doing more than smiling and flashing some leg for that chip?" Maria said.

"Have you talked to her?"

Maria shook her head.

"At least, Moyer got vice to kick the whole thing," Dominic said.

"Now he can hold this over my head forever. Everyone can because you know everybody knows," Maria said.

"Nobody cares. They got their own problems. Besides you get a lot of accolades for your success, but I'm sure there are plenty of people who are smiling to cover their envy, and you'll be more likable if you got some scars of your own," Dominic said.

"What does that even mean? Should I cut myself along the cheek with a knife? Would I be more likable than?" Maria said.

Dominic took a sip of his coffee and sat back in the chair. He had a lot he wanted to say, but he could tell Maria was working up to something that was really bothering her. He could tell by the pause in her speech. The way she looked down at the table. Closed her eyes. Gathered herself. She'd first done that when she was five and wanted to tell on herself. She'd broken a lamp, but Tommy had gotten blamed for it, and her guilt over his punishment had torn her up for a good hour before she screwed up the courage to be honest. She came into the living room and stood before him telling him some story about her day. Something unconnected and random and then the pause. The look at the floor. The eyes closing. The moment when she faced her fear.

Was anything more beautiful than a child showing the integrity a parent hoped they'd have?

"I'm just so stupid. I mean, how could I have not seen this coming? Her mother was a stripper and god knows what else, and I just assumed she was different," Maria said.

"What does her mother have to do with anything?" Dominic asked.

"You're a cop, I'm a cop. Our parents influence us," Maria said.

"Do they?" Dominic said.

LAS VEGAS *1965*

All he wanted was to be alone.

Dominic was sitting on the stairs when the taxi pulled into the parking lot. He pushed himself against the wall to try to hide from the headlights, but they flashed across him all the same. He put his head down into his hands and hoped whoever was coming home wouldn't be coming upstairs.

The taxi door slammed shut, and heels struck the pavement.

Dominic snuck a look.

The woman who lived three doors down. She had on a black jacket over a minidress and thigh-high boots. Dominic's father had told him not to speak with this woman and called her a whore, but the woman had always been nice to him, and his mother had frequently chatted with her, so she couldn't be all bad. Still, Dominic didn't want to anger his father, so as she approached, Dominic kept his head down.

She slowed as she saw him. Stopped in front of him and reached down and grabbed him by the chin. Her touch was gentle but firm, and she turned his face up to the light, so she could see what he had been trying to hide, the beginnings of a nasty black eye.

"Did your dad do that to you?" she asked.

Dominic pulled his head out of her hands. Looked away.

She let the silence draw out, waiting for an answer that wasn't coming.

"Have you eaten?" she asked.

Dominic didn't say anything.

"Come on. I'll give you some ice for that eye too," she said.

Dominic didn't move as she walked up the stairs, and at the top, she turned and looked down at him. Asked him if he was coming or what? Dominic didn't know what to do. He didn't want to anger his father further, but he was starving.

His stomach won out.

THE WOMAN'S apartment was neat but full. The closet was bursting with clothes, and magazines with pictures of beautiful women on the covers lined the table and piled up next to the couch. Everything had a place and was neatly positioned in that place, but every place was full.

The only thing full in the apartment Dominic shared with his father was the kitchen sink and the trash can. Things had been better organized and neater before his mother had left, but not by much, and not like this woman's apartment.

The woman had changed in the bathroom and came out in a black shiny robe that hung to her ankles. Her long blonde hair was in a ponytail and hung halfway down her back. She leaned against the fridge and crossed her arms. Looked Dominic over. Dominic was too young to understand the emotions spilling across the woman's face. He thought she looked angry, but anger was just a small bit of what she felt.

"Where's your mother? I haven't seen her for weeks."

"I don't know," Dominic said.

"I'm sure her being gone stings a hell of a lot more than that eye," the woman said.

Dominic didn't say anything. Just stared at the table.

"The soreness of that shiner lasts for a bit, but it'll go away. Next time he hits you, that's what I want you thinking about. How it hurts, but it goes away, and soon, you'll get used to it, and it won't even hurt much at all anymore. Eventually, you'll laugh right in his face when he hits you," she said.

"How long does that take?" Dominic said.

"Everybody's different, but I was twelve when it stopped hurting. Thirteen when I was brave enough to laugh," she said.

▭

MARIA LEANED back in her chair. She'd never seen this side of her father. The wounded side. But she was beginning to understand why he'd gotten along so well with people from the streets, almost all of them the product of broken homes.

"Sometimes we imitate our parents, sometimes what we become is a response to them," Dominic said.

"I always wondered why you never talked about them," Maria said.

"Some people ain't worth talking about. But I'll tell you this much, they both were people who worked in the respectable world, with respectable jobs, and they were both terrible people. But that woman who fed me that night, she worked at night doing things women aren't supposed to do for money, and she was much kinder than either of my parents," Dominic said.

How did her father always know how to fix everything?

Was there a manual he was reading that no one else had?

Maria's phone buzzed, a message from Harold: I figured it all out. Come by my house ASAP.

"Carla?" Dominic said.

"Harold. He wants me to go talk to him," Maria said.

"At this time?"

"He wants to tell me something about Tommy. Says he figured it out."

"Probably drunk and mooning over a picture of you," Dominic said.

"Get out of here with that," Maria said.

"He's been in love with you since the eighth grade. He was the only person more upset than your mother about you being gay," Dominic said.

"I should go talk to him. Maybe he really does have something worth listening to," Maria said.

"Don't go using that as an excuse to not deal with what really matters."

"And what's that?" Maria said.

"You know exactly what I'm talking about. Go home. Go talk to Carla. Give her a chance to explain," Dominic said.

"I don't know if I want to listen."

"It's not about what you want to do. It's about what you should do."

"Try not to be right all the time, will ya? It's getting kind of annoying," Maria said.

Chapter 36

Had she always been this scared and just not known it?

Maria stood in front of her door, keys in her hand, totally intending to go inside, but she just couldn't make her hands move. She couldn't remember any time in her life when she'd been so damned hesitant to do the hard thing. She'd always been the person who broke up a relationship, who argued with her parents, who offended someone for her willingness to say what she meant, but here she was, completely and totally paralyzed.

What had happened to her?

She didn't know, but she was damned if she was going to stay paralyzed another second.

Still, her hand didn't move.

Her father had been right, Carla deserved a chance to explain herself, but what was holding her back wasn't not wanting to hear. Maria was desperate to hear Carla had been unfairly arrested, desperate to hear the whole thing was bullshit, but what Maria was terrified of was Carla telling her that it was true. The truth would be followed up with explanations and justifications and promises to not do it again, and Maria was terrified she wouldn't leave even if it was true, that she'd find a justification to stay, and she'd turn into one of those DV victims who refused to leave an abusive relationship, women sticking around just looking for reasons to not believe the total and absolute truth. Maria knew how easy it was to judge women like that, and she had judged those women herself, but she also knew it was damned easy to say what you'd do until you were in the situation where you actually had to do it.

Carla opened the door. Her eyes were red from crying. She looked exhausted and miserable, and the sight of her made Maria happy, both seeing her and seeing her miserable. Then Maria remembered Michael's incredible smile.

Could Carla fake her emotions as well as Michael?

Maria hoped not.

"I've been calling you all day," Carla said.

"Work," Maria said, her voice flat.

Carla turned to go inside, the door left open.

Maria followed her and stopped in the doorway between the kitchen and the living room. She leaned against the frame and took in Carla wearing an oversized onesie pajamas with a panda bear hood. The table in front of the sofa had a pile of used tissues. The television was off, just a lamp on, no overhead. If Carla was staging a scene, she was doing an amazing job. Everything screamed depressed. Miserable. Heartbroken.

"Who told you?" Carla asked.

"I saw you in the interrogation room. Watched you in your little outfit shivering," Maria said.

"They let me go because of you?" Carla said.

"I had nothing to do with it. Of course, that won't keep my Lieutenant from hanging it over my head for eternity," Maria said.

"Can I at least explain? Please?"

Maria didn't say yes, but she didn't say no either.

"I've never sold my body, at least not like that. I danced for a while, but I've never had sex for money," Carla said.

"That's-"

"Just listen. I did take a thousand dollars off of a client. He was one of those assholes who looked at you like he owned you, and he offered me the chip to go to his room, and I said yes, but I was never going to his room," Carla said.

"That's a crime," Maria said.

"He's an asshole. He got what he deserved."

"So being an asshole means you can get stolen from? I have to tell the guys down at robbery because they've been arresting people for stealing from assholes for years. They'll be so relieved. You've just cut Vegas's larceny rate in half," Maria said.

"Are you done?" Carla said.

Maria wasn't done. She was furious. She wanted to storm out. She wanted to scream, but as she felt it, she realized that Moyer had been right. She'd been overcome with rage and grief and too busy stuffing it to even realize, and she was about to take it out on the one person she didn't want to take it out on whether she deserved it or not.

"Then a second guy did the same thing. The same offer, but something was off," Carla said.

"Off?"

"He had bad teeth, so I never said a word. I never said yes. I never shook my head. Nothing. I didn't even take the chip. He just put it on my tray and walked off," Carla said.

"So now you're saying the vice squad set you up?"

"Yes and no," Carla said.

"How can it possibly be both?" Maria said.

"What I'm saying is that if I hadn't gotten a bad vibe, I would have done the same thing all over again," Carla said.

"Are you seriously telling me that you would have robbed a second guy? Is this supposed to make me feel better?" Maria said.

"I'm not sorry for robbing that man. I'm sorry for embarrassing you."

"That's not the point. You lied to me. You stole. You don't do those things," Maria said.

"Is it really about that? Really? That asshole won't even miss that thousand dollars. He had a stack of them as high as my wineglass," Carla said.

"Now you're Robin Hood," Maria said.

"I'm not going to pretend to feel guilty for something I don't feel guilty about," Carla said.

Looking at her girlfriend, Maria knew she was telling the truth, everything screamed honesty, and all the anger just drained right away. She was so relieved she would have been ashamed to admit it out loud. She took two steps forward and collapsed onto the couch. Carla looked at her cautiously, hopeful. Maria shook her head. This discussion wasn't anywhere near done, but Maria didn't have the energy to keep fighting. Carla wasn't guilty of what vice had accused her of. Sure, she was guilty of something else, but Maria could find a way past that. She wasn't ready to tell Carla that just yet, though. This discussion would have to stretch on for days. Carla had to know that this couldn't happen again, but Maria was so relieved.

Maria's phone buzzed, another message from Harold: They found out I was talking to you. Please come soon.

"Who's that?" Carla asked.

"I have some work stuff to deal with," Maria said.

"You're not really going to leave right now, are you?" Carla said.

"Unfortunately criminals don't care if I'm having issues with my girlfriend or not," Maria said.

"Please don't leave me sitting here thinking about this. We have to work this out," Carla said.

"I think leaving you sitting thinking about it sounds wonderful," Maria said.

Carla started to cry. Not softly either. Heavy sobs that couldn't be faked, and Maria had that same mixed reaction, misery that the woman she loved was in pain and gratitude that she was miserable. Because if Carla was truly upset, there was hope, and Maria knew that she wanted to find a way through this.

"Look, this won't take long and the time in the car will give me a chance to calm down and when I come back, we'll talk more. Ok?" Maria said.

Chapter 37

One last conversation and then she was letting go.

Before pulling to a stop in front of Harold's house, Maria drove around the block twice, looking for signs of surveillance. Maybe Harold was just being paranoid, but if he wasn't, she wanted to know what she was walking into. All Maria saw though was empty streets and empty cars and darkened houses. So she pulled to a stop in front of his house and wondered how seriously to take all of this. On the off case Harold wasn't exaggerating, she decided to go in with her gun and flashlight and handcuffs.

If Moyer found out she was here, he'd probably put her up for some kind of disciplinary reprimand, maybe even demote her, and as she sat in the car looking at Harold's house, Maria knew Moyer was right, she'd been reckless, and for all that people wanted to claim that her father's rep had cleared the way for Maria to make detective, in reality, it had been Moyer who'd taken a shine to her, Moyer who'd pushed her to take the detective test, Moyer who'd gotten her plum assignments, so she could prove herself. Her father had told Maria she should slow down, Moyer was pushing things along too fast, better to build up to it slow, but she hadn't wanted to do anything slow, she'd wanted to achieve and achieve fast, and now where was she? Informally suspended, sitting alone in her own car, about to go talk to a suspect/witness who happened to be a lifelong friend rather than pushing him off onto the investigating officer. This was why a cop didn't investigate her own brother's murder. She ended up in situations like this. She should be home making Carla give her a foot massage rather than out here, but here she was.

She'd go inside. Have this conversation and give it all to Michael in the morning, and then, then she was going away for a few days. Maybe a week or two. Just her and Carla, and they'd work through this shit together, and her mother could keep coming up with baby names. Not that Maria planned on using any of them, but she'd at least let her mother rattle them off.

Maria got out of the car and headed for Harold's front door. She checked the street again. No cars. No people walking. Just a silent residential street late on a weeknight. Turning her attention to Harold's house, she saw that all the lights were out except in the living room. Then she noticed a shadow where the front door met the seam.

The door was ajar.

She clicked the flashlight on and attached it to the barrel of her gun. She pushed the door open with her left hand and aimed the light and gun into the house. The runner rug was bunched up against the wall, the coffee table toppled over, and a lamp broken in two on the floor.

Maria stepped into the foyer.

On the right was Harold's home office. Papers were strewn across his desk, and folders scattered about the floor. A chair had been knocked over sideways and the seat cut open. Stuffing poked out of the slit. Maria brought her attention back to the hallway.

Straight ahead was the kitchen. Two steps forward and on the left was the living room. Hanging on the wall to the right, new since her last time here, was a blown-up photo of Harold and Tommy while they were still in High School.

Maria inched forward.

At the doorway to the living room, she peered around the corner. The sofa was toppled over. The television stand pulled away from the wall. A painting face down on the floor with its paper backing slit open. But most interesting, the bookshelf against the far wall had been pushed aside and a doorway leading down to a basement was visible. Maria couldn't even remember Harold having a bookshelf, but she'd only ever been here once before two days ago, and she'd mostly been in the kitchen. Hadn't even looked at the living room, so Harold could have had a bookshelf. She just wouldn't have noticed.

Maria looked back towards the kitchen. She shone her light towards Harold's room, the last door on the hallway on the right. She didn't see or hear anything or anyone. Someone had searched Harold's house thoroughly, and the chance was good that if they weren't gone, they were down those stairs. They couldn't have heard her come in and nobody would be expecting her. She could surprise them, and she'd have the high ground.

Maria moved across the room slowly, stepping over sofa cushions and around the painting. Her senses were focused on the open doorway, but she heard nothing. Not even the creaking of the house. She looked down the stairwell. Wooden stairs descending into pitch black darkness. Maria brought the gun to bear and shone her flashlight down.

Saw a concrete floor.

Heard nothing.

She took a step into the doorway. Something made the hair on the back of her neck rise, a draft, a movement, then she heard pounding footsteps behind her. She tried to turn, but she couldn't get her gun around because she was blocked by the doorway, and two hands slammed into her back propelling her down the stairs into the darkness.

Maria tried to keep her footing, tried to run down the steps, but she missed one halfway down, and she brought her arms up to cover her face, and she slammed into the ground. Her gun skittered off across the floor, the flashlight illuminating dust motes.

The bookshelf slid into place sealing the doorway with a click.

Maria lay there gasping for breath, pain screaming up and down her side. Then she heard a low, guttural growl that turned into a snarl. She couldn't see anything. The snarling could have been on the other side of the room or right next to her. She couldn't tell. She heard nails clacking against the floor, and the snarling grew louder. Maria scrambled for her gun, expecting powerful jaws to tear into her any second. She dove but overshot her mark.

The gun was underneath her now.

The snarling was so close.

There was no way.

She pulled the gun from underneath her belly and spun around.

Maria saw nothing in the beam of the flashlight.

No dog. No wolf. No animals.

But the snarling continued.

The nails kept clacking against concrete.

Maria stood up and played the flashlight from one end of the basement to the other. She was alone, but along the wall were speakers. The animal sound was a trick, which meant it was planned, which meant-

"This would have been a lot more fun if you had forgotten your flashlight," Harold said, his voice tinny but triumphant coming through the speakers.

"This would be a lot more fun if you'd come down here," Maria said.

"Don't be angry at me. You should have cleared the house before inspecting the secret door, but you didn't, did you?"

"My partner knows where I am. They'll come looking for me," Maria said.

"Good luck to them in finding you. Did I mention the basement is soundproof? It's not as well designed as the original, but I did fine considering my timetable," Harold said.

Maria pulled her phone out of her pocket and looked at it. No signal.

"I've got jammers installed. No wireless signal getting in or out. You'll come out when I let you out and that'll be when you beg me," Harold said.

"You texted me to come here. They'll know it's you," Maria said.

"I'll dump your car somewhere. They'll think the same man who killed Tommy got you, won't they?"

The basement light clicked on. Maria didn't like what she saw. No windows, just concrete wall and dirt floor. Except in the far corner where a rug had been laid down. On top of the rug a mattress. Next to the mattress, a bucket. Next to the bucket, a dog cage.

"Not exactly my kind of decor," Maria said.

"Getting out is really simple. All you have to do is throw your gun into a corner. Take off all of your clothes and lock yourself against the wall with the handcuffs," Harold said.

Maria looked against the wall and saw a pair of handcuffs soldered to a hook.

"That's never happening," Maria said.

"Eventually you'll be so hungry and thirsty you'll be begging me to do what I want just so you can have some water and when you've broken down, when you finally realize how powerful and great I am, then I'll deign to let you serve me," Harold said.

"Deign to serve you? Were you always this fucked up or have you just been watching too much BBC lately?"

"Go ahead and look around. Get a feel for your situation and we'll talk again when you're ready to be more reasonable."

MARIA WENT quadrant by quadrant looking for weaknesses, openings, escape routes. What she found was a sealed tomb with cameras covering almost every possible angle. She climbed the stairs and felt around the doorway. Steel bars. Not even light coming around the frame. She pushed at the bookshelf, blocking the doorway, knowing that the effort was a waste of time and energy but hoping that incompetence would make her lucky.

No luck.

She was trapped, and it was her own fault, and she knew it, and that pissed her off more than anything else. How could she have been so foolish to let this happen?

"You always thought you were too good for me. Always loved to torture me with your smiles. We used to laugh together so much, but it was all a lie," Harold said.

"We were friends. Friends laugh together. That's what they do," Maria said.

"Yeah, yeah, yeah, you always had all the answers. You were always so fucking smart. Were you watching when I talked with your partner? Did you enjoy my performance? So easy to send you guys chasing after the shady Russian. Do you remember the time you told Tommy and I all the signs for when someone is lying?"

Had Maria told him that? She couldn't remember the conversation. An image popped into her head, her and Tommy and Harold sitting at some corporate restaurant on the strip. Her new to being a detective, them interested in hearing about the job. Was she imagining this because he'd prompted it?

"I remembered everything you said and wrote it all down when I got home and boy, did it come in handy. I practiced and practiced after Tommy died, knowing that eventually, you'd all come looking for information from me, and I knew I'd be able to create a scenario that ended with you right where you are. Who's smart now, bitch?" Harold said.

After Tommy died, he'd said. Not after I killed Tommy. He'd also said, they'll think the man who killed Tommy got you. Would he admit it if he'd been the one? Once she got out of this basement, she could beat the truth out of him, but there was only one way to get out of that basement and that was through Harold, and the only way she could get him down here was by giving him what he wanted.

But could she really risk it?

"And the look on your face in the casino. So concerned while all the time I was just winding you up so you'd do what I wanted you to do," he said.

"Fine Harold, you win," Maria said.

Maria threw her gun on the floor.

"You think it will be easy to overcome me when I come down there. You think I'm so weak that you can disarm me when you're handcuffed, don't you?"

"There's only one way to find out," Maria said.

"I'm more experienced at this than you can ever imagine," Harold said.

Maria pulled off her belt, turning as she did, so she could stick her hand in her pocket for her handcuff keys. She palmed the keys as she threw the belt aside. She started unbuttoning her shirt. She wanted to do it slowly, wanted to taunt him, something to build up the desire to make him lose whatever edge he might have, and also to have the time to stuff the handcuff keys in her bra, but the whole thing was so ridiculous and disgusting that she felt like she could vomit at any second, so she just got her shirt off as fast as she could. As she slid the shirt off, she whipped it up in front of her, hopefully blocking the camera as she slid the keys into her bra with her other hand. Then she kicked off her sneakers and yanked down her jeans. She threw the clothes on top of the gun, hoping he'd forget about it.

She stood there in her bra and panties.

"Take it all off," Harold said.

"A real man would want to take the last bits off himself," Maria said.

Maria moved to the handcuffs and inserted her wrists. Before locking them, she checked the height and her ability to access the keys. She wasn't going to have much time. She would have to unlock the cuffs while Harold was sliding open the bookshelf and on the stairs, and she'd have to get them both undone. Only unlocking one would leave her still pinned to the wall.

She hoped she could do it.

Hope nothing, she had to do it.

She clicked the handcuffs shut around her wrists and turned toward the stairs.

"I'm waiting," Maria said.

Chapter 38

The basement was cold and quiet.

She stood there, shivering. Listening to the creaks of the house and waiting for Harold. He let her wait. She couldn't tell how long it was, maybe five minutes, maybe ten. She couldn't trust herself to have an accurate sense of time in a situation so tense, but it felt like forever, and she realized he was waiting and watching. He wanted her to fuck up. To spring the trap too soon. To make a move out of impatience. She wasn't going to fall for it.

She focused on her breathing.

She listened.

She waited.

She calmed herself so much that she almost missed her chance. A click preceded the sliding open of the bookshelf. The track had been installed hastily and had a sticking point, and Harold had to pry it open and then push it over the imperfection. Two shoves, not one smooth one.

Maria dug into her bra. Pulled out the keys.

Harold slammed his feet into the stairs, the sound of the footsteps echoing in the basement. He saw himself as an all-powerful conqueror descending to a terrified prey, and that arrogance gave

Maria time to unlock one handcuff. If Harold had rushed down the stairs, she never would have had time to unlock herself, but his arrogance gave her a chance.

Now she needed him to make one more mistake.

She needed him to get close enough that she could knock him on his ass so she could get out of the other handcuff. If she could just get free, she knew she could take him. Maria turned toward the stairs, holding the handcuffs together, so Harold wouldn't be able to see that one was unlocked.

What she saw when he reached the bottom of the stairs shocked her. Harold wasn't dressed differently, jeans and a t-shirt just like always, nor did the gun in his hand bother her, Maria had seen and been around guns her whole life, and while she was certainly scared, she was also sure that she could take Harold's gun from him. He wanted her alive not dead. That would give her an opening.

No, none of those things bothered her.

The look in his eyes though.

The way he watched her.

The hatred.

The desire.

How had she not sensed this part of him earlier?

His energy was different, too, the way he walked. She could tell that Harold felt more alive in this moment than he ever did. The rush of this experience was more powerful than anything he'd ever stuck up his nose, and she knew as she looked at him, he spent all of his waking moments waiting for another time like this. A time when he was going to dominate and destroy.

Was that desire in everyone or just a truly deranged few?

"Your desire to be helpful, that's your weakness. All I had to do was make you believe that I was in danger, and you trapped yourself. You really see yourself as a protector, don't you?" Harold said.

"I am definitely the asshole of the year apparently," Maria said.

Harold took a step closer. Still too far away for her to spring and reach him before he could fire. She really needed him to be right next to her, so she could push the gun aside, but if she could distract him, she could attack sooner. But now, no. He was a good five or six feet away. For Maria, holding still as he ate her with his eyes was the most revolting and powerless she'd ever felt, and she had to fight against the urge to attack just so she could stop feeling that way.

Being rational was easy when the damaged party was someone else.

"Look around. This is the last place you'll ever see. I'm going to fuck every hole on your body and when I grow bored, I'm going to slit your throat right where you stand and bury you. So you'd better fuck like your life depends on it. Because it does," Harold said.

Harold took a step closer. Examined her up and down.

"I thought your stomach would be flatter. But don't worry, you'll lose that extra weight in no time," Harold said.

Maria tried to keep her face blank as she noted the distance. One more step would be on the outer range of a good idea. Two steps, ok. Three steps better. Could she last through more of this?

Harold walked away from her toward the dog cage.

Shit.

"Maybe Carla would be a good addition to the basement? What do you think? I want you all to myself for a week or two, but after that, after the attention has blown over, I should be able to pick her up rather easily. You, I had to trap, to trick. But her, I could easily overpower. Would you like that? Would you like to have her here with you?" Harold asked.

"Fuck you, Harold," Maria said.

"I could put her in here and fuck her right through the cage while you watched. How's that sound?"

"Like your dick could reach through," Maria said.

"Careful or I'll ram this gun up your ass instead of my cock," Harold said.

"At least, I'd feel the gun," Maria said.

Harold laughed, but it was an angry laugh. A sharp bark of frustration not joy. Maria was supposed to be terrified. He was supposed to be the conqueror, but she wasn't playing along. She was laughing at him, and his rage was building. He looked down at the basement floor, and Maria knew the difference between his fantasies and reality was driving him nuts.

He bullrushed her. Gun raised high above his head, so he could strike her with the butt.

Maybe if he was an athlete, Harold could have closed the distance quick enough, but he was a man in his late thirties who drank and smoked too much, and Maria had time to pull her hand free and strike his arm as he swung downward. He lost his grip on the gun and it slid across the floor. Harold's momentum crashed him into her, but Maria shoved him aside, and he careened off balance face first into the wall. He fell to the floor. Dazed.

Maria went to unlock the other cuff.

Harold pushed himself off of the ground. Shook his head.

Maria had the key in the lock and turned it. The handcuff came free.

Harold saw the gun about eight feet away and started toward it.

Maria pushed off of the wall with her foot, trying to close the distance.

Harold dove and his hands grabbed the gun. He turned toward her, but Maria lashed out with her right foot. The gun went off as it flew from Harold's hand. The bullet slammed into the ceiling, spraying wood chips.

They both went for the gun, getting tangled up and falling together. They rolled against the floor, and Harold's knee slammed into Maria's stomach. The air whooshed out of her, and she gasped for breath. Harold straddled her and reared back to slam his fist into her face.

Maria bucked her hips.

Harold's fist slammed into the floor. He screamed in pain.

Maria bucked her hips again and flung him off of her.

Harold tumbled to the floor. But Maria had thrown him toward the gun, and she saw it sitting on the floor just behind him. She spun around on her back and kicked with her left foot, connecting with his jaw. Harold's head slammed backward into the floor. But he was still conscious and saw the gun behind him.

Maria flipped over and pushed herself off the floor. She sprinted for her gun. When she was close enough, she dove headfirst for where she had hidden it under her jeans.

Harold shot as she dove, and the bullet went wide right, but since she had been diving, he thought he had hit her.

"You see bitch, that's what happens when you fuck with me," He said.

But Maria was too busy pulling her gun out from under her clothes to listen. As she aimed the barrel at Harold, she saw the look of confusion as he realized he had been wrong. He tried to bring his gun back to bear.

Maria shot twice.

She didn't miss.

Two red circles appeared in Harold's chest. One just below his left breast. One just above his belly button. He went to his knees. The gun clattered to the floor.

Maria approached, gun still out and up.

Harold looked up at her. A shocked look on his face.

"It was you who killed Tommy, wasn't it?" Maria said.

"Killed Tommy?" Harold looked like he was hurt more by the question than by the bullets.

Maria took everything in. Everything she'd learned in the days since Tommy's death. Everything Harold had said. Everything she'd failed to see, and the implication was terrifying. So terrifying.

"What did you mean by 'not as good as the original'?" Maria said.

"Fuck you," Harold said.

He got one last smile, one last momentary triumph before his eyes closed for good, and he fell face first to the floor.

Chapter 39

Where was the original?

As Maria drove to Tommy's house, she heard Harold's voice over and over inside her head, "It's not as good as the original." He had been talking about the basement dungeon, and Maria was both sure of what she would find when she arrived at Tommy's and hoping, praying, that she was wrong.

When Tommy's house was a few blocks away, Maria pulled onto a side street and parked behind a pickup truck. Her car hidden from anyone passing by. Maria walked down the sidewalk toward her brother's house. The night was cold and clear, the land lit more by the moon than by the streetlights. As Maria rounded the corner to Tommy's street, she stopped. Did she really want to do this? Alone?

Did she really even want to know?

Harold had hated her in a way that could only be described as evil. How had she entirely missed that side of him? How... Could her brother have had that side too? Tommy had never treated her badly, he'd only ever been protective and loving, and now, what was she suspecting of her own brother? She had to know. Not just because of what she might find out about her brother but because she was reasonably sure who the Desert Saint was, and the answer was in Tommy's house.

She quickened her steps.

Practically broke into a run.

She just wanted this night to be over.

TOMMY'S KITCHEN was how she had left it. The coffee mug her father had used sat rinsed out in the sink. The magazine her mother had been reading lay open on the kitchen table. Maria made her way into the living room and looked at the bookshelf. She heard her father say, "What does he have all these books for, he doesn't even like to read," and he was right, Tommy was not a reader, never had been, and Maria had wondered the same thing when she saw the bookshelf for the first time.

Why does Tommy have a bookshelf? He hates to read.

But what if a bookshelf was something else?

Maria tried to visualize what was on the other side of the bookshelf. She went back into the hallway and walked to what should be behind that wall and found a storage closet. She opened the door and saw shallow shelves lined with towels and linens. But the closet should be deeper. Why such a narrow space?

Maria went back to the bookshelf and started methodically moving her fingers along the bottom of each shelf, pressing up into the corners and along the side, but she couldn't find anything. She told herself she was being ridiculous, looking for a hidden passageway in her brother's house.

What did she think she was in a movie?

But Harold had said, not as good as the original.

If the original wasn't here, where the hell would it be?

She stepped back and looked at the bookshelf again. She started feeling along the edge where the shelf met the wall, first along the left side, nothing, then after pulling over a chair, along the top, again nothing, but a quarter of the way down on the right-hand side, high enough up that no one would touch it by accident, she found the indentation. She dug her finger in and heard the click of the latch releasing. She pulled the bookshelf out and slid it over and looked at the wooden steps descending into darkness.

She burst into tears.

She'd wanted to be wrong so badly.

Maria turned away from the bookshelf and pulled out her gun. She cleared the house, room by room. No one would be shoving her down any stairs again. She found stripped beds, empty closets and drawers, and furniture pushed into corners. But no people. Just Maria and the hidden basement.

She returned to the entrance and shined her light down.

Wooden stairs.

Concrete floor.

Maria went down slowly. At the base, she flashed the light around and saw the outline of objects. This basement was fuller than Harold's. Then she noticed the light switch. She flicked it on and what she saw tore her heart in two.

It wasn't the cage against the wall or the dentist chair with hand-cuffs welded to the arms that broke Maria's spirit. She had been expecting evil, and she was prepared for some kind of demented restraints. No, the evil wasn't what destroyed her. It was the studio with the tripod for a camera and the light blue backdrop that was behind each of Tommy's YouTube videos that laid waste to Maria's soul. There was a room upstairs, an extra unneeded guest room, perfect for a studio, but no, her brother had put his camera and his backdrop here because he enjoyed being here. He fed off of it.

How had she not seen this evil in her own brother?

What else was she blind to in this world?

The answer to that last question was evident in the lingering smell of bleach. Someone had scrubbed the whole basement clean and recently because not even a light coating of dust covered anything. Everything was gleaming. Everything but the floor around the dentist chair because the black hue expanding like a blob was definitely dried blood. Someone had come through and removed whatever evidence they could of death. Whenever someone found this room, there'd be the suspicion that terrible things had happened but very little hard proof. She grabbed the tripod and tipped it over to look at the top. The video camera used to make Tommy's videos and probably to record horrific acts was gone. A computer monitor sat on a desk, but the hard drive was gone, removed.

Could Harold have cleaned up? Probably not, especially since he'd been busy building his own dungeon. Maria doubted that Harold would have had the time. But the Desert Saint would have had the time that right after he killed Tommy. And he not only had a reason to want this area cleaned of any trace but also had a way of knowing that Tommy and Harold were not the men they appeared to be. Maria walked back to the stairs and took one last look around the room before flipping off the light and climbing back up into the world of the living.

THE HOUSE WAS as empty and quiet as she had left it. She walked out the back door and circled around the pool and looked off at the glistening lights of the strip. From this distance, everything looked so peaceful, no masses of humanity jostling against each other. Just lights against the black sky. She told herself she should call Michael. She shouldn't do this alone. No, she definitely had to do this alone. Besides, the Desert Saint wouldn't kill her. Unlike her brother, she'd never hurt anyone. She wasn't a predator, and the Desert Saint wasn't really a serial killer.

He was a vigilante, and he loved her.

She dialed her father's number, and he picked up after three rings.

"It's late, are you ok?" Dominic asked.

"I'm hanging in there," Maria said.

"How'd it go with Carla?" Dominic asked.

"It went fine, but that's not why I called. Harold tried to imprison me in a basement dungeon he'd built in his house," Maria said.

"WHAT? Are you ok? Where are you?"

"I'm fine. Harold's dead. It was the craziest thing. He tried to kidnap me so he could rape me. How could I have not seen how fucked up he was?"

"People hide their dark sides better than we'd like to admit. Are you still at Harold's? Do you want me to head over?" Dominic said.

"Stay home. I don't want to alarm Mom. Besides the crime scene techs are going to be awhile. It's a mess over here," Maria said.

"You sure?" Dominic said.

"You might want to keep her away from Tommy's house tomorrow, too," Maria said.

"Why?"

"We're going to go over it again. We're going to see if there are any hidden doors like at Harold's. Michael seems to think we'll find something, but I don't know. Did you see anything strange at the house when you were cleaning it up?"

"No, I didn't see anything. Just a house with a hell of a lot less furniture than it should have," Dominic said.

"I have to go, but I'll call you tomorrow once we're done going over Tommy's place again," Maria said and hung up the phone.

She'd baited the Desert Saint.

Would he fall for it?

DOMINIC HAD TAUGHT Maria how to shoot when she was nine. She started with a .22 and eventually moved up to a .38. By the time she was in high school, her father had her practicing with a .45, the kick practically knocked her over the first time she shot it, but those guns she had shot with were blurs in her memory. She could remember the heft of them in her hand. The shock of the recoil. The smell of the gunpowder, but she couldn't visualize those guns.

There was a gun she remembered vividly, though.

She was maybe ten or eleven, and she'd been snooping around the garage while she waited for her mother to finish dinner. Her father had an old dresser there. Something from a previous house, the paint peeling, the wood cracking at the corners, her mother was always trying to get him to throw it out, but he wouldn't. Said it wasn't hurting anyone in the garage. Said it was holding up the wall for us. Her father liked to say things like that when he was being unreasonable and knew it, like when a pair of jeans he liked started to show a hole. He'd say it was just air conditioning. It was his way of saying I'm not throwing it out.

Maria was fascinated by the drawer mostly because her father had told her and her brother to stay away from it. Maria opened the top drawer and saw old newspapers. The second drawer had records. One near the back had a colorful sleeve, and she pulled the drawer open as far as she could to get a better look, but a thud stopped her.

Something was under the drawer.

She slid open the bottom drawer and reached in and felt along the bottom of the middle drawer. A gun was there in a holster bolted to the bottom. She pulled the gun out. A dark black .22 with a white Fleurs de Lys symbol on the handle. Maria thought the gun was beautiful. Then the headlights of her father's car flashed through the windows on the garage door, and Maria put the gun back and slid the drawers shut and ran inside.

Maria never brought the gun up with her father, but somehow he must have known she'd found it because when she went back the next day to look at it, the drawer slid open smooth and easy with no blockage. The gun and the holster were gone, and Maria never saw them again.

Her father had guns everywhere in the house.

Why had he been hiding that one?

ABOUT THIRTY MINUTES after the call, Maria heard a car pulling into the driveway. She was still standing on the other side of the pool watching the bright lights of Las Vegas glitter in the darkness. A part of her felt elated, and she knew this was the part of her that was addicted to the job, to the validation of being right, of being dogged and determined and catching killers.

How much was being right this time going to cost her?

The headlights of the car shone down the side of Tommy's house and then clicked off.

A car door opened and slammed shut.

The garage door slid open.

A door in the kitchen creaked, and a light clicked on.

Maria moved so she had a good view of the living room.

The hallway light clicked on.

Then the living room light.

Dominic came into view. His gray hair sticking out from under a black baseball cap. He headed for the bookshelf and reached for the indentation. He pushed the bookshelf aside and headed down.

Maria came around the pool and opened the backdoor quietly. She made her way to a chair facing the bookshelf, and she sat down and waited for her father to come back upstairs.

Chapter 40

Dominic knew something was wrong as soon as he hit the basement.

The room didn't feel right. Maybe if he hadn't spent hours in here trying to figure out how to get everything out, he wouldn't have noticed the difference, but he sensed right away that something was off. He stood there at the base of the stairs trying to place what was wrong. Was it the air, less musty than it should be? Dominic moved from one end of the basement to the other, looking for signs that someone had been here, and then he saw the tripod indentations, slightly off. The legs had been moved.

And he realized the call had been an elegantly laid trap.

He smirked, partially impressed by how cooly his daughter had pulled it off, partially angry at himself for falling for it. How could a man feel pride, fear, and relief all at one moment? Dominic hadn't thought it was possible but standing in that basement, that's what he felt, three contradictory emotions jostling around. Returning to the stairs, he stood there for a long brief second, hand on the rail, one foot on the lowest step, and he breathed in long and deep. This moment was the last moment before everything was going to change between him and his daughter and he wanted to enjoy it.

He saw her as a five-year-old at the beach, the one time his wife had been able to convince him to go, Maria with sand clinging to her chin, running up to him with a sea shell whose center had a hole, and Maria held the seashell up to her face and peered at her father, giggled and ran back to look for more. That little girl had grown up to be one hell of a cop, and Dominic couldn't be more proud.

No parent wanted their child to know how deeply flawed they were. Dominic had maintained the veneer of excellence for so long that he dreaded the look on his daughter's face. But neither was he a man who shied away from difficult situations, so he grasped the banner and started up, step by step, his feet getting heavier and heavier as he rose and as he reached high enough to see through the doorway, there she was, sitting in a chair waiting for him.

Dominic wondered if she was feeling that sense of satisfaction that he always felt when he solved an important case. That mixed feeling of accomplishment and regret. Regret that the puzzle was over and fear that another challenge would never come as challenging as that one. Did she feel that? He thought she probably did because whereas Tommy was a mix of his mother and that piece of shit pimp who'd fathered him, Maria was all Dominic.

"Did you forget anything down there? You knew deep down inside that you hadn't. You've always been so careful, but that nagging doubt made you come look one last time," Maria said.

Dominic headed across the room to a chair facing Maria and sat down. He could probably play all this off, pretend he'd discovered the room by accident. But she wouldn't believe him, and eventually she would find out he'd been out of the house at all the times the Desert Saint was killing people. For all the things he'd done wrong in this life, he'd never lied to her face, and he wasn't about to start now.

"And here I was thinking you stood up for me at the precinct because you thought I could take care of myself. But that wasn't it at all, was it? You just knew I wasn't in any danger," Maria said.

"Everybody knows how capable you are," Dominic said.

Maria rolled her eyes and looked away. Shook her head.

"Maybe I should have figured it all out earlier, but why would I think the Desert Saint was my father? The Desert Saint killed Tommy, so my father couldn't be the Desert Saint. Why would he kill his own son? Then I found out that Tommy wasn't really your son just like tio Tomas wasn't really anyone's uncle and then Harold locked me in that room and he told me that his room wasn't as good as the original and as I drove over here, I started to put the pieces together. You see, I thought Naomi was you working your way through your grief. A broken bird that you could save since you couldn't save Tommy. But that wasn't it at all. Tommy was the client who attacked her. And somehow she told you the story, and you knew who it was. And it was more than just a young woman who needed help, so much more," Maria said.

Dominic tried not to smile, but he couldn't quite keep the pride off of his face.

"She reminded you of mom," Maria said.

Yes, Dominic thought, she did remind me of your mother, but that wasn't why he helped her. She could have been a six foot blonde from Iowa with a heroin addiction, and he would have done this. Because it needed to be done. But would telling Maria that make it easier or worse?

"It was the keychain, wasn't it?" Maria said.

Dominic didn't say anything.

Maria sat there with a calm, patient look on her face. The we have all day look, and Dominic wondered what the point of silence was. What was left to protect? She already knew everything. Maybe if he explained it right, Esperanza would never have to know.

"They drugged and handcuffed her, but she woke up earlier than they planned right in front of the chair that you're sitting in. She saw the doorway to downstairs open. She heard Tommy and Harold planning what they were going to do and the idiots had not only left the keys right on the table in front of her but also hand-cuffed her in front," Dominic said.

"The Alaska key chain?" Maria said.

"She unlocked herself and took off. Went to the shelter. The nuns introduced me to her. Whatever drugs they gave her messed with her memory. She couldn't describe the men who attacked her because she couldn't remember them, but she remembered the key chain," Dominic said.

Maria let out a sharp breath, like she'd been punched in the stomach.

A part of her was dying, and Dominic couldn't decide whether finding out about her brother or finding out about him was what was killing her. A revelation like this was harder for people like him and her, people who staked their identity on being able to look into people's souls. How else could you really decide if someone was lying or not? When the evidence wasn't there, how did you decide? By looking into their souls, and that's what she had done, she didn't have any evidence tying Dominic to anything, but she understood his soul, and she'd figured it out even though the realization was tearing her in two. But her brother, she hadn't seen that one coming at all. That had to make her doubt everything in this life.

How was Dominic going to get her through this whole?

She needed to understand why killing Tommy was necessary. She would never forgive her father for this, but maybe she could understand enough of the why to be able to live with it.

"I tried to raise him right. Really, I did. I taught him the same as I taught you, but he ended up just like his father. For Christ's sake, your mother gave him that key chain when we got back from our cruise. He was using a gift from your mother to lock up women so he could rape and kill them. A gift from your mother," Dominic said.

"So the tokens, the things you left, they were the evidence that led you to them?"

"Fifteen," Dominic said.

"Fifteen?" Maria said.

"That's how many recordings there were. Those bitcoin transactions, people were buying porn from Tommy. Real rapes. Maybe it started as fake rapes, Tommy in a mask and Harold filming but somewhere along the line things got darker. Maybe they figured out they'd make more money if the films were more authentic looking, maybe they just got bored, but they were really raping women. You could see the fear in their eyes, and Tommy stopped wearing a mask. The camera wouldn't go above his chin, but you could tell, there was no mask. What do you think they were doing with these women afterward if they weren't even afraid of showing their faces? The last video I saw he was choking this woman and her lights went out. She was just gone," Dominic said.

"So you had to kill them?"

"You have to know who's redeemable and who isn't."

"And you get to decide who those people are?" Maria said.

"It was never like that," Dominic said.

"Never. What about the nurse?"

"Her husband staged it," Dominic said.

"But you definitely killed him when you probably could have arrested him," Maria said.

"When you are clear-eyed about everything, when you can really see how someone is and how the circumstances are, then you can do what you need to do. But you have to be sure, you have to be careful, you have to be in control," Dominic said.

"What is all this you? You have to be sure? You have to be in control? Are you trying to give me advice on how to be a killer?" Maria said.

"No, it's just, when you do these things, when you face up to these people-"

"You can't say 'I' can you? You're dissociating," Maria said.

"What? Get out of here with that."

"Then say it, say I," Maria said.

Dominic looked at her, but he didn't say anything. He was so tired. Tired of everything, and the way his daughter was looking at him made him feel so bad that the only thing he could think would come close to that feeling of utter despair would be if she died.

"The man from last night. Preston Millicent," Maria said.

"He was trash," Dominic said.

"That's really how I figured it out. You didn't kill him because of who he was. You killed him so I would know that Jack and Rebeka were innocent," Maria said.

"If you'd ruined Jack's reputation for nothing, your career would have been shot," Dominic said.

"My career? Are you serious right now?"

The iron inside Maria came out. Everything about her stiffened, her back, her face, her shoulders. She stood up and looked straight at her father. He knew what was coming next. He could see the training taking over.

"Stand up please, sir," Maria said.

"Seriously?" Dominic said.

"Dominic Varela, you're under arrest for murder. You have the right to remain silent, anything--"

"Just hold on a sec. Ok, just a second," Dominic said.

"Stand up please, sir," Maria said.

"Or what? You going to shoot me?" Dominic said.

"My father wouldn't make me shoot him. At least, I don't think he would."

"I just, I just couldn't let him go on like that," Dominic said.

"We could have arrested him."

"And how would that have worked out for your mother? Knowing what her son was capable of? Is it better for you now that you know everything? I did nothing once and a good person died. She looked out for me when no one else would and she died because I did nothing. I couldn't just go on doing nothing," Dominic said.

"What are you talking about?" Maria said.

Chapter 41

Las Vegas 1965

The ham sandwich on a paper plate looked like a steak to Dominic.

The woman sat across from him. Lit a cigarette. Dominic picked the sandwich up and took a bite. His father had given him an egg and some toast for breakfast but nothing since then. Only the memory of his mother swatting him with a spoon when he ate too fast kept him from swallowing the sandwich whole.

"Not sure what your mother ever saw in your father. Strange how people end up together. You can tell your mother used to be a catch. It's still there if you can get past the hunted look in her eyes. But your father, he was never anything but walking trouble. Of that I'm sure," the woman said.

Dominic took another bite of the sandwich. Watched the woman smoke her cigarette.

"The thing is, some people are just decent to their core and can't help but be helpful, and most people will do the right thing if you motivate them properly, but a certain set of people, it don't matter what you tell em or what you give em, they're always going to be a big pile of shit. Don't waste your time with people like that.

It's just lost time that could be spent on someone worthwhile," she said.

Dominic waited for her to say something more, but that was it. She sat there smoking, blowing small tight rings before taking another slow drag. She smoked her cigarette like she was drawing energy from it, a long slow pull of power from the tip to her.

"How do you know which type of person someone is?" Dominic asked.

"Experience. Painful fucking experience," she said.

There was a knock at the door.

The woman walked to the window and peered outside. What she saw confused her. Dominic could see her rolling something over in her mind. She walked back across the room to her closet and reached into a purse and pulled out a small black handgun.

Another knock at the door.

"Just a second," the woman said.

The woman placed the gun in the pocket of her robe, and then she returned to the door. Took another glance through the window. She double checked the chain and then opened the door enough to look through.

"Well Big Al, isn't this a surprise?" she said.

"I just had to see you," Big Al said.

"I don't generally entertain at home," she said.

"I promise to give you a bonus. I just had to see you right now," he said.

"Just a second," the woman said.

She closed the door. Looked around the apartment. Looked at the boy. She was running things over, thinking it through. Dominic felt like he'd been let into some secret adult world that had always existed, but he hadn't been allowed to see.

The woman made a decision, something switched, her energy changed. She adjusted her robe, so the front showed more skin, and pulled the chain off the door and whipped it open. She looked vibrant and alive in a way she hadn't while talking with Dominic, and she was standing differently. One leg forward, smooth skin sticking out from underneath the fabric.

The man in the doorway was tall and wide, and he had a nose that was crooked like the noses on boxers. He had on a dark suit, the tie loosened, and in one hand was a bottle of whiskey. In the other hand was a white plastic flower. He handed it to the woman.

"You're so sweet," she said.

"That your kid?" the man said as he looked at Dominic.

"No, he's the neighbor's boy," she said.

The woman motioned for Dominic to go.

Dominic looked at the sandwich, half eaten.

"Take the whole plate. Bring it back tomorrow," she said.

Dominic picked up the plate and headed for the door.

"Let me freshen up real quick for you, sweetie," she said. The woman gave Dominic a wink and then headed towards the bathroom.

As Dominic headed for the door, the man barely looked at him. All of his attention was focused on the woman, and he'd changed. In the doorway, he'd looked like any other man in a suit, but something in the way he looked at the woman was off. Dominic was even with the man and looked him up and down and dangling from the inside pocket of his suit was the end of a piece of rope. Who puts rope in a suit jacket? Dominic stopped in the doorway. Something was wrong.

The man saw Dominic staring at him and pushed him out of the doorway.

"Go home, kid," the man said as he shut the door in Dominic's face.

Dominic stood there, plate in his hand, looking at the door. What should he do?

The door to Dominic's apartment opened, and his father stuck his head out.

"What the hell are you doing talking to that whore? Get in here," his father said.

DOMINIC WAS UP and out of the apartment early. The woman's plate in his hand, the sun barely peeking over the horizon. Dominic was worried about waking the woman up, but the look on the man's face the night before had haunted Dominic's dreams.

At the woman's door, he knocked. No one answered.

Dominic knocked again. This time harder. No sound. No rustling. Nothing.

Dominic tried the knob, and the door opened.

The woman was lying on her bed. Her body on its side, right arm hanging limp across her naked torso. A white rope, the same rope Dominic had seen in the man's suit pocket, was wrapped around the woman's neck, and her eyes were a bright red and looking right at him.

AFTER THE POLICE SHOWED UP, Dominic stood around, waiting to speak with the detectives. The first patrol officer on the scene had listened to what Dominic had to say, but he had listened in the way adults listen to children, half believing, half not. The detective, though, seemed interested. He walked up and squatted down with a notebook in his hand.

"They said you saw something," the detective said.

The door to Dominic's apartment opened up, and Dominic's father came out. He had on his uniform for his gas station job, and he looked like he'd just gotten out of the shower.

"What are you doing talking to my kid?" the father said.

"We're just asking him what he saw," the detective said.

"He didn't see nothing," the father said.

"We can let him tell us, can't we?" The detective leaned down and looked Dominic right in the eye. "What did you see?"

Dominic was about to open his mouth when he felt his father's hand on his shoulder pulling him away from the detective.

"He's my kid, and I'm telling you he didn't see nothing. Whore got what she deserved anyway," his father said.

THAT NIGHT, when his father passed out in front of the television, Dominic returned to the woman's apartment. The body was gone, but the room still reeked of death. The flower the man had given her sat on the kitchen table. Dominic took the flower and then made his way across the room to the robe that hung from the bathroom door. As he got closer, he could see the bulge in the pocket, and he reached his hand in and pulled out the gun.

It was small and black and had a white Fleur de Lys symbol on the handle.

⸺

DOMINIC HAD NEVER TOLD anyone that story. He thought that he'd take that experience with him to the grave, but here he was dumping it all on his daughter, and he could see the indecision and the pain just piling up inside her. This life could be damned unkind, and right now, life was tearing a hole through his little girl, and he was the one doing it to her.

"Jesus, Dad, I'm sorry. I'm sorry your father was an asshole. I'm sorry that someone killed your friend. I'm so sorry you had to live through that. But what are you asking of me? That I just look the other way? Is that what you expect me to do? You taught me to do everything right, and now, now you want me to... Really? How can you ask that of me?" Maria said.

She turned away from him and looked up at the ceiling. She was right. How could he ask her to do that? What the hell was the matter with him? Nobody in her family was who they portrayed themselves to be, and now he wanted to make her have a hidden life too. No, he couldn't do that to his little girl. There was a way to end this. A way to tie up all the loose ends without making her betray who she was.

Chapter 42

How could someone so damaged do so much good?

Maria wondered how anyone could overcome a trauma so profound at such a young age. He'd always been so evasive about his youth, and now Maria was truly beginning to understand why. Could she arrest her father? Could she let the man who killed her brother go free? Was she going to be able to live with herself either way? She just didn't know what to do, and the one person her whole life she'd depended on to talk things over, asking him wasn't an option.

"I'm sorry. I never meant for it to end up here," Dominic said.

He'd have to give up the gun, and she'd have to bury it somewhere in the desert, somewhere so far away so remote that no one would ever find it, and she didn't know how she'd be able to face him, but could she put her own father in prison? No, no, she couldn't do that, and she doubted she'd be able to be a cop anymore either because how could she face her coworkers knowing what she'd hid? She'd have to give it up, go work security for a casino or who knows what. Maybe do something totally different. She'd figure it out, but now she had to deal with this.

Was she really going to have to give up her whole life?

Yes, yes, she was. She'd find something else. She'd build a family with Carla. She'd do something. Something that didn't involve being a cop.

"The thing with Carla, let that go. She's got a good heart," Dominic said.

"Now is not the time for life lessons," Maria said.

"There's a way to do this where you're being honest but protecting the people that matter. Just take the time to think this one all the way through because you're going to have to finish it," Dominic said.

Finish it? What the hell was he talking about? He shifted behind her, the rustling of cloth against the chair, and Maria came fully back to this moment in this room standing a few feet from her father, and she knew what he planned to do.

"I love you," he said.

She spun and reached for him.

But Dominic had already stood up and turned away from her. He had the gun, the little black .22 pointed at the side of his head, and he pulled the trigger. The crack of the gunshot was minuscule compared to the pain the sound unleashed. Dominic crumpled onto the chair, body twisted at a weird angle, face planted into the cushion, arms spread.

The gun dropped to the floor and spun towards Maria. Settled a few feet away.

And she understood what her father had meant because the Desert Saint always shot his victims twice. If she was going to protect her mother and his reputation, she had to pick up that gun and shoot her father in the head, and if she was going to do this, she had to do it now before blood stains told a story different from the one Dominic wanted told.

Did she want to tell that story?

She saw her mother's face flushed with pride as she talked about the Time magazine cover. She saw the way her mother sat as her husband told her Tommy was dead. She heard her father comparing Tommy to his pimp father, and Maria realized her mother had never lied to her father about Tommy. The only people lied to had been the children.

Dominic had offered his daughter a way out of this that didn't involve giving up her life.

That didn't involve destroying her mother's faith in her husband.

Was she going to take it?

Maria reached down and picked up the gun.

She aimed it at her father's head.

She pulled the trigger.

WHAT FOLLOWED WOULD FOREVER BE a blur for Maria, actions taken by her, but from a distance. She hurled the gun down into the hidden basement and closed the door. She opened the scrapbook Tommy had of her father's news clippings and picked one at random. Removed the plastic veneer and placed the clipping on her father's hand. Then she went out into the backyard and walked back down the street to her car and drove back to Harold's.

She called in Harold's death. Waited for patrol cars and crime scene units to come by.

Michael and Moyer showed up. Michael was all business, taking over the scene. Moyer was distant, his concern and his anger fighting with each other. In front of them, she called her father, but no answer. So she called her mother, who told her Dominic had gone out, she didn't know where. She called her father again. Moyer wanted to know what was up.

"Nobody knows where my father is," she said.

"We'll find him," Moyer said.

Finding Dominic didn't take long, a patrol car passed by Tommy's and saw Dominic's car in the driveway. The officer looked in some windows and saw the body, and Moyer was the one who sat Maria down and told her that a body had been found at Tommy's.

Maria didn't wait for an explanation. She ran to her car and took off.

By the time she arrived at Tommy's house, cops were everywhere. She ran up the driveway and pushed aside the patrol officer, who tried to keep her out. When she hit the living room, it felt like she was seeing it for the first time, and she went to her knees and sobbed. Before long, Michael was running into the house and helping her up, walking her outside.

Moyer too, standing a few feet off, trying to hold back his own tears.

Michael was trying to comfort her, trying to find something worth saying, but he just kept tripping over the words, and the thing was, all the times Maria had sat with the loved ones of victims, she'd always felt like she knew what to say, we're going to get this guy, we're going to do justice, but nothing could really fix that loss, nothing, not words, not actions, nothing. The loved ones had nodded along and grabbed onto her words like they meant something not because they did but because drowning people grab an anchor if that's what they find. Drowning people can't see anything other than that they're drowning.

And Maria was drowning.

But one thing brought her up for air.

She needed to go tell her mother.

Chapter 43

Where in the hell was Dominic?

Esperanza sat at the kitchen table. She hadn't even noticed her husband leaving. Then the call from Maria had come in, and now Dominic wasn't here and wasn't answering her calls. What the hell was going on? She wanted to light a cigarette right at the kitchen table so he'd have to smell it when he came back. What was he doing worrying her and her daughter so?

Headlights flashed through the window as a car pulled into the driveway.

Esperanza ran to the front of the house. Her daughter was getting out of her car. Esperanza had never been so disappointed to see her own daughter. The only car she wanted to see pulling into that driveway was Dominic's.

Maybe he had gone for a long drive.

He liked to do that. Drive out into the desert. He thought the miles and miles of emptiness were soothing. Esperanza thought all that emptiness was anything but soothing. The further and further she went from civilization, the more and more anxious she became, but he'd enjoyed his lonely night drives, usually when a case was really bad or something was bothering him, and he wanted to think.

Tommy's death had left an emptiness in all of them. Maybe taking a long drive in the desert was a reasonable response. As reasonable as any other.

Esperanza opened the front door of the house and watched her daughter walk up.

Maria looked deathly tired.

"Still nothing from your father? He hasn't been answering my calls."

Maria didn't answer, but Esperanza was so caught up in her thoughts that she didn't notice her daughter's silence. She turned back towards the kitchen, and Maria followed.

"I think it's the magazine cover," Esperanza said.

"Magazine cover?"

"The proof came today. The journalist sent it ahead so your father could see it. It's there." Esperanza motioned to an end table where the cover was.

Maria picked it up and looked at it, a photo of Dominic in the desert, the sprawl of Las Vegas and the lights of the strip in the distance behind him.

Esperanza thought the photo caught the essence of Dominic because he was of Las Vegas, he straddled the old dusty desert town and the new glamourous corporate mecca, and she told him as much, but he hadn't said anything. Just put the photo down and went about his day.

"Something about the photo bothers him, so I think he went on a drive," Esperanza said.

"A drive?" Maria said.

"He's always liked to drive out in the desert when things are bothering him. I thought you knew," Esperanza said.

"Did he do that much?" Maria said.

"No, not much. Maybe when a case was really bothering him, he'd go. He more or less stopped when you were born. I don't think he liked leaving you home alone in the house. I think he wanted to be here protecting you," Esperanza said.

Esperanza sat down at the kitchen table and looked at her phone. Nothing.

"You know the service out there is spotty and since he always answers when I call, but now I can't get a hold of him, and seeing as how upset he's been since Tommy died, I figure he's out on a drive."

Her daughter sat across from her, and Esperanza noticed the determination on her face. Something was bothering her daughter, something she wanted an answer to, something she didn't think Esperanza would want to answer. The first time she'd seen that look was when Tommy told Maria there was no Santa Claus, and her daughter came to ask her mother if Tommy was telling the truth. No tears. No fear. Just a quiet determination to get the truth. Back then, it had been so cute.

Now the look sent a chill up Esperanza's spine.

"I want you to tell me about the first time you met Dad, and I don't want to hear the sanitized version," Maria said.

"He took me to the movies," Esperanza said.

"In a paddy wagon full of hookers," Maria said.

So that was it. She'd finally figured it all out. But what had brought this realization on?

"I always liked being called a working girl better. Felt more fitting," Esperanza said.

Maria shook her head. Leaned back in her chair.

"Is anybody in this family who they claim to be?" Maria said.

"Claim to be? How else do you think a young woman from a tiny little town in Mexico who couldn't speak but four words of English got across the border? Claim to be? I thought you were a detective. How did you not figure this out years ago?" Esperanza said.

Maria started to open her mouth. She wanted to tell her mother that she shouldn't have said it like that, she shouldn't be judging her mother, but Esperanza cut her off and kept going.

"I wanted to tell you because I have never been ashamed. I had two choices: work the fields or spread my legs. I took option two because I could. That decision brought me here. That decision gave me you. You have to understand I was so lost when Tomas disappeared. I had no bank account, no papers. I didn't know how to pay rent or bills. I didn't even know who owned the house we lived in. I spoke just enough English to get a man to invite me to his hotel room, and to be honest, with the way I looked back then, I didn't need much English for that. So what was I going to do? Where was I going to go? And your father, he came and took me in, and he told me he was going to look out for me. And you know what I did? I hocked his television, and I went back out to the streets because I knew I was pregnant, and I figured as soon as he found out he'd cast me aside, so I should grab something and go first, and he rode up and asked me where his television was, and the first thing I noticed was that he wasn't angry. He thought it was funny. Like, of course, I sold his television, why wouldn't I do that? And I realized this was a man who accepted me for who I was, who didn't judge me, who wasn't going to try to control me, and I decided right then and there to trust that man, so I told him I was pregnant. And he said, raising that child alone will be hard. Why don't you let me help? I started crying right there, and I got in his car and it was the last car I ever hopped into, and it was the best decision I ever made, and he didn't want you to know how we started. He wanted you to maintain your innocence. Sure, the job makes you see a whole mess of misery, but it's there. It's not in your home. He wanted to keep your home clean, and I said ok. I didn't agree. I didn't want to hide anything. But I owed him that much and now here I am, telling it all to you anyway," Esperanza said.

Esperanza picked up her phone. She tried Dominic again. Nothing. Right to voicemail.

"I'm sorry I'm not the woman you thought I was but-" Esperanza said

"No, Mom, I'm sorry. I found out Tommy wasn't his a couple of days ago and I thought you had lied to Dad, and I was so angry, and the thing is, I should have known better. I should have known you love him too much to lie to him like that," Maria said.

"Just don't tell your father you know. He spent all this time keeping it from you. He's going to be furious with me for telling you," Esperanza said, and as she talked, something in her daughter's face changed, and Esperanza knew.

"Wait, why are you here? You never come over this late? What happened?" Esperanza said.

Maria started to speak but couldn't get out the words. Tears streamed from her eyes.

"No, no, no," Esperanza said.

"The Desert Saint killed him, and I need you to understand something. I'm going to do everything I can to catch him, but we don't have much to work on, and we'll probably never find him," Maria said.

Chapter 44

Las Vegas 1973

Dominic was seventeen and on his own.

He rented a room above a tavern paid for by money made working at a gas station, the same gas station where his father had worked before he'd fallen down the steps drunk and never gotten back up. Dominic had found him there, the second dead body he'd had to see before the age of twelve. This one hadn't made him as sad as the other, but with his father's death, Dominic would never have the chance to ask about his mother. His parents had gone out one night and only his father came back. He'd said she'd abandoned the two of them for some cowboy in a casino, and being a boy, Dominic had no choice but to accept what his father said, but he'd thought a day would come later in life when Dominic could find out the truth.

Now, he'd never know.

An aunt in Los Angeles had taken him in, but that had only lasted a couple of years. Dominic didn't like LA. Too many cars. Too many people. He missed the desert, so he'd gotten on a bus and come back and gotten hired at the gas station. The owner, a tall, wide man who wore a cowboy hat every day, had given him an advance so Dominic could rent the apartment. Just like that woman had said the night she died. Some people are just decent to their core and can't help but be helpful.

Dominic was just waiting out the two more months until he would be eighteen, so he could join the military, and while he waited, he worked at the gas station during the day and spent his nights at his window above the tavern listening to people hoot and holler and play the jukebox and shoot pool. Dominic liked to sit and watch them walk in and then stumble out. He knew he'd never be a drinker, but these people were interesting to him. He'd sit at the table cleaning the .22 he'd taken from her robe and watch people come and go.

Then the black Cadillac showed up, and the man stepped out of the car.

Dominic approached the window, pushed his nose right up against the glass.

The man circled around a group of men walking out of the tavern. The men were singing some song whose words were only understandable to them, and the man chuckled as he passed. Dominic couldn't hear anything though, not the men in the street, not the song on the jukebox, Dominic could only see the woman giving him the sandwich on the plate, telling him that pain passes, telling him to bring the plate back tomorrow, and then the look on the man's face as he watched her go into the bathroom.

Pure evil.

Dominic's dreams had been haunted by that man's face and the woman's corpse on the bed ever since. Every time he closed his eyes, he saw this man watching her go into the bathroom and every time he woke in the middle of the night in a cold sweat, the woman's corpse, rope still around her neck, was what chased him from his sleep.

Dominic needed to kill this man.

In a box in the closet was the flower the man had given her. Dominic retrieved it and put the gun in the waist pants of his jeans, the shirt untucked and covering it. He went downstairs and eyed the man's car. Long and black and parked diagonal from the bar and right under a streetlight.

The light would have to go first.

Dominic needed three rocks to take out the light, the first and second throws missing badly, the third hitting the target, mostly through luck. But the effort took almost an hour due to all the comings and goings. As the time passed, Dominic's frustration grew, and he was sure the man would leave before Dominic was ready. But the man didn't come out of the tavern.

Dominic returned to his steps and waited.

And waited.

The clapping of the door against the frame woke him, and the man came into view. He was drunk, but not stumbling. He walked slowly, hands in his pocket, looking up at the sky. Then he stopped in the middle of the street and looked up at the crescent moon.

The world stopped.

On that street, at that moment, there was the man, Dominic, and the moon. Nothing else moved. Nothing else made a sound. Nothing else existed.

The man was focused on his car. Digging his keys out of his pocket. He didn't hear Dominic's steps on the asphalt. But he did see Dominic's reflection in the car window. The man turned around. Squinted his eyes to try to get a good view of Dominic, but with the light out, all he could see was a shadow for a face and a hand holding a gun. The man put his hands up in the air, but in a mocking way. This gun was not the first gun to be pointed at him, and he doubted a boy so young, so scrawny, could really pull the trigger.

"What do you want? Money?" The man asked.

Dominic didn't reply.

"If you're going to rob me, you'll need to speak. What's this your first time?" The man said.

The gun shook.

"I was scared my first time, too. Don't let it be so obvious. You have to hold the gun steady or people won't be afraid of you. Like how I'm not afraid. Now listen, you can't rob me. But you come downtown to Harris Automotive sometime next week. My name is Al Deltoro. You ask for Big Al, and I'll give you some work. We'll see if we can make a man out of you. Now scram," the man said.

He turned away from Dominic and put his key in the door. Clicked the lock open. The car door came open. Big Al put a hand on top of his car and started to step in.

"Why did you kill her?" Dominic asked.

Big Al smirked. Looked over his shoulder.

"Which one?"

And there was the look again, the look Dominic had seen eight years earlier, the wolf inside the man. Big Al turned back to his car. He didn't see the barrel of the gun stop shaking, nor did he notice the calmness that came over Dominic as he took careful aim and pulled the trigger.

The crack echoed down the street.

The man collapsed slowly, first against the car, then sliding down the door to the asphalt.

Dominic took a step forward to be sure.

The man's right arm spasmed.

Dominic jumped backward. Startled. Almost ran off.

Gathered himself instead.

Shot one more time. The man settled to the ground, his body descending deeper as if the asphalt was pulling him into an embrace.

Dominic looked around. No one but him, and the body was in the street. He leaned closer to be sure the man was dead. Nothing but the deepest silence possible. Dominic took the flower out of his pocket and threw it onto the ground next to Big Al. Then he turned away and headed back across the street, around the side of the saloon, and up the stairs to his apartment. He sat there in the dark waiting for the police to come, sure someone saw him, sure someone would turn him in, but no one had seen him, and Big Al had a list of enemies longer than his arm. The police figured it for a mob killing and didn't even interview any witnesses.

Dominic held onto the gun and the memory of the man sliding down the side of the car, and was sure he'd done the right thing by avenging the death of the woman who fed him and given him advice on how to survive. He'd learned more from sitting with her for five minutes than he learned in a decade with his father, and he was determined to never be someone who didn't act again.

⊏⊐

THE DESERT WAS cold but well lit by the half-moon.

Maria plunged the shovel into the dirt and lifted up the blade. Flung the dirt aside. She was sweating heavily, and the perspiration was practically freezing on her back. Michael was right, she needed more exercise. She put the shovel against the ground and leaned on it. Looked at Carla sitting cross-legged on the trunk of the car. Al Deltoro's case file open on her knees.

"So you figure this guy, Big Al, was his first one?" Carla said.

"Antoinette suspected him of killing some of her girls, and that's what set him off, you know? Finding that woman dead. A woman who probably worked for Antoinette."

Maria turned back to the hole. It was almost deep enough. Her forearms were already burning, and she wasn't looking forward to filling it back in. She hoped that part would be easier.

"Well, this was definitely an interesting start to our vacation," Carla said.

"I'm sorry, I just... I just couldn't bear this alone," Maria said.

"Nor should you."

"He used to come out here. Him and a body and a shovel. How could he do that?" Maria said.

"He was trying to protect people," Carla said.

"But he was a cop. He could have arrested them," Maria said.

"Could he have really? You complain all the time about how hard it is to get convictions now. Imagine forty years ago."

"He shouldn't have done it. Not like that," Maria said.

"Maybe not. But I'm not going to judge him, and I'm pretty sure I don't ever have to hear another comment about my mother."

"Now you bring that up, really?" Maria said.

"I told you I was coming back to it. Did you really think I'd forgotten?"

Carla jumped down off the trunk and reached her hand out for the shovel.

"You don't have to help. I just couldn't do this alone."

"If I wait for you to finish, we'll never get to go on vacation." Carla took the shovel and leaned down, dug it into the dirt. "Besides, I'm the one who actually goes to the gym in this relationship."

Maria pulled the gun from her waistband. She walked around Carla and looked at the hole. Maria knew why she was hiding this gun just as she knew why her father had turned it on himself, but she was supposed to do the right thing, and hiding evidence wasn't the right thing. Maybe she should just turn it in. Let her mother deal with knowing the truth. Sure, it would tear her apart but could it really be any more difficult than what she had already gone through.

Carla grabbed the gun from Maria's hands and threw it into the hole.

It settled with the dull thud of metal against dirt.

The white Fleur de Lys symbol glowed in the moonlight.

"Whatever conflicted feelings you have about this, your mother has suffered enough in this life, and how long will Naomi last in that house if she figures out who it was that tried to kill her? There's not enough therapy for anyone to get over this one. Some things are just best buried," Carla said.

Carla turned to start filling the hole, but Maria reached for the shovel.

"I'll do it."

Acknowledgments

Writing a book is never a one person affair. I'd like to thank Ingrid for her helpful critique of an earlier version, and Mike for pushing me to publish.

About the Author

A.M. Pascarella is the author of the Desert Saint and the forthcoming A Family Man: Maria Verla Mystery # 2. A.M. Pascarella splits time between Las Vegas and Miami.

The author can be reached at pascarella@bayroadpublish ing.com. If you are interested in joining the mailing list to be notified of upcoming publications, let us know.